Whiskey on Our Shoes

Tonya Preece

CHAMPAGNE BOOK GROUP

Whiskey on Our Shoes

Published by Champagne Book Group
712 SE Winchell Drive, Depoe Bay OR 97341 U.S.A.

~ ~ ~

First Edition 2022

pISBN: 978-1-957228-76-1

Cover Art by Sevannah Storm
Illustrations by Chloe Preece

www.champagnebooks.com

Version_1

To Tim.

Chapter One
Eva

A thrill races through me as I decide to ignore the wigs on my dresser and run a brush through my own hair. I don't need a disguise when I leave the house today. I'm going out alone. No driver. No security. And no celebrity family members.

The opening riff of "Welcome to the Jungle" blasts across the upstairs landing from my brother's room. Lor's favorite Guns N' Roses song is a good sign his physical therapy didn't suck for a change.

Hopeful, I set down my brush and go peer through his half-open door.

He's sitting in his hospital bed, playing air guitar. I'm sure he misses playing for real, but I cringe at the memory of the last time he tried. He got so pissed at the pain and weakness in his hands that the acoustic wound up on the floor with its neck cracked.

The song ends, and I call from the doorway, "Hey, you must be feeling—"

"Fan-freakin-tastic." He gives me the smirk I know well.

Not much else resembles his former self, though. His face is thinner, and his shaggy blond hair cropped shorter. Last year, during the filming of a Polly's Poison music video, one of his drunken pyrotechnic stunts led to a spinal injury and burns. He's forty, twenty years older than me, but he looks even older from a hard and fast life as a guitar god.

He lowers the volume on the next song and motions for me to enter.

His room, like the rest of his huge house, makes me think of a Hard Rock Café. Concert posters, photos, and guitars hang on every wall.

"You're still going somewhere, right?" he asks.

"Desperate to get rid of me, huh?" Smiling, I perch on the edge of his bed. "I'm leaving soon, but I don't wanna be chauffeured. Could I borrow a car?"

His scruffy, unshaven face brightens. "Take the Lamborghini. It's a sweet ride."

"Too recognizable." I don't want to be spotted in one of his poison green custom cars.

"Dammit, Eva." He shakes his head. "Stop letting Mom's paranoia freak you out."

"I'm trying. See, no disguise." I point at my wigless head.

"Nobody in Austin's gonna bother you."

He's told me this more than once in the two weeks since I moved in with him, but it's not easy to let go of how our mom taught me to stay anonymous. One of her obsessive fans tried to kidnap me when I was three. Although I don't remember it, the story haunts me to this day. Besides, I *like* being unknown in this family of celebs.

"And, while Mom's gone," Lor adds, "you don't have to worry about Crazy Carla."

Carla's the latest celebrity gossip reporter who tracks Mom. She's probably in L.A. where Mom's doing a commercial for a new cosmetic line.

"I understand but let me take baby steps. I'll drive the Challenger. It'll blend in better."

"Boring." He rolls his eyes and nudges me off the bed. "Go raise hell for the both of us."

"Ha! That's your style, not mine." I lean in and kiss his cheek. "Be back in a few hours."

"Take your time."

I stop in the doorway and glance back at him. He's looking at his phone and doesn't notice me pausing to watch him. For a moment, I consider staying. He's bound to be bored. I should keep him company, shouldn't I? We could play cards or watch TV.

No. I better go. When he asked me to live here, we made a deal: he'll stay sober, and I'll venture out on my own. This is my chance.

With a sudden surge of independence, I descend the long marble staircase and exit, leaving behind the safety and seclusion of Casa Lor.

Chapter Two
Alex

My classes are done for the day, and I head for my dorm, playing a voicemail from a missed call.

"Hi, Alex." The speaker doesn't identify herself, but I'd know the voice anywhere. It's the one that lured me into what I thought was the best time of my life—and left me in ruins.

I stop on the sidewalk. My gut churns, but morbid curiosity keeps the phone to my ear.

"I miss you," she says, low and sexy, like she thinks it'll work. "Call me, okay?"

"Not a chance, Angie," I mumble and block the unknown number.

What the hell would we talk about? We haven't spoken in months.

Revulsion ripples through me. I shake it off and check messages for my errand service business. There's one from a person named Lor, which sounds fake, but whatever, it's work.

I message the customer to say I'm available now, and they reply right away.

> *Hey, man, thanks for the fast response. I need you to meet with a guy at Kudos Café near Lake Travis. He'll give you a package to bring to me.*

This sounds fishy, but I send a response.

> *As long as it doesn't have anything illegal or hazardous.*

No worries. What should I tell my guy you look like?

I'll be the tall guy in a dark blue shirt, jeans, and cowboy boots. Please confirm your agreement to my terms and conditions, and an invoice for prepayment will follow.

Cool. I'll text further instructions once you have the package.

Within minutes, his credit card payment goes through and damn, he included a twenty-*five* percent tip. I need him as a regular customer.

I arrive at the café early and order a soda, knocking out some reading for my marketing class while I wait. Right on time, a guy approaches me, carrying a plain brown bag with handles. He has spiky blond hair and ear gauges. His neck tattoo is a...steampunk penguin? I stifle a laugh as he eyes my boots.

"Are you picking up for Lor?" he asks, and I nod. The bag's heavier than I expected, and the top's taped shut.

"Tell Lor I said hello." The guy leaves before I can even ask his name.

I text that I have the bag, and Lor sends me a residential address that's ten minutes away.

Enter NINE9999 at the security gate. Drive to the house, ring the bell & ask for Jojo. Tell her you need to hand-deliver the package to Mr. Jenson.

I'm intrigued and make the short drive with the bag on the front seat.

A little guardhouse is unoccupied. The code opens the gate onto a long, brick-paved driveway lined with perfectly landscaped shrubs and trees. A mansion ahead has a five-car garage and a balcony across the whole second story. Most deliveries, often for older folks, are to quiet neighborhoods and apartments. This place blows my mind.

Why didn't Mr. Jenson send a butler for this errand?

I park in front of the house, grab the bag from my passenger seat, and ring the doorbell. Sweat trickles down my back. I feel out of place. I'm a small-town guy in jeans and have never stepped foot in a house this big. The door's opened by a woman in a dark blue suit.

"Hello, you must be Alex."

"Yes, ma'am." I remove my cowboy hat with my free hand. "Are you Jojo?"

"I am." She waves me into a huge foyer. "Mr. Jenson only informed me he was expecting company a moment ago. Would you like something to drink?"

"Oh, no thanks. I don't want to impose. If you'll just take me to him, I'll—"

"Of course." She leads the way up a massive, winding marble staircase overlooking a living room where platinum records and guitars are on display. Maybe I should recognize who this Lor guy is, but I can't put my finger on it.

Jojo shows me into a room where a man's sitting in a hospital bed. His hands and arms are scarred. I've seen scars like those before, from burns.

He glances up from an iPad as Jojo and I approach his bed. "The biographer's here," she tells him.

I squint, taken aback. "Um, excuse me ... what do you mean, bio—"

"Excellent." He sets the iPad aside and eyes the bag in my hand.

"I'll leave you two gentlemen to the task at hand," Jojo says and leaves.

"What *task* was she talking about?" I ask the man, more uneasy by the second.

"Oh, don't pay any attention to her." He waves a dismissive hand. "You're kinda young, but this could still work. How are your acting skills?"

Chapter Three
Eva

I browse through a few clothing shops at a galleria but don't buy anything. My shoulders are so tense from this new, undisguised solo experience, there's no way I could enjoy trying anything on.

Heading back to Casa Lor, I stop at a place called Austin Creative Repurposing. I've read about it online, how they use recycled stuff to make art, and I want to check it out for myself.

A bell chimes as I enter, and a few people look my way. My skin prickles from the familiar fear of exposure. There's no way anyone here would guess who I'm related to. Too bad my heart doesn't understand that logic. It hammers away in my chest. I run my fingertips along the edge of my wig to check that it's on right, but *duh*, no wig.

I glance around to get my bearings. ACR is a furniture showroom and art gallery. The air's a bit musty, with a hint of tobacco. The scent, mingled with furniture polish, reminds me of pleasant days at my grandparent's house in San Diego, and I relax.

A tall woman in a red ACR shirt greets me. "Holler if you need help with anything."

"Thanks." I clear my throat, embarrassed by the waver in my voice. "I'm just browsing."

There's a wall hanging with piano keys mounted on a long, painted board. It's simple yet elegant. On another wall, several doors hang sideways with cutouts for photos. In between the doors, there are window frames made into shadowboxes. They're above a table display of vinyl records that've been heated and molded into cool decorative bowls. Mixed in with The Rolling Stones and Metallica records is one for my dad and uncle's band, The Fabulous Undertakers. Nobody here knows my connection to them either. I trace the familiar record label with my fingertip. The design accentuates the band's nickname, FU.

The tall woman, whose name tag says Nadine, walks around with another woman and young teenage girl. Mother and daughter, I assume. It sounds like Nadine's giving them a tour.

"Everything's one of a kind," she says. "Artists and furniture makers obtain supplies from our warehouse, create new pieces, and sell them on consignment." She points to a clawfoot tub. "This is the work of a volunteer." One side is sheared off, and it's lined with padding.

"Oh cripes, art skills aren't required, are they?" the woman asks. "Jenny has none."

The girl's eyes shoot daggers at her mom, and Nadine says, "No ma'am, but we do hope volunteers have an interest in repurposing things otherwise destined for a landfill."

The girl rolls her eyes, and her mom scolds her in a hushed voice.

"I'll give you a moment," Nadine tells them. Stepping in my direction, she grimaces.

"Yikes," I mutter. "Sounds like they don't get the point of this place."

"Nailed it." She sighs.

The girl breaks away from her mom, storming out. The mother huffs and calls to Nadine, "We'll have to get back to you later, okay?"

"No problem." Nadine waves. Once the mother's gone, Nadine introduces herself to me as the co-owner. "Since you seem to appreciate, or at least understand, our goal here at ACR, by any chance are *you* interested in volunteering?"

"Um…" Put on the spot, I falter, but I'm grinning. Something about this place makes me feel like I belong. "What would I be doing?"

"Come on, I'll show you the warehouse."

We exit through a back door and cross a parking lot between the showroom and another building. "These are donated supplies." She points to rows of shelves, neatly labeled, holding stuff like paint, bolts of fabric, and bins with craft supplies. "Volunteers sort and stock, rearranging as needed." Bricks, lumber, tiles, and metal are stacked on the other side.

"Everything's so organized." I'm impressed.

"Thanks. We try. My stepdaughter, Blair, did the setup. What do you think of joining us? We'd love your help."

This would take time away from being with Lor, but *he's* the one who insists I get out more.

I bite my bottom lip for a second, then say, "Yeah, I'll give it a try."

"Yes! Let's go to my office, and you can complete a volunteer application."

The simple form only takes a few minutes. Since I've kept my identity disassociated with the celebrities in my family, I don't worry much about using my real name.

Nadine schedules me to volunteer on Tuesdays and Thursdays and sets a red shirt on her desk. As I reach for it, her eyes zero in on my left hand and widen in shock. Surprisingly, a lot of people don't notice my left index finger's missing. I'm prepared to brush it off as a childhood accident, but she doesn't ask.

Instead, she looks away and opens a file cabinet. "One more form. A liability waiver. How old are you?"

"Twenty."

"Good, no need for a parent to sign."

Whew. That would've sucked. Mom's signature could end my anonymity. Sloane Silver is a household name, like Heidi Klum.

"Are you a college student?" Nadine asks.

"No." Fact is, one gap year led to another, and I have no clue what to do with my life.

On my way to the exit, Nadine takes me through an area of the showroom I didn't notice earlier. I stop dead in my tracks. There's a guitar on display, decorated with colored glass mosaic tiles arranged in intricate patterns. Nadine traces a green tile. "The artist found the guitar beside someone's trash near the lake. In the right hands, one person's trash becomes another's art."

I touch the back of the guitar's neck. The burred texture of cracked wood confirms it. *I* was the one who threw this guitar out, at Lor's insistence. And here it is, transformed.

Checking the price tag, I say, "I'd like to buy this."

Her eyebrows rise in surprise. "Awesome. I'll ring you up. Bonus, there's a volunteer discount, albeit small."

Once I've paid for it, I carry the guitar to the Challenger. The glass tiles make it heavier. I carefully place it across the backseat. Before starting the car, I check my phone for the time and see a message from Lor's personal assistant, Jojo.

> *Did you know your brother's having*
> *someone write his biography? The writer's*
> *here, meeting with him.*

Frowning, I reread the message. There's no way Lor finally agreed to let someone write his bio, not while Polly's Poison wants to keep a lid on his condition.

Abandoning plans for a drink at the nearby café, I hurry home. At Casa Lor, there's a black truck with a UT longhorn symbol on the bumper. I park beside the truck, grab my purse, and sling the ACR T-shirt over my shoulder on the way to the front door. Up the stairs, two at a time, I rush into Lor's room.

"Whoa, Eva." He sits up straighter. "You're back already?"

I take a deep breath, relieved he isn't drinking. "What's going on? Who's this?" I gesture at the guy in the room holding a cowboy hat.

"Alex," Lor says. "He's here to work on my biography. Alex, my sister, Eva."

A strangled sound escapes my throat. Lor must've lost his freaking mind, telling this stranger who I am. He's usually more careful, even if he doesn't agree with me wanting to stay unknown. His eyes widen. "Shit, I'm sorry."

Sorry doesn't help now. I could run out, but the damage is done. It's best to draw the attention away from myself. I set my purse on the bed and ask Lor, "A biography, huh?"

He says, "Yeah," but Alex shakes his head.

My body tenses, thumbnail digging into my scar. Lor is nothing if not consistent. Despite his good intentions, he's the king of self-sabotage.

Unfortunately, now we have an audience.

Chapter Four
Alex

Lor was explaining this biography nonsense when a beautiful girl rushed in. He introduced her as his sister, Eva, and her face became beet red. Now she looks pissed.

Her eyes bore into me, and she asks, "Are you even a writer?"

"No." I give Lor an apologetic frown.

"Dude!" He groans. "You caved so easily."

"I'm just here to make a delivery," I tell Eva. "I don't know anything about him."

"Delivery of what?" She marches over to me. "Where is it? Is it booze?"

Uh, oh. My gaze darts to the bag on the floor near my feet. She goes straight to the bag, rips the tape off, and takes a bottle from it. Great. I've brought booze to an obviously unwell man.

Eva glares at me, then at him. "We had a deal."

He flashes her a shit-eating grin and attempts to swipe the whiskey. "Eva, give me the damn bottle."

She steps out of reach, turns on her heel, and heads for the door. I follow, wanting to convince her not to shoot the delivery guy, but she stops and spins around, smacking into me.

Hard.

The bottle slips from her hand. I drop my hat and hook an arm around her waist, pulling her out of the way right before the glass breaks on the hard floor. The amber liquid spreads into a puddle. My arm stays around her, and she doesn't move.

She gazes at me with the prettiest green eyes. My pulse races.

Time stands still.

Until Lor wails, "Nooo!" He cusses at us but doesn't get up. The wheelchair on the other side of the bed makes me wonder if he even can.

I cough into my hand to cover a gag on the strong liquor smell and reluctantly take my other arm from around Eva. A red shirt draped on her shoulder falls to the floor. It has a logo, something called ACR. I grab for the shirt, but she snatches it first. The hem drags through the liquor on the floor, splashing some on her right shoe and the toe of my left boot.

Jojo runs in and grimaces at the spill and broken glass. "Is that whiskey?"

"Yeah, and by the way—" Eva gestures at me "—this guy is *not* a writer."

Jojo frowns at me, obviously disappointed, and I insist, "*I* didn't say I was."

"He's right," Jojo tells Eva. "DeLorean said it."

DeLorean? Lor must be short for DeLorean. Isn't that the name of a car?

He's sitting there with his arms crossed, scowling. Jojo shifts her annoyed frown from him to the mess on the floor. "Where's Stella when we need her?"

Eva cups her hands around her mouth. "Stelllaaa," she hollers in the direction of the open door.

Her Marlon Brando impression from *A Streetcar Named Desire* is spot on. I laugh without thinking. She silences me with a jaw-clenched stare.

Damn, she's beautiful. It sucks she's mad at me. I wouldn't mind getting to know her.

I pick my hat up off the floor, and Eva whispers something to Jojo. The two of them look at me and back at each other.

"What should we do?" Eva asks her, loud enough for me to hear.

"About what?" I butt in, tired of being treated like this is all my fault.

"Security." Eva retrieves her purse from the foot of the bed. "How'd you get in the gate?"

"He texted the code to me." I gesture at Lor, or DeLorean, whatever his name is.

"Great, now I'll have to change it." Eva rolls her eyes.

"Let's discuss this elsewhere." Jojo indicates for Eva and me to leave the room with her.

Downstairs, Eva gets right in my face, or she tries to. She's quite a bit shorter than me.

"You said you don't know anything about him," she says. "Is that true?"

"Yes. Why would I lie about it?" I look around and realize the platinum records on display say Polly's Poison on them. "Ohhh. I didn't recognize *him*, but I've heard of the band. I mean, who hasn't, right? So, you're his sister? What's wrong with him?"

"Whoa, there, cowboy," Jojo says and pushes through a set of swinging doors. Once again, Eva and I follow her. This time, into a huge kitchen. There's a guy in a chef hat with earbuds in. He waves cooking utensils around in each hand, as if directing an orchestra.

He sees us and removes the earbuds. "What's going on?"

"Hector, three iced teas, please," Jojo says.

"Say what?" Eva plants her hands on her hips. "This isn't a social call, Jojo. This guy—" she jerks a thumb in my direction "—brought whiskey to Lor. He isn't here for iced tea."

"Excuse me." I straighten my posture and challenge Eva with a glare of my own. "*This guy* has a name. It's Alex. And I didn't know I was bringing him *whiskey*."

"Where did you get it from?" she asks and sits on a barstool.

"Good question, whiskey boy." Hector points a spatula at me. "You twenty-one?"

"No. Mr. Jenson arranged for a guy to meet me at a café. He had a…penguin tattoo."

Eva props her head on her hand. Her long blonde hair falls to the side in a silky curtain.

Jojo pats her arm. "I'll get an NDA."

She leaves the room, and I wonder what the hell I've gotten myself into here.

Doesn't NDA stand for non-disclosure agreement?

Hector rounds the end of the bar to place a hand on Eva's shoulder. "Is Lor okay?"

"He didn't drink any, but he's pissed I dropped it." The fight has left her, and she looks like she might cry. It makes my chest kinda tight.

I step closer to her. "Listen, I'm sorry about this. I'm just a UT student making some cash on the side with an errand service business. The whole biography bit was something Mr. Jenson sprung on me when I got here."

She tilts her head and looks at me, her expression difficult to read. "I guess it isn't your fault for being lured here under false pretenses."

I feel an inch tall now. She might as well have called me gullible.

"Problem is," she continues, "you saw and heard things you

shouldn't have." Her serious tone gives me a chill.

"Okay, so…what does that mean?" I ask.

"It means, now we have to kill you."

Chapter Five
Eva

Alex takes a step back toward the swinging kitchen doors and takes a phone from his pocket.

Worried he'll call the cops, I hop off the barstool and walk toward him, hands up to show I'm harmless. "I was kidding," I say.

He freezes, shoulders back. His chest is broad. A brick wall. That's what running into him upstairs felt like. His arm had gone around me, strong and warm, pulling me out of the way and—*whoa*. Heat creeps into my cheeks, despite the coolness of the kitchen.

Squelching the impulse to fan myself, I shift my focus to Alex's face. There's a spark in his deep blue eyes, like he caught me ogling him, and my whole face ignites. Damn fair skin.

What the hell am I doing? This guy poses a threat to mine and Lor's privacy. He could blab what happened here to everyone.

So why am I thinking of his warm, spicy scent?

I clear my throat. "We wouldn't kill you. Right, Hector?"

"You're safe, man." Hector hands us each a glass of tea.

Alex's posture relaxes some, but he doesn't take a drink. He watches me sip mine. I switch from holding the glass with my left hand to my right and wonder if he noticed I don't have a left index finger. If so, he's hiding his reaction better than Nadine at ACR did.

He pockets his phone. "Okay, what shouldn't I have seen or heard?"

"I'll let her explain it," I say as Jojo breezes back into the kitchen, NDA in hand. There are perks to having Lor's personal assistant on the premises.

"Have a seat, Alex." She sets the papers on the bar. "This is a standard non-disclosure agreement. The band's keeping DeLorean's injuries private while he's recovering."

Alex shrugs. "Fine. I won't tell anyone. I don't even have any idea what's wrong with him."

Jojo hands him a pen. "Good. By signing this, you *also* agree to not mention anything of DeLorean having a sister."

"Why?" His eyes snap to me. "Don't people know he has a sister?"

"No," Hector tells him. "She works hard to stay anonymous. You must forget everything about her." His tough guy act warms my heart, but he's no bigger than me, with not much more muscle.

Alex, on the other hand is clearly shredded.

"Don't worry. I can keep a secret." His eyes are full of understanding.

"Great." I gesture to the NDA. He breaks our gaze and reads it. And I mean, he really reads it, like word for word. Finally, he signs it and hands it to Jojo.

"Thank you, sir," she says. "Eva, will you see Alex to the door please?"

A splash mark on his left boot catches my eye as we walk through the foyer. I point at the dark spot. "Oh no, some of the whiskey got on you. I can have Jojo arrange to replace them."

"No, it's fine." He stops at the door. "But maybe I could get *your* number?" From the way his Adam's apple bobs with a swallow, I sense he surprised himself as much as me.

"Um..." I'm tempted, but *what* is happening? He's supposed to leave and forget me. I need to forget him. Our lives are so different. "I'm not sure it's a good idea." I open the door.

Disappointment flickers in his eyes. He nods and goes past me, through the open door. Heading for the black truck, he puts his cowboy hat on and glances over his shoulder at me with what could only be described as a wistful smile. I almost grin back but decide not to encourage him.

After he drives away, I move the Challenger to the garage and retrieve the guitar from the backseat. Returning the damaged instrument to the main house feels wrong. Instead, I lug it to the much smaller guesthouse nobody uses and lean it in a corner of the living room. Back in the main house, I plan to chew out Lor but halfway to his room I stop, too disgusted to deal with him yet. He had some nerve bringing a stranger here and saying what he did in front of him.

That cowboy better keep his word. Time will tell.

Chapter Six
Alex

I enter my dorm room after classes on Thursday and Graham, the guy from across the hall, is at my desk. Like this is *his* room. It might as well be. He's always in here with his buddy Sean, my pain-in-the-ass roommate.

"What happened to you?" I ask Graham, whose elbow's resting on an ice pack.

"Weight room injury." He overdoes it and hurts himself almost every time he works out.

I set my backpack on my desk. "Lay off the weights for now. Stick to cardio."

"That's what *I* told him." Sean, lying on his top bunk, lobs a tennis ball at the ceiling.

"How am I ever gonna bulk up like you guys?" Graham whines.

"Takes time," I remind him. "You think I got like this overnight?" If these guys only knew how scrawny I was just a couple years ago.

Sean's ringtone plays, "Boom Chicka Wow," and seconds later someone knocks on our door. "Come in," he yells, and tells Graham and me, "I'd clear out if I were y'all." His conquest-of-the-week sashays in. He tosses the tennis ball at me.

I catch it and throw it back, hitting him in the head with a satisfying *whack*.

He flips me off as the girl climbs up to him.

Graham follows me into the hallway. "Man, Sean gets all the babes. We don't stand a chance."

"Speak for yourself." I bristle. "I'm not looking for a chance with any of them."

"Damn, what are you, a monk? Have you even been with anyone since Ang—"

"*Don't* say her name." I should've never mentioned Angie to him.

At least he doesn't know the whole story. I'm still paying the price for falling into her web of lies. My grades tanked last semester from being involved with her. Now, I'm on academic probation and need to turn it around before my folks find out.

Graham unlocks the door to his own room. "Wanna kill time in here for a while?"

"Not today." I keep walking down the hall.

My phone pings with a message from my cousin, Cassidi.

Can you help me move some furniture? I'll feed you dinner.

Sure, but why? Are you moving? The semester's not even half over. Is everything okay?

Everything's fine. I'm not going anywhere. Natalie moved out to live with her boyfriend. Her room's bigger, so I want to swap before I find someone else to move in.

Ah, ok. I'm on my way.

I wish I could take the vacant room, but the timing sucks. Cassidi probably needs someone to split rent with now, and I'm stuck with that asshat Sean through May.

On the way to my truck, my best friend Brady sends a text.

Bored. Let's hang out.

Gotta help Cass with something at her apartment. Meet me there?

Hell yeah.

Brady has a longstanding crush on my cousin.

When we meet in the parking lot of her apartment, Brady says, "I'm ready to leave the friend zone with Cassidi. Help me, okay?"

I laugh as we walk toward her place. "You're on your own with that."

"Thanks for nothing." He punches my arm.

Cassidi opens her door.

Brady puffs his chest out. "Hope you don't mind the extra help. I didn't want Alex to hurt himself doing the heavy lifting alone."

I put him in a headlock, and Cassidi rolls her eyes and laughs.

Inside, I set my phone and keys on the kitchen counter.

Cassidi shows us what she wants to have moved into in the empty room. After we relocate the dresser and desk, we take apart the bed frame. "I'll order pizza," she says, leaving the room.

As Brady and I reassemble the frame, I tell him, "I met a girl. But I'm not sure I'll see her again."

"Hope she's at least *close* to your age. I don't get your deal with older women."

"Your mom didn't mind the age difference."

He stops what he's doing and glares at me. "That better be a joke."

"Yeah, idiot. I've only been with *one* older woman. Why do you act like it's a thing for me now? And for your information, the girl I met is my age. Or close to it anyway."

"Where'd you meet her?" He takes one end of the box spring. "Is she hot?"

"Smokin'." I grin, and we position the box spring on the frame. "It's a weird story, but she's cool. And funny." I stop there because Cassidi walks in. I've already kind of broken the damn NDA terms; better not make it worse by telling my cousin about Eva.

The three of us work in silence for a few minutes until Cassidi grumbles. "Looking for a new roommate's gonna suck. Nobody I know needs a place, and I've never had to live with a stranger." She shudders.

"How'd you know Natalie?" Brady asks, positioning a bookshelf against the wall.

"We met in a summer program for business school. Things were great, as far as being roommates. But then she started going out with this guy, Harrison Winchester *the Third*. The name says it all, doesn't it?"

"Says what?" Brady asks, but I know the answer. Cassidi sees the world through one filter.

True to form, she answers, "The name says money. In his case, old money. The kind that gets passed down, generation to generation." She shoves a stack of books on a shelf with a loud *thunck*. "Harrison asked Natalie to move in with him rent-free, as if *he's* even paying a cent for that fancy condo. At least he's willing to cover her share of this place for as long as she was supposed to be here."

Brady helps her refill more of the bookshelf. "It's nice you're not left hanging for rent."

"I guess. Gives me time to find someone new."

I'd mostly tuned them out, focused on moving her hanging clothes from one closet to the other, but I pause with a realization. "Hey, Cass, what if I moved in here? I mean, I can't until the semester's over, but—"

"What a great idea!" Eyes wide, she tosses a set of sheets onto the bed and squeezes my arm. "I can't believe I hadn't thought of it."

"Awesome." Brady fist bumps me. I'm surprised *he* didn't offer to move in. I bet he'll be over here a lot under the guise of hanging out with me.

"Thank you so much, Alex." Cassidi hugs me. "You're a lifesaver."

"Sweet." I help her put the sheets on. "Now I just need a real job."

"There's a waiter opening at the restaurant," she says. "We could wait tables together and make fun of the snobby, rich customers and celebrities. On second thought." She pauses and gathers her hair into a ponytail. "Never mind. I wouldn't wish the job on my worst enemy."

"Why do you work there if you hate it?" Brady asks, putting a desk drawer back in place.

"I don't hate everything about it. The tips are good. And those people are entertaining *sometimes*."

She works at a posh, downtown restaurant. Ironic, considering the chip on her shoulder about the rich and famous. It stems from her mom abandoning her at fourteen to follow a wannabe actor to Hollywood.

I don't want to wait tables *or* celebrity bash. "I'm gonna apply for campus jobs."

"Sounds good. Oh, here—" she hands me my phone "—you left it in the kitchen and got a call. I answered it without thinking."

"You what?" I scowl. Family or not, I don't like people handling my phone.

"Sorry." She grimaces. "It was a girl. I told her you were busy, and she hung up. Are you seeing someone new?" She gives me a wary look. Besides Brady, she's the only person in my life who knows of the Angie fiasco, and she's been overprotective ever since.

"No." My blood boils. Was it Angie again?

"I think the caller ID said Jenson," Cassidi says.

Jenson? That's Lor. "Wait." My breath hitches. "A *girl?*"

"Yeah. She didn't give a name."

Could it have been Eva? As soon as I let myself think it, I push it away. Maybe Jojo called to make sure I've kept my mouth shut. Or, it *might* have been Eva. And I missed it.

"Let's watch *Eighth Moon*," Cassidi suggests. Brady readily agrees.

"Y'all start without me," I say. "Jenson's one of my delivery service customers. I should return this call now." I step outside and press the name Jenson on my phone screen.

There's no answer, only a standard voicemail recording. I disconnect without leaving a message. Once again, I replay what happened a couple of days ago. One of my favorite parts was when I pulled Eva out of the way so the bottle wouldn't fall on our feet. Mad as she'd seemed before that, I was surprised she didn't slap me. Instead, she placed a hand on my chest to steady herself and left it there a bit longer than necessary. It's why I asked for her number, hoping the attraction was mutual. Could this missed call mean I'd been right?

Chapter Seven
Eva

I toss Lor's phone onto my bed, shaky with embarrassment. Calling Alex did *not* go as I'd hoped, but I can't stop thinking of him. He was more genuine and real than anyone I've ever met. And he saw *me*. Not the sister of a guitar god, or some random girl hiding in disguise.

But a girl answered his number and said, "He's busy right now."

It must've been his girlfriend, and that makes him a jerk for asking for my number, but I guess I'm a jerk too. I swiped Lor's phone to keep him from arranging more deliveries.

Bummed, I slump downstairs. Hector is in the kitchen mincing garlic. A pot of pasta sauce simmers on the stove. "Mm, smells good." I drop onto a barstool.

"Looks like you need a drink." He points at a pitcher of tea on the counter. Before I have a chance to pour any, the doorbell rings, which is odd in and of itself since a person needs the code to pass through the gate—oh *damn!*

I didn't change the code after Lor gave it to Alex last week. I dash from the kitchen. Jojo beats me to the front door, opening it to a busty woman in a costume worthy of a Vegas showgirl. The woman has a bunch of balloons, and she's yelling at a man beside her who's holding several leashes.

"Get those things away from me," she yells as small gray and white critters scamper and tug at the ends of the leads. They scurry so fast I can't tell what type of animal they are.

The man throws his head back in laughter, and some of the leashes escape his grip.

Jojo screams bloody murder, waving her arms at the animals charging toward her.

Hector runs out of the kitchen. "What the hell?" He rushes to Jojo as the animals run wild in the living room. I chase after one of them, managing to stomp my foot on a strap. It's tethered to…some kind of weasel? But why? For the love of God, *why?!*

"Hello, hello! The ferret circus has arrived!" the man yells like a carnival barker. "Sorry, those got away. Give me a minute to round them up, and we'll start the show." Instead of remedying the chaos he's created, he laughs at Jojo, Hector, and me as we scramble around, grasping for leashes.

After a few minutes of this madness, music floats down from upstairs. I freeze in place, realizing the balloons the woman was holding have floated to the high ceiling of the foyer. And she's gone. I understand now. These stupid ferrets were a distraction. And it worked.

Leash in hand, I move toward the stairs. The ferret runs ahead of me and into Lor's room where Def Leppard's "Pour Some Sugar on Me" is playing on the stereo. The showgirl's doing a striptease. Lucky for me, she isn't *au naturel* yet. *Un*lucky for me, Lor has a bottle of Jack Daniels. The lid's off, and he wipes his mouth with the back of his hand. He laughs and points at the weasel gyrating at the end of its leash, like it's dancing. I might think it's funny, if I wasn't fuming mad as I pry the whiskey away from him.

"You need to leave," I yell over the music at the nearly naked woman. "And take this with you." I shove the leash into her hand and turn the stereo off.

"Sorry," Lor tells the stripper and laughs. "The killjoy spoiled it, just like I predicted."

"It's all good, sir. Thanks for paying in advance and for the generous tip." She gathers her clothes and leaves. The dancing wonder—the ferret, not the woman—left a parting gift on the floor. Stella will love cleaning that.

Lor leans his back against the propped-up pillows. His face is smug, eyes glassy.

I set the whiskey aside. He only got a few swallows, but some of his meds intensify the effect of alcohol. I want to shake him, slap him even.

How did he arrange for this without his phone? His iPad's on the nightstand. I should've removed every device.

Seething, I take my phone from my pocket and call Jojo. "When you're done with the three-ring circus, you might wanna join me up here. The stripper brought Lor a bottle of J.D."

Jojo arrives a couple of minutes later, her hair a mess, clothes askew. "How bizarre. A ferret circus! I've never heard of such a thing."

"I think Lor just invented it." I show her the bottle and gesture at Lor, who looks asleep.

We call Dr. Blankenship, Lor's private physician.

"I'll be there shortly," he says in a monotone. Nothing Lor does seems to surprise him.

I thank him and hang up. "I can't believe Lor did this."

"I know. I'm sorry." Jojo tucks the bedcovers around him, like he's a sleepy child.

Dr. B arrives and checks Lor's vitals, determining there's no need for an ER visit. "Just keep him as calm and comfortable as possible."

Jojo shakes his hand. "Thank you for coming."

"Anytime." He gathers his things. "Eva, would you accompany me downstairs?" In the foyer, he says, "Lor's at a higher risk of secondary problems now."

Secondary problems?

"Because of the alcohol?" I ask, a tightness in my chest making it hard to breathe.

"Alcohol could cause complications, of course, but I'm also concerned about his refusal to cooperate with therapy. Were you aware he fired his latest physical therapist?"

I blink rapidly. "I had no idea."

"He *must* follow the recommended regimen if he expects to walk again." Dr. B's expression oozes concern.

Hot saliva fills my mouth, like I might hurl. The room spins.

"Eva!" Dr. B catches me by the arm as my knees buckle. He guides me to sit on the foyer bench and presses a palm on my forehead. "You almost fainted." He checks my pulse.

"I'm okay." My head clears a bit. "A little lightheaded. Haven't eaten much today, and then this happened with Lor. Everything's so…" I grimace.

"I understand. Sorry I laid more at your feet."

"It's okay. I needed to know. It's part of why I'm here, to help him recover." I rub my thumb along the thin scar where my left index finger used to be.

Dr. B notices, and his brow furrows again. "Is your hand bothering you?"

"Oh, no, it's just a nervous habit." I flatten my hand beside me.

He's familiar with the abridged version of what happened and has commented in the past on the remarkable plastic surgery, but I don't like how I've drawn his attention to it now.

I rise and open the door. "Thanks again, Dr. B. I'll talk to Lor about this."

He gives me a tight smile. "Call if you need anything."

Closing the door behind him, I lean on it, crushed under the weight of this quasi-parental role I've unwittingly taken on. Resentment forms a lump in my throat.

Hector enters the room. "Let's get you something to eat." He puts a comforting arm over my shoulders and leads me back to the kitchen.

Getting ready for bed later, I'm restless and realize I can't stand to be in Casa Lor, sharing the same roof with my self-sabotaging brother.

I take my computer and some clothes to the guesthouse and text Jojo to let her know I'll sleep here from now on.

Chapter Eight
Alex

The call from Lor's phone remains a mystery. I resisted calling the number all weekend.

Monday, when I'm done with homework, the gym, and running errands for customers, there are no more distractions. Curiosity wins.

I'm alone in my dorm room and give the number a call. A man answers on the first ring.

"Mr. Jenson?" My stomach drops, disappointed Eva didn't answer. "Hi, this is Alex, the errand runner you hired last week. Sorry to bother you. I missed a call from this number. Did you...or someone else there try to reach me?"

"Not me. I couldn't have. Eva stole my phone and I just got it back a little while ago." He sounds pissed, but my hopes rise. "Hang on." His voice becomes muffled. I think he says, "For Eva."

My palms sweat as I wait for what feels like an eternity.

There's a shuffling noise.

"Hello?" Eva sounds hesitant.

"Eva? This is Alex."

"Oh...hi." Her voice falls flat. Not the reaction I'd hoped for, but I forge ahead.

"I was at my cousin's the other day, and she took a call on my phone from this num—"

"Wait, your *cousin*?"

"Yeah, her name's Cassidi. I don't know what she was thinking. I mean, we're family, but who answers someone else's phone like that? Right?" I chuckle.

"Right." Now she sounds amused. "What kind of person would do such a thing?"

"Says the girl who stole her brother's phone," I tease.

"Ugh, I felt like I had to, after what he did. Have you ever heard of a ferret circus?"

"A what?" I take in her voice and the music of her laughter as she the tells me a crazy story about weasels and balloons and a stripper. Talking to her is going better than expected.

"Your brother's a trip," I say during a pause. "Did he drink any of the whiskey?"

"Yeah, unfortunately, *that* time he managed to." She sighs.

I mentally kick myself for making her sound sad. "I'm sorry, Eva."

Silence stretches out on her end. I worry I've blown it.

Then she says, "So, um, I called the other day because I had second thoughts on *not* giving you my number."

"You did?" I sit up fast and hit my head.

"What happened? It sounded like something fell."

"That was my hard head hitting the bottom of my roommate's bunk." I rub my forehead.

"Are you okay?" There's a laugh in her voice. God, I hope to see her laugh in person.

"I'm fine. Uh…what made you change your mind about giving me your number?"

"I guess you're pretty trustworthy."

I keep hearing a beep on her end. "Do you need to answer another call?"

"No, but I should probably take Lor's phone back to him."

"Okay, yeah."

"Bye, Alex. I'll text you my number."

A few minutes after we hang up, my phone rings. Unknown number. Eva must've decided to *call* from her own phone, not text, which is great. "Hello, again," I answer, a bit eagerly.

"Hi, Alex." It's a female voice, but not Eva's. "I miss you and want to see you."

Shit. My stomach roils, and I break into a cold sweat.

"Hello? Alex, are you there? Say something. Don't you miss me?"

I disconnect without saying a word and block yet another number.

Chapter Nine
Eva

I'm curled up on a sofa in the main house living room. The book I was reading before Jojo brought me Lor's phone has fallen on the floor. I don't bother getting it and just lie here, still giddy from talking with Alex. It's such a relief the girl who answered his phone was his cousin.

I'll take the leap and send him my own number, but not quite yet. No harm in making him wait a bit so I don't appear desperate. And I'll still be careful with how much I reveal to him. What if he gets starstruck over my family? I'll always wonder if he's interested in me or just them.

As I wait for what I hope is a respectable time to pass, my eyes fix on Lor's collection of playing cards—all jokers—under a big piece of glass on the wall. They're from foreign countries, and some look wicked, like they're leering at me. They give me the creeps.

I sit up and face away. Lor always brought a little something back from overseas tours and loved telling stories of his obscure finds. The one thing he's never talked about is the framed postcard of a city street in Budapest that sits on a small table against the wall.

"Someday, I'll explain it," is the only thing he'd said when I asked about it once.

Lor's phone vibrates again. I go ahead and text my number to Alex and take Lor's phone to him.

He's sitting in bed, reading something on his iPad.

"How's it going?" I ask, unsure what his mood will be like.

"Shitty," he deadpans and gestures for me to sit in the chair beside his bed.

On the sofa across the room, Jojo sits awfully close to Darnell, Lor's new physical therapist who's also a nurse.

Jojo stands and smooths out the crinkles in her dress. "I feel like having some coffee, don't you, Darnell?" She gives him an expectant look.

"Coffee does sound good." His voice is deep and rich, and his hand grazes the small of her back as they leave the room.

Lor and I exchange amused glances.

"You know they're hooking up, right?" I ask Lor. "Or if they haven't, they will soon."

"Good for them, as long as they don't do it in here." He laughs, catching my eye. I hold his gaze. Is he testing *my* mood, as well? Looking away first, he says, "I ordered some books for you last week. Have they arrived yet?"

"Yesterday, while you were napping." I move some stuff aside on his nightstand, uncover a couple of books, and hold them up to show him. One is titled *How to Get a Teen-age Boy & What to Do With Him When You Get Him*, and the other, *Pole Dancing to Gospel Hymns*.

Lor's eyes bulge. "Eva, why'd you put 'em there? Someone might think they're mine."

"Then the joke would be on you. *Ha.*" I hand him the books. "Where did you find these?"

"eBay rabbit hole." His hours of boredom lead to obscure online purchases.

Sometimes they're nice surprises, like the autographed album of my favorite band, California Nine, but I could've done without the glitter bomb that came with it.

"This is great." He flips through one of the books. "But wait, there was supposed to be a third book. It had a dinosaur on the cover."

"*All My Friends Are Dead.* That one's cute. Thanks, I'll keep it."

"Hey, so uh…Jojo told me you moved to the guesthouse. I should've suggested it in the first place. It gives you a little more independence."

"Yeah, I need a place…to myself sometimes."

"Should I have Jojo bring in an interior decorator?" he offers, but I tell him no. I've slept better there than I ever did in the main house and don't want to change a thing.

"What else is new with you?" he asks.

"I'm volunteering at a repurposing center. Oh, and I bought a Prius. It's a hybrid. Go ahead, bring on the tree-hugging jokes."

"Nah." He shrugs. "Whatever makes you happy, Eva. Go for it."

"Thanks, but…you don't make it easy to be away from here." I wring my hands in my lap, tired of dancing around the elephant in the room.

After a moment of quiet, he says, "I'm sorry for last week. I got some news that I…didn't handle well."

"What?" I scoot to the edge of my seat, leaning toward him.

"Polly's Poison found a new guitarist. They're ending the hiatus without me."

"Oh, Lor, I'm sorry." I take one of his hands.

"Replacing me was inevitable." He shrugs. "But it stung worse than I expected."

"I know but promise you won't do anything like that again. Remember our deal?"

"I promise." He squeezes my hand.

"And don't fire Darnell, dammit. You'll walk again, but you have to put in the work."

"I will."

~ * ~

At ACR, Nadine and I are unloading a trailer of leftover lumber scraps from a construction site when a truck towing a tiny house rolls to a stop in the parking lot. The driver, a woman with short gray hair, gets out. "Howdy, folks."

Nadine greets her with a hug. "Sue, this is Eva. She's our newest volunteer."

"Hi, Eva." Sue shakes my hand. "I love to see young people interested in repurposing."

"Looks like you're ready to hit the road." Nadine gestures at the tiny house. "Blair's not home from college yet. She'll be sad she missed you."

"Yeah, but she and I keep in touch. I've sent her photos of the house. Let me show y'all inside." She gets a stepladder from the truck bed, and we use it to climb onto the tiny porch.

Inside, I'm reminded of the close quarters of a tour bus, but this has a kitchen, mini appliances, a ladder to a loft bed, and a built-in bathroom shower stall.

I take a seat in the kitchen nook, my mind and body relaxing in the small space. A new sense of contentment washes over me, making me aware how restless I've been lately. This stranger's tiny house feels more like home than the wide-open spaces of Casa Lor, or even the guesthouse.

"Where are you headed?" Nadine asks Sue, and I tune back into the conversation.

"I'll travel some, then park it on my brother's property in Arizona. This is about two hundred square feet, and it'll serve this old lady just fine."

"You aren't an old lady," Nadine chides. "Old ladies don't have adventures like this. But these walls are a little bare. Shall we visit the showroom for a few décor items?"

"I *have* had my eye on a couple of 'tiny' things." She and Nadine go to the showroom, and I finish unloading the lumber.

My phone vibrates in my pocket. I take it out, and my heart races at the sight of Alex's name. I duck into the warehouse and answer, "Hey, Alex."

"Hi, Eva. What do you have going on today?"

"I'm volunteering." With my free hand, I open a box on the sorting table. "At ACR."

"Oh yeah? I know the place. Maybe I could meet you there. I'll be done with classes at three. We could walk to Kudos Café. Can I buy you a cup of coffee?"

"Make it a soda, and you're on. Meet me here around four."

The excitement in his voice as we say goodbye gives me a thrill that lingers as I work on sorting donated supplies.

Around the end of my shift, I wander to the back of the warehouse to see what Nadine's husband, Hank, is working on.

He unrolls an old Metallica concert poster, lying it flat on a big table and using little bean bags to hold the corners down. The paper's warped and discolored.

"What happened to it?" I ask.

"A buddy of mine used to run a music store that went under years ago. Some of the stuff was in storage and got water damage. We hated to throw it away, and I have a mixed media idea. Let's see what else is in there." He points at a box with more posters.

We check the rest of them, and they're so cool. There's one from FU's tour when Polly's Poison opened for them years ago. It's in bad shape, having suffered more water damage than most of the others.

There're also posters of '80s movies and celebrity models. Cindy Crawford, Christie Brinkley, and the very one I'm named for— Linda Evangelista.

The final supermodel poster I unroll is in great condition, not damaged at all. The model's dress shows every curve. Her alluring "come hither" expression would make anyone feel like they're getting a personal invitation into a perfect world of beauty and ease.

Hank lets out a low whistle. "That's Sloane Silver, isn't it?"

He has no idea, and I'm not telling him, but that's my mom.

Chapter Ten
Alex

"Excuse me, where could I find Eva?" I ask a tall lady working at ACR's front counter.

"She's in the warehouse. Are you Alex?"

"Yes." I grin, unable to hide my happiness that Eva mentioned me to someone.

"You can go out there. The building across the parking lot."

My eyes have to adjust as I walk into the dim warehouse. Nobody's in this part of the building, but voices come from the back. I wipe my clammy hands on my jeans and head toward them. There's Eva, as beautiful as I remembered. She takes my breath away.

"Hey, Alex." Her voice is light and sweet. "This is Hank, one of ACR's co-owners."

"Nice to meet you, sir." We shake hands.

Eva passes a rolled-up poster to him. "Could you hang on to this one for me?"

"Sure, and if I don't see you again before you leave, have a good evening."

On our way out, Eva quietly says, "Keep in mind nobody here knows I'm Lor's sister."

"It's like you live a double life," I tease, and she makes her eyebrows dance.

In the showroom, she introduces me to Nadine, the tall lady, and gives me a tour.

"My dad has a workshop and builds furniture sometimes," I say. "I help him whenever I can. It's one of his hobbies, but he's never done anything with reclaimed wood."

"That's what this place is all about." The hint of pride in her voice is cool.

She's quiet on our way to the café. I'm at a loss for words until I ask, "How's Lor doing?"

"He's okay. We talked. He promised no more schemes."

I'm glad and also thankful one of those schemes led to my meeting Eva.

At the café, we choose a small table by the window and sit across from each other. A server takes our drink orders.

"How long have you lived in Austin?" I ask.

"A few weeks."

"Oh, not long then. Where'd you live before?"

Her eyes narrow, and she hesitates.

"Sorry," I say. "I know you don't want people knowing much about you."

"It's okay. I'm not *from* anywhere. I've moved around a lot." She smiles, like she's trying to assure me I didn't upset her. I appreciate that.

The server brings our drinks. "Is there anything else I can get you folks?"

"No, thanks," we answer together.

Eva peels the paper from her straw, and I notice her left index finger is…not there, but there isn't a stump. Her hand's like an optical illusion. There isn't even a knuckle where the finger would be joined to her hand. It's fascinating, but I try not to stare. We sip our Cokes, and I act like I didn't notice anything different.

"I'm glad it was just your cousin who answered when I called," she says. Her cheeks redden. "A girl answering your phone made me think it might've been your girlfriend."

"No, there's no girlfriend."

The glimmer of relief on her face is the encouragement I need. "I have a confession. The night we met Hector told me to do something I haven't been able to do."

Suspicion—or dread—fills her expression. "Uhhh, what?"

My heart's gonna pound through my chest. "Eva, I haven't been able to forget anything about you, much less *all* about you." I hold my breath and wait for her reaction.

Her face breaks into a slow grin. "Smooth." She chuckles.

"Thanks. I try." I bow my head in acceptance of her sarcastic compliment. "Seriously, I'm glad you called the other day."

"Truth is, I've been…well, I want to know you better."

Yes! "What would you like to know?"

Her left hand is on her glass now, and her right hand rests on the table in front of her. She flattens the straw wrapper and crinkles it back up. "Are you from around here?"

"I grew up in Florence, a small town an hour and a half north of here."

"What year are you in at UT?"

"Sophomore. How about you?"

"No plans for college yet. For now, I'm trying to be around for Lor."

I lean forward and place my hand beside hers. "He's lucky to have you. Y'all seem close."

"I like to think we are, even with the big age difference." She curls her pinky around my thumb, and it's the touch I've craved. The warm softness of her skin, sliding across mine, sends sparks of electricity through me. I press my hand under hers, palm to palm.

Her chest rises with a deep breath, like she feels the same sparks, and we watch each other across the table. It's like we're in our own little world, just the two of us.

A clatter from the café's kitchen breaks the spell, making Eva startle, but she doesn't pull away. She rubs the calluses at the base of my fingers. "What are these from?"

I shrug. "I guess I've had them most of my life, growing up on a ranch and working outdoors. But most recently they're from lifting weights at the gym." My thumb traces the almost invisible scar where her left index finger's missing. "What happened here?" I quietly ask.

Chapter Eleven
Eva

I shiver at the gentle grazing of Alex's thumb on my hand scar. "I lost it in a shark attack," I joke, but his face pales in horror. *"Kidding,"* I'm quick to say.

His shoulders sag, and he laughs. "You had me for a sec there. What really happened? Tell the truth."

The truth? I've never told anyone the whole story, but I'm strangely compelled to be transparent with Alex.

"Lor accidentally closed a hotel door on my hand when I was five," I admit. "He was drunk and didn't know I was behind him. For some reason, I put my hand on the hinge side of the door. My finger was severed."

Alex's smile fades. "Eva, I'm sorry."

"I don't remember the pain. What I *do* remember is, by the time Lor realized what happened, my finger—which was lying on the floor—had gotten stepped on *twice*. Once by him and again by his ditzy girlfriend. She was also drunk. I think she screamed more than I did."

"Why couldn't it be reattached?"

"It got left behind when Lor freaked out and drove me to the hospital. Drunk. The nurse asked where the finger was, and Lor fainted, right there in the ER. It's a wonder he didn't hit his head on anything." For some twisted reason, the memory's kinda funny to me now, and I laugh. "He was only out for a few seconds, but everybody forgot *me* and was falling all over themselves to help him."

"At least you're able to laugh about it now. I can see the headline: 'Guitar god—out cold in the ER.' How did you stay anonymous with all that happening?"

"My mom arrived, and she must've paid the doctors and nurses off." I proceed to explain how Mom insisted on reconstructive surgery so I wouldn't have a stump. "The surgeon amputated what was left of the finger, knuckle and all, and removed the bones connecting my index finger to my thumb. Then, he connected the bones at the base of my thumb to my middle finger."

"It's cool-looking." He takes my hand in his and studies it. "I didn't even notice you're missing a finger until I watched you unwrap your straw a few minutes ago."

"You have a great poker face. Doesn't it gross you out?"

"No." He slides his fingers between mine, entwining them. It sends pulses of excitement racing through me until they settle, warm and buzzing between my legs. I squeeze my thighs together and try not to sound breathless as I change the subject. "What kind of music do you like?"

"Country mostly. You?"

"My favorite band is California Nine."

"They're like…emo, right?" His nose scrunches.

"Yeah." I laugh. "But I think they prefer to be called pop punk."

He takes a drink. "I listened to some Polly's Poison since meeting y'all."

"And? Are you becoming a fan?"

He ducks his head a bit. "Not my thing."

"Mine neither," I admit.

"But I *can* appreciate his guitar skills."

"Yeah." I'm sad those days are over, at least for now. "He was talented."

"Do you mind me asking what happened to him? I won't tell anyone."

"Polly's Poison was filming a music video. There were pyrotechnics involved, and he was wasted. Tried to do something stupid and fell from a scaffolding that was part of the set. He has a spinal injury. Plus, you saw his burns, right?"

"Yeah. Do the doctors think he'll walk again?"

"Hopefully. With time, the nerve damage from the burns could heal."

Alex's phone chimes. "I'm sorry, but I've gotta go. There's a study group I kinda forgot about."

"Oh, okay." I try to hide my disappointment we can't spend more time together.

As we're leaving, he says, "This is where Lor arranged for me to meet the penguin tattoo guy who gave me the whiskey."

I laugh. "What a coincidence. That was the first day I went to ACR. I wonder if you were at the café at the same time I was down the street."

The fact we ran into each other later that day feels…serendipitous.

"We might've crossed paths sooner than we even knew," he says, like he's thinking the same thing. He takes my hand, and my stomach does somersaults.

Chapter Twelve
Alex

I want to stop right here on the sidewalk and kiss Eva, but it's too soon. It's safe to say I'm already in over my head with her, though, as evidenced by the dumbass move of forgetting the finance study group. I *cannot* afford to bomb Thursday's test.

Eva and I approach my truck in the ACR parking lot, and I reluctantly release her hand.

"This was fun," I say. "I'll talk to you later, okay?"

"Yeah, good luck with the study group." She waves on her way to a silver Toyota Prius.

The sun bathes her hair in its rays, making her look even more radiant. Everything in me wants to stay, hang out with her more. But it's time to put my nose to the grindstone, as Dad would say. At least I'll have time off for spring break soon. Maybe Eva and I can have a real date.

~ * ~

I bust my ass the rest of the week, working hard in every class. The finance test was killer, and I'm relieved it's done. I want to kick back in my room and call Eva to ask if she wants to go out next week but as I approach my dorm room, there's a sock on the door handle.

I silently curse Sean and head for the library. On the way, I call Eva.

"How was the test?" she asks.

"I think I did all right."

"It's good to hear your voice." She sounds so damn sexy.

If only she could see the smile she puts on my face. "I much prefer your voice to Professor Lipshutz's."

"Lipshutz?" She laughs. "For real?"

"Yeah, you know how some people have thin lips? All he has is a horizontal line for a mouth. And he doesn't talk loud enough, so we have to watch his mouth, like we're reading his lips. It's not easy when the guy doesn't *have* lips."

The sound of her laugh soaks into me. "Hey, next week is spring break," I say. "I'll be in Florence at my parents' house, but could I take you to dinner one night?"

"I'd like that."

After we hang up, I've got a bunch of pent-up energy. More like too much Eva on my mind. Wish I could talk with someone about her without breaking her trust or the NDA. It's weird to be back in a situation where I have to keep quiet. When I was with Angie, she'd said, "People won't understand, with our age difference and all."

And I'd agreed. Of course, I learned later she had other reasons.

Chapter Thirteen
Eva

Friday, I receive an email from Sue, the lady with the tiny house. I'd asked Nadine how she was doing, and she shared Sue's contact info with me. I enjoy reading her Tiny House Adventures, as she calls them. This time, she sent pictures of the Grand Canyon. I envy her independence and adventurous spirit.

I reply to her, and Stella knocks on the guesthouse door. She has a package that came for me in the mail. It's DVDs—seven seasons of a show called *Buffy the Vampire Slayer*.

I carry them to the main house and to Lor's room. When he sees me, he turns his phone over, screen facedown. Jeez, I hope he isn't planning something crazy again.

"Thanks, Captain Random." I show him the box of DVDs.

"You'll love the show. Let's watch it now."

I don't have any plans today, and something tells me I should keep an eye on him. I pop the first disc into his DVD player. He scoots to the side of his hospital bed, making room for me, and we watch *Buffy*.

He was right; the show's great, and I love to hear him laugh so much, even if it's at my expense for freaking out at jump scare moments.

"Have you watched the whole series?" I ask after the second episode.

"Years ago. There's another show called *Angel*. A spinoff. I'll order those next." He yawns, and it isn't the first time.

"You should rest." I stand and smooth out my rumpled clothes. "Is there anything you need before I return to the guesthouse?"

"Are you going anywhere for the rest of the day?" There's a

weird gleam in his eyes.

Suspicious, I narrow my eyes at him. "What an odd question. What are you up to?"

He shrugs. "Just wondering if you'll be around. There might be another surprise for you today. Don't worry. It has nothing to do with ferrets or strippers."

An hour later, Mom calls me. Was this Lor's surprise? "Hi, Mom!"

I'm anxious to tell her about Alex, but the first thing she says is, "Come see me in the main house. We're here for a visit."

"What? For real?" I jump up and head over.

Bursting into the house, I greet Mom with a hug and inhale her familiar perfume. Her hair is perfectly styled, as usual. She's either wearing a pushup bra, or she got a boob job. She looks way younger than fifty-seven, but I haven't seen her in weeks and, for the first time ever, I notice wrinkles around her eyes and mouth.

The house is full of people. This must be what Mom meant by "we're" here—it's The Fabulous Undertakers and part of their entourage.

"There's little Eva," someone shouts, and I'm lifted off my feet by my dad and uncle, FU's guitar player and bassist.

They go by the stage names Spike and Ike, which is what I call them. They're identical twins, ten years younger than Mom, and are so alike most people can only tell them apart by their tattoos. Ike has a couple; Spike has a lot, including a sleeve.

"I can't believe you're here!" I exclaim.

They set me down, and I hug Spike. His familiar cinnamon scent takes me back to all those hours at his side in recording studios.

"My turn." Ike kisses my cheek, and his rough stubble reminds me of how wishy-washy he is on growing out a beard.

"You've got a little something on your face," I joke.

He tweaks my nose and kisses my cheek. "Baby girl, it's good to see you."

Mom watches us, beaming her multi-million-dollar smile.

The elevator dings and there's Lor, being pushed in his wheelchair by Darnell. Mom hugs him, and he waves at the others in the room. They begin approaching, saying hello. "Glad you're here," he says. "Make yourselves at home."

I notice the bus driver and a roadie are bringing in luggage. If they're staying here, how will we make sure Lor doesn't drink? People are stocking the bar at this moment.

I search for Jojo, but I'm intercepted by Johnny, the drummer.

"Eva!" He gives me a big hug and introduces me to a redhead named Rhonda, referring to her as his girlfriend.

I wonder how long Rhonda's been around. Ever since losing his wife ten years ago to a lethal drug and alcohol combination, Johnny's gone through women like crazy.

"Nice to meet you," I say to Rhonda and ask Johnny, "Are Toby and Talina here?"

"They're in there." He points toward the kitchen.

Jittery with excitement, I step through the swinging door and spot Johnny's kids at the bar, noshing on some of Hector's leftovers. I tap them on their shoulders. "Hey, you guys."

Talina, a few weeks older than me and sporting spiky purple hair, squeals. "Eva! This is going to be a blast. We're staying with you for a whole week."

"A week?" Some warning on this would've been nice. I've spent a lot of time with these two in close quarters. It was mostly fun, but not always easy.

Toby, who's eighteen, shoulder bumps me. "We're crashing in the guesthouse with you. This place is the bomb. What have you got here, like ten bedrooms?"

"Counting mine in the guesthouse, there's nine."

"Ha! *Nine.*" He taps my left hand, reminding me that Nine—as in only nine fingers—was a nickname for me that he tried to make stick when we were kids.

A blonde I don't recognize speaks with Hector in Spanish. "Who's she?" I ask.

"Missy, your mom's 'lady's maid,'" Toby says.

Huh. So, Mom got a boob job *and* a maid. A lot has changed while I've been in Austin.

Jojo enters, the picture of calm, as if the house *hasn't* been invaded by an additional dozen people. "When did you find out we'd have company?" I ask her.

"A couple days ago. Your brother wanted to surprise you. I've hired extra kitchen and maid staff. And don't worry, Lor swears he won't drink, and Darnell will be here most of the time."

This eases my mind. "Great. Sounds like you've got it under control."

Jojo gives my arm a gentle squeeze and leaves, saying, "Everything will be fine, Eva. Oh, and Rob has placed some guys in the guard house."

Talina grumbles, "Ugh, *Rob.* Babysitting us has been added to his security duty."

"Y'all are getting into so much trouble you need a babysitter?" I tease.

"Y'all?" Toby laughs. "I take it you didn't hear about Talina sinking a boat?"

"No! When? Where?"

Talina rolls her eyes and laughs as Toby says, "At a party in New York. Talina and this other girl took the neighbor's boat out on the water to set off fireworks—"

"Leftovers from New Year's," she interjects.

"And a bottle rocket went off in the wrong direction," he continues. "It caught another boat on fire and sunk it. Thank God nobody was hurt." He frowns at his sister. "But you're damn lucky you weren't arrested."

"No kidding. What'd Johnny say?" I ask.

"Dad freaked and grounded me. What a joke. I'm almost twenty-one!" She saunters away, calling for Baxter, the roadie she hooks up with off-and-on.

"She's a wild card lately," Toby says. "A few nights after the fireworks incident, she snuck out of the hotel to hang with some people she'd met at the party. Yours truly tagged along to make sure she was safe, but Dad's *girlfriend* narced on us."

"The redhead?"

"Rhonda. I bet she won't be around much longer. She expects Dad to act like a parent. Kinda late for him to start now. You know what it's like. None of our parents act much like parents."

"My mom did all right by me," I say in her defense, but I *do* know what he means. Mom was never much for parental supervision. And Spike and Ike—whom I consider equal father figures—haven't played big parenting roles either, other than doting on me and trying to spoil me.

"I guess your mom's been better than my dad," Toby says. "Plus, you had a nanny."

"She wasn't a nanny. Vanessa was my governess. I nicknamed her Govern'Essa."

"Nanny. Governess. What's the difference?" He takes the last bite of lasagna on his plate.

"A governess is also a teacher."

Talina swings back in. "Can we see your place, Eva?"

I lead them to the guesthouse, which isn't much compared to the palatial main house, but there's plenty of room for me. A kitchen, small living room, and a bedroom and bathroom.

"You can share my room with me," I tell Talina. "We'll stick

Toby on the pullout sofa."

He takes a six-pack of beer from a duffle bag he brought in, and Talina turns on my stereo, cranking up a rap song. My quiet space has been officially invaded.

Chapter Fourteen
Alex

My brother, Devin, is the only one home when I arrive in Florence on Friday afternoon. He's slouched on the couch with a beer— not something our parents would approve of, but that never stops him.

"What's up?" I ask, carrying my bag in. "Didn't expect you to be here."

"I moved back in yesterday. I'm between jobs. And girlfriends."

"What's-her-name kicked you out, huh?"

"I left because *I* wanted to." He gets up and follows me to my old room. "I was tired of her nagging me. You know how it is, right? Oh wait." He taps his temple. "What am I thinking? You wouldn't know since you've never even had a girlfriend."

He doesn't know about Angie. Scratch that, he knows *about* her, like *who* she is, but not that I was with her. He and I met her at the same time last summer. We worked on her ranch together until Devin quit after two weeks.

"What, no comment?" he taunts. I ignore him and unpack a few things. He runs a hand through his shaggy hair. "Poor Alex. Still haven't been laid. Have you even been kissed?"

My jaw tightens, and I don't say a word, determined not to let him chip away at the confidence I've gained over the last year. He blocks the doorway as I go to leave my room. I square my shoulders and shove past him, back into the living room.

"Oooh, you gonna beat me up?" His eyes skim my arms and chest with a glimmer of realization.

I'm no longer the weakling he loves to bully. And he's out of shape, looking more doughy than muscular.

Before I do something stupid, I leave the house, saying, "I forgot my phone in the truck."

He steps onto the porch and watches me with a smirk on his ugly mug.

Screw this. I'm not going back in there with him while no one else is home. I get in and drive off. Devin shoots the bird at me. Real mature.

Mom teaches at the middle school, and I head over there to surprise her.

"Alex!" She hugs me. "Good to see you, but I'm on my way out. Gotta pick up your sister."

"Want me to pick Lena up for you?"

"She'd love that, and y'all should head straight home. I'm making your favorite dinner, and I want some help. You better hurry. Lena worries if she's the last one to be picked up."

I make the five-minute drive to the high school and spot my sister, Lena, with a group of other kids. As soon as I park and get out, she runs and throws her arms around me. I lift her off her feet in a hug and swing her around, loving the sound of her laughter. She has Down syndrome, high functioning.

"Alex, what are you doing here?" Her big, round eyes are full of happy surprise.

"I'm on spring break for the next week. Did you think I wouldn't visit to make sure my little sis is staying out of trouble?"

"More like *you* need to stay out of trouble." She takes me to meet her friends. They seem like good kids, and I'm glad they're nice to Lena. Not everybody is.

On the way home, my phone chimes with a text. I ignore it, and Lena grabs the phone off the seat and asks, "Who is Angie?"

"What?" I almost swerve off the road. "Nobody. Give me the phone." I reach for it.

"You're not supposed to use the phone and drive," she says with authority.

"I won't. But come on. Let me have it."

"Bossy much?" she jokes but hands the phone to me.

I slide it under my thigh, feeling like it'll burn through my jeans from whatever poisonous text Angie sent that Lena could've seen.

I arrive at the house and read the message.

> *This is Angie. We should talk. You can't ignore me*
> *forever. I think of you all the time. I'm sorry for how*
> *things turned out, and I want to make it up to you.*

Make it up to me by leaving me alone.

I hit send and block the number. Yet again.

Beside me, Lena sighs. "You're mad. What's wrong?"

"Nothing for you to worry about." I smile to assure her, and we get out of the truck.

"Devin moved back in." Her tone's grave as she points at his blue truck.

"Don't worry. I'll try to get along with him."

Later, after Mom's delicious dinner of chicken and dumplings, Dad shows me a dining table he's building in the barn. "Your mom has wanted me to do this for years. I'll surprise her with it next Saturday in time for a dinner party she's been planning. I'll need your help to finish it in time."

"Sure, I'd love to help while I'm here. But, uh…I do have some plans. I met a girl, and I'm planning to go out with her sometime next week."

Dad's eyes widen, and he nods, as if to hide surprise. Since he doesn't know I was in a relationship before, I think he worries about my lack of dating experience. A moment of awkwardness sets in, and he pats me on the back. "Let me know what your schedule is. I might take time off from work, and we can knock out some chores around here."

Brady texts about meeting up with him and some friends of ours from high school. Good thing I brought my best boots and cowboy hat. We go to Cedar Park Dance Hall, thirty minutes from Florence. The dance hall's having an "All Country Music Night," and some of the girls from our class are here, including Jessica. She and I went to senior prom as friends and have been close since elementary. As we dance the Texas Two-Step, she keeps staring—at *me*. A couple of times she starts to say something and stops.

"Why so serious tonight?" I ask.

She glances around us, her forehead creased with worry. "I heard you'd been…with an *older* woman."

I freeze in place, but the room spins. I'm off balance and queasy.

Jess blushes, but she can't possibly feel as awkward as I do. I leave the dance floor. She tries to grab my hand, but I head outside for some air.

"Alex, I'm sorry." She follows me. "I wasn't even sure I believed it, but you're…there's something different about you. It made me think what I heard must be true. It is, isn't it? I can tell."

I try to put the brakes on the panic train and bank on the possibility she hasn't heard the whole story. "Who told you? Was it

Brady?" I'll kill him.

"No! As far as I could tell, the people I heard it from don't know you personally. What I overheard gave me the impression it was someone who knew...the woman you were with."

Oh shit. This is bad. "What did you hear?"

"You're gonna make me do this, aren't you?" She grimaces.

"You brought it up, so *yeah.*"

"Okay, okay. Several months ago, two women in the café were in a booth behind me, talking about a friend who had a fling with a younger guy named Alex. Something was said of him being from Florence and graduating a year before last. You were the only Alex in our class. I figured it was you."

I bet it was Angie's friends Michelle and Sydney. I met them once and had a feeling Angie mentioned me to them. "What were they saying?"

Jessica sighs. "They were saying there's only one reason a teenage guy would be with an older woman like that, and you probably got *quite* the education. This is embarrassing."

She's embarrassed? I'm the one whose face is on fire.

We lean against the wall, silent. Sex was a big reason I was with Angie but not the *only* reason. We had a relationship. We also did other boyfriend-girlfriend stuff, but not in public anywhere around Florence. If I'd only known what I was getting myself into.

Hell, who am I kidding? Even if I'd had a crystal ball, I would've hooked up with Angie. There I was, spending tons of time alone with a hot, older woman who was seducing *me.* Was it worth it? Maybe at first, but not with the way it ended. Talk about a recipe for small town scandal.

Jessica breaks the silence. "Remember in ninth grade, Brady got pantsed by a junior?"

I laugh, despite my sour mood. "It was a *bad* day for poor Brady."

"And the time Kayla puked in the lunchroom after she and Kristen had been drinking vodka from Sprite bottles?"

"Gross, don't remind me." I shudder. "I was in the splash zone."

"Oh, Trey and I got caught skipping class in eighth grade."

"What were you doing?"

"Making out in the janitor's closet." She giggles. "Your mom's the one who caught us."

"What? She never told me."

"Good, I'll have to thank her next time I see her. Oh, and senior year, Sam fell asleep on the bus home from a game and talked in his sleep about the cheerleader he was sitting with."

My sides ache from laughing. "Why are you telling me all this?"

She stands in front of me, hands on my shoulders. "Because, dumbass, you aren't the only one who's done something stupid or embarrassing. Don't be so hard on yourself."

"Easy for you to say."

Dread twists in my gut at the idea of more people knowing about Angie and me. It has to stay buried, or I can forget my parents ever being proud of me again.

Chapter Fifteen
Eva

I slowly awaken from a dream about Alex. His deep blue eyes gazed into mine, and our lips met in a slow, soft kiss. As the dream slips away, I stretch and open my eyes, confused to find Mom standing over me.

"Come on," she whispers. "I've missed you. Let's go shopping."

Talina's sound asleep on the other side of the bed, and I whisper back, "I need a few minutes to get ready." Now, I'm wide-awake and crawl out of bed, excited to spend the day with her.

"Don't forget—"

"A disguise? Duh." Like I could *ever* forget it if I'm going somewhere with her.

She blows me a kiss as she leaves.

We meet in front of Casa Lor several minutes later, where a black SUV from Jojo's favorite car service awaits. We climb in behind the driver and one of Rob's security guys.

"Eva, this is Missy." Mom gestures to the blonde in the back row, the one Toby and Talina said is Mom's lady's maid.

"Hi." I brush a long strand of the brunette wig over my shoulder and nod at Missy, curious how much she knows about me.

"Nice to meet you, Eva. Your identity's safe with me," Missy says, as if reading my mind.

I thank her and relax into the leather seat.

"It's admirable, how well you've remained anonymous," she adds. "I've seen lives and reputations destroyed by the media."

What she said rings true, making me think of Toby and Talina's mom. She wasn't famous, just the wife of a rock drummer, but when the celebrity press got wind of a relationship she'd had with a teacher in high school, her past became painfully present.

I was seven at the time, and the whole thing strengthened the resolve Mom instilled in me to stay unknown. I'm not hiding anything in my past, but that wouldn't stop fans and the media from expecting my life to provide entertainment value. It wouldn't stop them from fabricating stuff, either.

I shake off the dreary thoughts and tell Mom, "Catch me up on everything."

She rubs her hands together and dishes out details of what happened with the band since I've moved in with Lor.

With a twinge of jealousy at what I've missed, I ask, "What was the latest prank?"

"Ike got Spike really good. He decked out his bunk with Justin Bieber stuff. Plastered the wall with posters. The bed had a Bieber throw pillow, a Bieber blanket. The best part—rose petals around a Bieber doll, like a shrine or something. You have to see it to believe it." She opens her phone's camera roll and hands it to me.

I scroll through the photos and laugh. Mom joins in, and the sound of our giggles fills the SUV.

"Oh, Eva, I wish you'd been there." Her face is flushed from laughing. She leans against my arm. "But tell me, what's the latest with you?"

"I've been volunteering at a repurposing center."

"What's that?" She straightens and rests against the door.

I tell her about ACR, and soon the SUV turns onto a boutique-lined street. The driver announces our arrival at downtown Austin's 2ND Street District. He and Bruce, the security guy up front, discuss special prearranged accommodations for private entrances to certain boutiques.

Checking that the wig hides all my blonde hair, I ask Mom, "Who am I today?"

Her head whips around, and she gasps. "I almost forgot. How about…Bella?"

"Works for me." I slide on a pair of oversized sunglasses, and she puts on a floppy, wide-brimmed hat.

She's told me before how being spotted in public doesn't concern her unless there's a chance of me getting drawn into the attention. On the few occasions I've shown up in snapshots with the celebs in our family, I looked slightly different each time, thanks to various disguises. And in those rare photos, I'm in the background, facing away from the camera.

Managers and salespeople create a subtle barrier between us and other shoppers, but my goal is to be invisible to *them* as well. Not so easy when they give us the royal treatment behind the scenes. I trust they won't take pictures or video, but a lot of my energy's spent pretending to be someone else. I'm rusty at avoiding curious stares. It's more exhausting than I remembered.

As Mom browses from display to display, I find it easier to stay engrossed in a game on my phone. Staring at the screen, my face is shielded by the tresses of the brunette wig.

"Earth to Bella." Mom waves a hand in front of my eyes. "Isn't it cute?"

I glance at a summer dress she's holding. "Yeah, it's nice," I say, and my gaze falls right back to my phone. She must not notice my lack of excitement and moves on to another dress, chattering non-stop.

"Ooh, Bella, check this out." "Hey, Bella, I could see you in this." "Bella, do you like this dress?" She won't stop, and I have an absurd sense of not being *me* anymore. How the hell should I know what Bella likes?

The next time Mom calls me Bella, I wince and squeeze my eyes shut.

"Are you okay?" Mom touches my arm.

"I'm not feeling well." I press my fingers to my temples.

She guides me into a curtained dressing room. "Try not to puke or faint or anything." She lingers by the entry, eying me warily. "Are you good now?"

"I will be. You should keep shopping. I just need a minute." I sit on a bench in the small space.

"Maybe you're dehydrated. I'll have someone bring you a drink."

I close my eyes and lean on the wall, craving the freedom I've enjoyed without Mom.

My heart sinks, though. I love Mom, and I've missed her, but is this what Lor means when he talks about me finding independence?

"Excuse me, miss, are you Bella?" someone says.

I open the curtain. There's a lady, mid-twenties, offering me a bottle of water. Grateful, I take it, and she has an eager, starstruck look in her eyes.

"It must be cool to hang out with Sloane Silver, huh? How do you know her?"

"She's a friend of my mom's." I take a long, cold drink.

"Wow, where're you from?"

Cornered, I mutter the first thing to pop into my head. "I'm from

Budapest."

Her eyebrows rise, probably from disbelief since I don't have an accent.

Oops. I stand. Time to leave.

The lady moves aside, and Mom's standing there, the color drained from her face. She stares in my direction, her eyes glazed over.

I approach her. "What's wrong?"

She startles and snaps out of whatever made her look like she'd seen a ghost. "Oh, nothing." Her gaze flits to the lady. "We're good here. Thanks for your help."

The lady makes herself scarce as Mom shoos me back into the dressing room and closes the curtain.

"Eva, what made you think of…that place?" Mom whispers.

"What place? Oh, Budapest?" I shrug. "It came to mind because of the postcard. The one in Lor's living room." I note the clenching of her jaw as she turns away. "Does the postcard mean something? When I asked Lor, he wouldn't say."

"If he didn't tell you, it must be private." She faces me again, with a tight smile. "You've hardly shopped for yourself today, and I want to buy you *some*thing. Try these on." She hangs the dresses she's holding on a hook in the dressing room.

I absentmindedly flip through them, waiting for her to leave before I strip.

"Ev—Bella," she whispers. "*Why* are you checking price tags?"

I shrug. "I guess it helps me decide if something's worth it or not."

"*Worth* it?" She eyes me, head to toe, like I'm a stranger. And I do feel strange. Maybe she doesn't know me anymore. Do I even know myself?

I go through the motions of trying on the dresses to humor Mom. She insists on buying me a couple of them, but her smiles no longer reach her eyes.

Returning to Casa Lor, she stares out the window, her mood as dark as the tinted glass. I ride beside her, subconsciously scraping a thumbnail on my left hand's scar until it's raw. I don't ask Mom what's wrong. I shouldn't push. But now, more than ever, I want to ask Lor about the postcard again.

Chapter Sixteen
Alex

After helping Dad work on fences, I walk back to the house. I'm sweaty and hungry—and shocked to discover my truck's gone, but my brother Devin's truck *is* here.

I run inside and Lena hands me a piece of paper with Devin's sloppy handwriting. "Devin left you a note."

It says: My truck wouldn't start. Borrowed yours.

"What the—where'd he get a key to my truck?" I ask.

"Kitchen."

Oh yeah, Mom and Dad have spares for our vehicles in a kitchen junk drawer. They're for emergencies or whatever, *not* borrowing without asking. This screws my plans to drive into Cedar Park. I wanted to shop for a new shirt for my date with Eva.

I shower and hope Devin's back by the time I'm done. He isn't.

What could be wrong with his truck? He drove it yesterday.

I find his spare key in the drawer and try it. The engine starts, no problem. What's he up to?

It goes against my ideas of respecting boundaries, but I search his truck. The glove box has vehicle registration paperwork, a phone charger, some pawn shop tickets, and a pack of cigarettes. As I debate whether to "borrow" Devin's truck, my own pulls into the driveway.

Devin parks and gets out. "Thanks for letting me borrow your truck."

"I didn't *let* you borrow it. And your truck fired right up for me." I can't pass on the opportunity to taunt him and add, "Do Mom and Dad know you smoke?"

His head rears back in alarm. "What were you doing in my truck?"

"It isn't even *your* truck. The registration has your ex-girlfriend's name on it."

"So what?" He grabs a fistful of my shirt. "I bet yours has Angela Forsythe on it."

Adrenaline spikes through me, but I fight to keep my face neutral. It's true I bought my truck after working at Angie's ranch last summer, but Devin's comment implies he suspects something more.

"My truck is in *my* name." I square my jaw at him. "I paid for it. Unlike you, I can finish a job."

"Yeah? I bet you were Angie's punk-ass boytoy. You'd hook up with an older woman, wouldn't you, mama's boy?" He pats my cheek.

Something in me snaps. I ball my fist, rear back, and sink it into Devin's doughy gut. Air whooshes from him. He doubles over, coughing.

"I knew it." He manages a maniacal laugh. "I figured something was going on when she called me."

"She called *you*? Why?"

He hocks a loogy and spits. "She asked if I knew why you won't talk to her."

Shit. He must be lying. But why? How would he even come up with such a thing to lie about? It's so specific. "What'd you tell her?"

"I said, 'Hell if I know.' *My* question is why's she calling you at all?" He sneers.

I need a second to think and turn away, getting into my truck.

Before closing the door, I tell him, "She wants help again for this summer." It's believable, even to me, and I mentally applaud myself for thinking on my toes.

"Why are you ignoring her calls then?" he asks, hands outstretched.

"None of your business, but I have *other* summer job plans. Don't take my truck again." I drive off, hoping he'll keep his mouth shut about whatever he *thinks* he knows.

~ * ~

At dinner, Devin sits across from me, aiming devious smirks my way. The idea of him insinuating to our parents that something went on with Angie kills my appetite.

Lena, who's talked non-stop through dinner, raises her voice. "I'm going to the senior prom, and I want Alex to take me."

"Hey, why are you asking *him*?" Devin asks. "I could take you."

She eyes him dubiously. "Alex has a nicer truck, and he'll look better in a tuxedo."

Laughter erupts from everyone—except Devin.

"I'd be honored to take you," I tell Lena.

The doorbell rings, and Dad goes to the door. He returns with worry on his face and a couple cops at his heels. One of them, Pete, graduated with Devin. He says, "Apologies for interrupting. We have questions about the black truck out front. It's yours, right Alex?"

All eyes fix on me. My heart wrenches at the shock and disappointment on Mom's face.

"Yes, sir." I wrack my brain for what this could be about.

"Could you tell us where you were this morning?" the other officer asks, and across from me, Devin goes pale. He eases back in his chair, like he can shrink away.

"I was here, helping Dad with fence repair," I say.

"Until eleven, when I went into town for more supplies," Dad confirms.

"Did you drive your truck anywhere this morning?" Pete asks me.

I tell him I haven't, but Lena chimes in with, "Devin drove Alex's truck this morning." If she hadn't said it, I would've, and now everyone looks at Devin. A film of sweat covers his forehead.

"What's this about?" Dad asks him.

Devin won't meet his eyes.

"A bunch of small appliances and electronics were stolen from a storage unit," Pete says.

"The surveillance camera shows Alex's truck entering and leaving," the other officer adds and eyes Devin. "We need you to come with us to the station for further questioning."

Other than widening his eyes and flaring his nostrils, Devin doesn't move.

Dad stands and nudges his shoulder. "Let's go, son."

They leave, and Mom gets up. "Alex, can you stay here with Lena?"

"Yeah. I'll be here," I say. Mom squeezes my shoulder as she passes behind me.

Lena wrings her hands. "Is Devin being arrested?"

"I don't know," I tell her, nervous too. Nobody in our family has ever had cops show up asking questions before.

Mom and Dad return much later, without Devin, and they head straight for their room. I guess he *was* arrested because I overhear hushed conversations from their room about bail and lawyers. They emerge from their room late the next morning.

Dad pockets his keys. "We've got to tend to a situation with your brother."

Mom has tears in her eyes and hands me some money. "Who knows when we'll be back. Here's some money. Take your sister to lunch."

Lena bites her lip and paces the living room after they leave. "Devin's in trouble. Is it my fault? I told the police about the truck."

"You didn't do anything wrong. Try not to worry. Where do you want to have lunch?"

"The Florence Café." She claps, her mood brighter.

As we buckle up in my truck, I notice she's wearing lipstick, and it's a mess. I hand her a napkin and pull the visor down in front of her, tapping the mirror. "Here, you might want to—"

"It looks bad, doesn't it?" She frowns. "I gotta learn to put it on right."

"Why do you need it?"

"Girls wear makeup to make themselves pretty."

"You're beautiful with or without makeup, Lena."

This makes her happy. She wipes most of the lipstick off. Once we arrive at the café, I discover why she may have tried to put makeup on. One of the boys she introduced me to at her school the other day works here.

The boy calls out, "Hello, Lena," and approaches to take our order.

"Hi, Brandon." She gives him a sweet smile.

They chat, and after he walks away, I ask, "Why don't you ask *him* to prom?"

She swats at my arm and giggles. "Girls aren't supposed to ask guys out."

"You asked *me*."

"You're my brother! Besides, Brandon already has a date."

"His loss then. But maybe he'll save a dance for you."

Terror crosses her face. "Oh no, will you teach me how to dance?"

"What do you want to learn?"

"Tango. No, the Macarena. Or waltz."

"I don't know any of those. How about the Chicken Dance?"

"No!" She slaps her hand on the table for emphasis. "No Chicken Dance."

"All right, I can teach you the Texas Two-Step."

When we return home, Dad's truck is there. Lena runs inside. As I open my door, I receive a call from Eva. "It's been a crazy couple of days," I tell her and stay in my truck for privacy.

"Is everything okay?"

"Just...family stuff. My brother got into some trouble."

"I'm sorry. I didn't know you have a brother. Is he okay?"

I rub my temple and wish I hadn't mentioned Devin. "I think he'll be okay. I also have a sister. She's seventeen."

"Are you getting to spend some time with them this week?"

"Yeah, but what I'm really looking forward to is spending time with you."

"Ooh, someone's feeling cheesy," she teases and laughs.

I laugh with her but say, "Hey, I'm serious. I can't wait to see you."

"I'm looking forward to it. What's the plan?"

"Dinner Tuesday. I'll pick you up at six."

"When you arrive, you won't need a gate code. There'll be a guard to open it."

"Why the heightened security?" I ask.

"Um...we have some houseguests." That was vague, but I don't question it.

I look up as Dad leaves the house. Devin's behind him, a duffel bag in hand. They stand at Devin's truck for a moment, saying something I can't hear. Devin gets in his truck, and Dad goes to his. They drive away separately.

"Alex, are you there?" Eva asks.

"Yeah, sorry, Eva. I've gotta hang up now. See you Tuesday, okay?"

We hang up, and I go inside, a little shocked Mom and Dad must've kicked Devin out. I find Mom at the kitchen table, wiping her eyes with a tissue.

"What's going on?" I ask and sit beside her.

"I keep wondering, what did we do wrong? As a first child, he was our guinea pig. I made his life too easy. Did too much for him."

"Mom don't blame yourself. He's an adult."

"Yeah, but it's hard. A mother wants the best for her kids." She covers my hand with hers. "Thank you for staying on track. I'm proud you're doing well in college."

She wouldn't thank me if she knew how bad I did last semester. I shift in my seat and hope she doesn't notice my face flush with shame.

"Your dad mentioned you have a date this week," she says, thankfully changing the subject. "What's her name?"

"Eva." It feels good to say her name. I hope it isn't a betrayal of her trust. "She's beautiful. Blonde hair and green eyes. And she's got a great sense of humor. She's so cool, Mom. She volunteers at a repurposing center where they sell furniture and art made from recycling and reusing stuff."

"How interesting. I hope you have a good time on your date, and we can meet her sometime."

Chapter Eighteen
Eva

Wherever Spike and Ike are, there's sure to be a party, and Casa Lor's like a hotel, with people coming and going at all hours.

Ike enters the kitchen with his arm around a woman I don't recognize.

"Oh, great, *she's* here," Mom mutters and grips her coffee mug in both hands.

"Eva." Ike is beaming. "I'd like you to meet my girlfriend, Ingrid."

I shake hands with Ingrid and struggle with hiding my surprise. I had no idea Ike has a girlfriend. It's something Mom should've mentioned.

"This is my first time in Texas." Ingrid has a European accent. "Ike picked me up from the airport this morning." She's like a younger, taller clone of Mom.

"We met in New York." Ike hooks an arm around her tiny waist. They're adorable together.

Mom averts her eyes and stares out the window, and now the changes I've noticed make more sense. Granted, Mom's in a romantic relationship with Spike, but she's used to having equal attention from Ike. The three of them are weirdly co-dependent.

A loud crash outside interrupts my thoughts.

The four of us hurry out the front door and follow the loud stream of expletives emanating from the right side of the mansion. I stop short at the sight of a tour bus trailer that's backed into—my car! The driver's side of my new Prius is smashed in, the windows broken.

"What the hell!" My heart leaps into my throat as I rush toward the mangled vehicle. At the same time, Spike and Curtis, one of the band's bus drivers, scramble from the bus and approach me. "How did this happen?" I ask, catching a whiff of pot.

"Oh shit." Ike whistles. "What have you guys done?"

"I was trying to back up along here," Curtis says. "This is my fault—"

"And mine," Spike says. "I was riding shotgun and didn't check the mirror for him like I should've. Eva, honey, I'm sorry."

"For being high or for wrecking my car?" I'm not an idiot— growing up around bands, drugs are part of the scene, but I've never seen these guys do them. Alcohol's their usual vice.

Spike grimaces with an apologetic look and doesn't answer.

"I can't drive it like this," I complain. I've taken the week off from ACR but need a way to get there next week. I'd rather not use Lor's black exhaust-spewing Challenger again.

"We'll have it towed to a body shop. It'll be fixed before you know it," Spike says.

Mom pats my arm. "Eva don't worry. We can always buy you a new one."

I tear my gaze from the damaged car and glare at Mom with incredulity. I'm not sure why it pisses me off that buying a new one is Mom's go-to. "I don't need a *new* one. Just…fix it." I walk away.

Dazed and hoping for a moment alone, I retreat to the guesthouse.

Toby's on the sofa. He quickly shuts off the TV. "What's wrong?"

"Curtis and Spike wrecked my car. They backed a trailer into it."

"Is that what that sound was?"

"Yeah." I collapse beside him and fight back tears.

"Crap. Don't cry. What can I do? Oh, there's ice cream. Hector stocked your fridge." He jumps to his feet, but I pull him back.

"I won't cry." I lean on his shoulder. "It's only a car, right? Distract me. Put the TV back on. What were you watching?"

"Promise not to laugh?"

"I can't promise anything but tell me."

"*World of Dance*." His ears turn crimson.

"Go ahead and turn it back on." I prop my feet on the coffee table, and we watch the show together. "So, dancing, huh? Is this something you're interested in doing?"

"Very." He stares at the screen. "I want to be a backup dancer, like on a team. I mentioned it to Dad. He said, 'That's for bubblegum-chewing pop stars.'"

I make a disgusted face. "Ugh, what does he know about anything?"

"Besides hard rock, not much, but my cousin works at Millennium Dance Complex in L.A." He points at the screen. "She said she'd give me lessons."

"You should. Don't let your dad steal your joy."

Toby gives me a funny look at first, then nods. "You're right. I'll find a way to bring it up with Dad again." He pauses the TV and tilts his head toward the door. "Hear that?"

Someone's strumming a guitar outside. I walk over and open the door. Curtis is on his knees, giving me sad puppy dog eyes. Behind him, Spike plays one of Lor's guitars. He and Ike sing the chorus of their song, "Little Eva," and it tugs at my heartstrings. I'm a sucker for slow, emotional songs. This one's the best.

"A tow truck is already on the way," Curtis says. "Do you forgive us?"

"Okay," I say, unable to stay mad at these guys.

He crushes me in a hug.

Spike hugs me next. I hold my breath against the faint smell of pot in his long hair.

~ * ~

Tuesday afternoon spirals into a wardrobe crisis. I've changed clothes three times for tonight's date, unable to decide what to wear and with what shoes. I wish Talina was here to help, but I don't know where she is. I've searched the main house for Mom and can't find her either.

Spike calls and tells me to come out front of the main house. As soon as I open the door, he says, "Surprise! Look what we got for you."

Yikes! It's a huge, shiny new, red truck. Spike, Ike, and Curtis stand beside it, grinning.

"It's your early birthday present," Ike says. "Happy twenty-first!"

I lean against the doorframe, lightheaded. This must be a joke. They wouldn't buy me a great big honking truck without talking with me first, would they? I search their faces. They're serious.

Speechless, I try to return inside, pretending the truck was a hallucination, but they gleefully drag me back out and off the porch. They're so proud of themselves, listing the truck's awesome features. It has a crew cab, tons of shiny chrome, leather seats, moonroof, backup camera, NAV system, and satellite radio. The hulking beast gleams dark red. They get points for picking my favorite color, but how could they think I'd want a truck like this?

Spike hands me the key fob. "We wanted you to have something Texas-sized."

"I thought the Prius was being repaired," I say in a small voice.

"It is, and you'll still have it if you want," Ike says, "but we want you to have this."

Lor, wheeled outside by Darnell, whistles. "*That* is a bad-ass truck."

"Did you have something to do with this?" I ask.

"I knew they were planning it. I told them to buy one with a diesel engine."

Ike drapes an arm over my shoulders. "Do you like it?"

I hate to act ungrateful when they're clearly hopeful I'll be gaga about this gift.

"Yeah, um, it's nice," I say. "Any idea how many miles per gallon it gets?"

"Who freakin' cares?" Lor asks.

"*I* do. Is that such a crime?" My irritation disappears the instant a black truck heads up the driveway. Alex! I run onto the porch, panicked. "Listen, you guys, the truck is *great*. I love it, but I've got a uh—my friend's here to pick me up. I have to go." I need them to get lost. I'm not ready to introduce Alex to them, but he's already parking and emerging from his truck, and *holy cowboy*! I never expected to be so attracted to a guy in western jeans and boots.

"Hey, what's *he* doing here?" Lor pauses, and a devious grin spreads across his face. "Oh, I see. You're going on a *date*. Hey guys, Eva's got a date!"

"Gee, thanks, Lor, for announcing it to everyone," I mumble and leave the porch to greet Alex who's looking around, probably wondering why there's a welcoming party.

"Hey." I smooth my hands down the sides of the dress I guess I'll be wearing on our date.

"Are these the guests you mentioned?" Alex asks me as Spike and Ike approach.

"Yep. This is...Spike and Ike." I gesture at the curious faces of my dad and uncle.

Alex does a double-take—*of course* he recognizes them as The Fabulous Undertakers, but he recovers quickly. "Hi, I'm Alex. It's nice to meet you."

Spike gives Alex an exaggerated, firm handshake. He and Ike are both puffed up, like they want to appear bigger next to Alex, who has several inches on them.

I introduce Alex to Curtis and explain, "He's one of the tour bus drivers for FU. And you remember my brother Lor, of course." I point toward the porch. Alex greets Curtis and waves at Lor, who waves back and smirks.

I clear my throat. "I need to run to the guesthouse for something, then I'll be ready." Unwilling to leave Alex standing here. I take his hand and squeeze. "Come with me."

We pass through the main house. "Are those guys friends of your brother's?" he asks.

"Um, yes. Oh—what's this?" Rose petals litter the floor inside the guesthouse.

Confused, I follow the trail leading to my room without considering that Alex is following right behind. He sees what I do: Baxter, the roadie, stretched out on my bed, naked except for the corner of the sheet covering his crotch.

"Baxter, what the hell?" I recoil into the hallway.

Alex's face has paled. "That's *your* room?"

"Yeah, but this isn't what it—"

"Dammit, Eva!" Baxter yells. "I thought you were gone. I was waiting for Talina."

"I need something from in there."

"Gimme a sec."

Some of the color returns to Alex's face, and I press a palm to his chest. "I'm sorry for this. Baxter's a roadie, and Talina's the drummer's daughter. She's been staying in my room."

He puts a hand on mine and coughs into his other, covering a laugh. "I understand now."

"You can come in," Baxter says.

Rushing through the room, I grab my purse and phone. "I have no idea where Talina is, and I'm taking *this* with me." I take a bottle of champagne from an ice bucket beside the bed. "And do me a favor. Burn the bed when you're done." As I usher Alex through the door, I think better of what I said and yell back to Baxter, "You know I don't really mean *burn* it, right? But replace the sheets, would ya?"

Alex's laugh is a relief. I'm glad he understands Baxter wasn't waiting for *me*. Alex brushes a hand down my arm. "Ready?"

"Yes. Get me away from this crazy place."

He points at the champagne in my hand. "Are we bringing that with us?"

"You want to?"

He laughs again. "Sure, why not?"

Chapter Nineteen
Alex

It's safe to say finding a naked guy in your date's bed isn't the best way to begin the night, but the situation was hilarious once I understood the naked guy wasn't waiting for Eva.

We return to the driveway, and the rock stars are gone.

"That was...unexpected," I say as I open the passenger door for Eva.

"You're telling me." She climbs in, her red dress showing her legs off nicely.

On my way to the driver's side, I also admire the red Ford F350 King Ranch truck parked nearby. Man, what's it like to have so much money?

"Are you hungry?" I ask and start my truck.

"Starving."

"I know a good steakhouse. You're not a vegetarian, are you?"

"Ha! No, I'll take steak over tofu any day." She holds up the bottle of champagne. "What should we do with this?"

"I have an idea."

I pull in at the first convenience store I see and buy a bag of ice. As I carry it to the truck bed where I have a cooler under the retractable cover, Eva hops out and hands me the bottle.

"Do you always prepare for your dates to bring their own champagne?" she jokes.

I laugh. "The cooler's for bottled water when I'm working with my dad on the ranch."

Her eyes linger on my biceps as I lift the cooler into the truck bed. Her impressed expression is a total turn-on. I hope the night goes well. I sure want to kiss her.

After placing our orders at the steakhouse, she asks me about my family.

"My dad's in the insurance business, and my mom teaches middle school English. They have a small ranch in Florence that's been in the family for generations."

Her eyes sparkle as she listens. "And didn't you say your dad builds stuff?"

"Yeah, he's building a dining room table to surprise my mom. I've been helping him."

"Sounds fun."

"When he talks about retirement, it always circles back to building stuff."

I'm about to ask what her parents do when the arrival of our salads interrupts the conversation. We both instantly grab our forks and drag our red onions and cucumbers to the edges of our plates, which makes us laugh.

"Hey, something we have in common." She raises her water glass, and I clink mine with her in a toast.

"What's your major at UT?" she asks.

"Business management." It's tough to sound excited. My parents pushed me into it, but I don't know what else I want to do, so I go along with it for now.

"Is it hard?"

"Harder than I expected," I admit. "And, since you shared a secret of yours, I'll tell you one of mine. I tanked my first semester. I'm on academic probation." Worried what Eva will think of me, I hold my breath.

"That sucks." Her voice and expression hold no judgment, just sympathy.

"My parents don't know. I didn't want to disappoint them. My brother does that enough for both of us. I'd hate for them to think I'm following in his footsteps." It feels good telling Eva this stuff. Hopefully, she'll trust me more for being transparent. "Thank God, I'm back on track this semester."

"I wonder if I'd be cut out for college." Her cheeks redden. "Nobody in my family went."

"Well, what kind of things are you interested in?"

"Lately, tiny houses." She chuckles. "But what college major would that be?"

"Hmm, good question. Architecture? Or maybe environmental

science."

"Ugh, I almost failed every science class. It didn't matter what tutor I had." She talks with her hands, animated. Adorable.

"So, tiny houses?" I need a distraction from how soft her lips look. "Tell me more."

"I met a lady at ACR who had one built, and I love the minimalism. Sounds crazy for someone living at Casa Lor, right?" The way she says Casa Lor cracks me up.

"Where did you live before?" I take a drink.

"Nowhere," she says, almost sadly. "I've moved around a lot. Have you traveled much?" she asks me as the waiter serves our entrees.

"I used to visit my grandparents in Oklahoma every summer. Otherwise, I've never left Texas." I'm embarrassed by how boring my life must seem.

"Texas *is* pretty big."

I appreciate her attempt to downplay my lack of travel experience. "What's your favorite place to visit?"

Her eyes light up. "California. I love the PCH."

The waiter refills our drinks, and I take the opportunity to google PCH on my phone.

Chapter Twenty
Eva

Alex sets his phone back on the table, screen facing up.

"Were you googling PCH?" I ask, unable to hide my amusement.

He turns red but grins. "I had no idea Publisher's Clearing House was in California."

"No, I meant Pacific Coast Highway," I clarify.

"I know that...*now*." His foot nudges mine under the table. "Why's the PCH your favorite?"

"I love how you can drive with the ocean on one side and mountain views on the other." I can almost smell the salty air as I describe the 17 Mile Drive and Big Sur. "San Francisco is awesome, too. Golden Gate Bridge and Alcatraz. Are you an outdoorsy person?"

"I grew up on a ranch, so to some extent, yeah, but I'm not much into hiking or camping."

"Me neither, but California's redwood forests are incredible. And most of the beaches are gorgeous, with powdery sand and brilliant blue water."

Blue like your eyes, I think to myself. His lips are gorgeous, full and smooth. Now I can't stop thinking of kissing them.

"What else do you like about California?" he asks.

"San Diego. My grandparents live there." I sigh happily.

By the time we finish eating, I've talked more than I meant to about places I've been. I hope he doesn't feel like I'm showing off.

"Your life sounds amazing," he says, paying the check. "Mine's boring."

"Not boring. Normal. I could use more normal in my life, believe me." I glance at my phone and show him texts I've received from Lor in the last hour. Pictures of clown couples. Together. In compromising positions.

"What the…" Alex grimaces.

"That's my brother's twisted humor." I tap the screen, deleting the photos. "He knows I hate clowns, and I guess he figures what better way to interrupt my date than to send pictures of clowns experimenting with the Kama Sutra? Promise you'll never send me clown pics."

"No way. I swear. Does he do that kind of thing a lot?"

"Yeah. One time, when he was pissed at me, he spammed my phone with pictures of *homicidal* clowns."

Alex's eyebrows rise. "Homicidal?"

"They were wielding blood-spattered axes." I shudder at the memory.

"Gross." He drinks the last of his water. "Hey, are you ready to leave? I have something less morbid to show you."

"Okay. You've got me intrigued."

To my surprise, he takes me to a drive-in theater playing old movies. We sit on the tailgate and face the big screen.

"I didn't know Austin has one of these. But then again, there's a lot I don't know about Austin," I admit.

"We'll have to do something about that." His eyes linger on me, and my heart flutters. Is he asking me out again? I hope so. In fact, I never want this night to end.

Goonies is playing, and we've missed most of it. *Raiders of the Lost Ark* is up next.

Alex spreads a blanket on the tailgate. I spot the cooler in the truck bed and grab the champagne. "Champagne's my favorite. It's the only alcohol my mom ever *let* me have and only on New Year's and special occasions."

He watches me open the bottle, and I realize I've been presumptuous. "I'm sorry, is this okay with you? Do you even drink?"

"Sometimes but I've never had champagne."

"Here's to firsts," I cheer, holding the bottle out to him.

He lifts his chin, inviting me to take the first drink. It's ice-cold, and the bubbles tickle my nose. I shiver from the cool night air. He rubs his hands up and down the goosebumps on my arms. I want his hands exploring more than just my forearms, and I want him to kiss me. For a second, I think he might, but then he doesn't and my heart sinks. Instead, he walks to the cab for a jacket and drapes it over my shoulders, enveloping me in scents of leather, the woods, and his aftershave.

Heaven.

The second feature begins. The bottle sits between us, and we take turns sipping. After a while, he sets it aside and scoots to close the gap between us. "Is this okay?" he quietly asks.

All I can do is nod, my breath stolen by a surge of electricity from the delicious feel of his body pressed to mine—shoulder to shoulder, hip to hip. He holds my hand and, every so often, our fingers rearrange in minor ways. The glide of his skin against mine sets off new rounds of fireworks that warm my core. Halfway through the movie, he puts an arm around me. I snuggle to his chest and wonder if he can tell the effect he's having from my erratic breathing.

"Eva," he whispers. I turn my face to him. He's looking at my mouth, as if silently asking to kiss me.

I answer with a light touch of my lips on his. With his free hand, he cradles my face. His other hand finds its way under the jacket to rest on the small of my back as his lips move over my mouth. At the gentle brush of his tongue, I eagerly part my lips. The kiss deepens until we're both breathless.

"Even better than I imagined," he murmurs once we part for air.

Lightheaded, I nip at his bottom lip. He tastes good, a mix of champagne and the restaurant's after-dinner mints. I'm dizzy and exhilarated, flying high with no desire to land. My fingers glide around the back of his neck. He makes a sexy noise like a quiet growl and brings his mouth back to mine.

The movie turns into a blur in the background of us making out, but he never pushes for more. He doesn't paw at me, trying to cop a feel like some guys have, but *I* have trouble keeping my own hands off *him*. His arms. Shoulders. Chest. Neck. He's solid, strong, and responsive— his every move in tune with mine.

We gradually slow things down. His lips are red. I touch my own. They're pleasantly puffy and tingle from grazing against his facial stubble. In the flickering light of the drive-in screen, he soothingly kisses the corners of my mouth.

On the drive home, I hold his hand the whole way, savoring every second.

Casa Lor comes into view, and I'm surprised at the sight of my early birthday present. I'd forgotten it for a while. "There's Big Red, the monster truck," I mutter as Alex parks and cuts the engine.

He laughs and scrolls through pictures on his phone. "*That's* a monster truck." He shows me a photo. The truck's tires are massive, easily as tall as me.

"True. At least they didn't buy me one of those."

"Who? Wait, the truck's *yours*?" His jaw drops. "Don't you have a Prius?"

"It got hit by the tour trailer. It's being repaired, but the truck is Spike and Ike's early birthday present to me." Damn. Now, Alex will probably ask—

"Uh, Eva, why is rock royalty buying you such an extravagant present?" He draws his words out, like he's working on a puzzle in his head. "Is it just because they're friends of Lor's?"

"No, but it's complicated." A lie would suck after the great night we've had. I cover my face.

"Are you okay?" he asks, and I feel his hand on my shoulder.

Straightening, I look over at him, then down at my lap. "I'm worried it's going to be too much for you. My life is...it can be...overwhelming."

He stares at me, confusion in his eyes. "Eva, who are Spike and Ike to you?"

I breathe a quiet sigh. "My dad and uncle."

Alex blinks a few times and chuckles, as if in relief. "Okay. I sure didn't anticipate that. Um...how do you tell them apart? They're so similar."

"Spike has a tattoo sleeve. Ike doesn't."

"Which one's your dad?"

Again, I don't want to lie and blurt out, "I don't know."

His eyes narrow, and his head leans a bit to the side. "I'm sorry, what?"

"I don't know which one is my dad." I cringe at how ridiculous it sounds. "Alex, this is something *very* few people know—"

"Of course, I'll add it to the list, but I don't understand. Why don't you know?"

"It's probably Spike, but there's a chance—like a one-night stand chance—*Ike* is my dad." With a deep breath, I launch into the sordid explanation. "One night, my mom thought Ike was Spike, but Ike didn't understand. He thought she crawled into his bed because she and Spike had broken up after a huge fight. There was lots of drinking involved if that makes things clearer." I note his shocked expression. "This is super embarrassing. My life is too much."

"Hey." He takes my hand. "Don't be embarrassed."

"But you look horrified."

"I'm not. Surprised, yes... I need a moment to process."

"Okay. It *is* a lot to drop on a person."

"Where's your mom now?" he asks. "Do you ever see her?"

"Oh yeah, they're all good together—but not like a threesome!"

I grimace. "What I mean is, everyone gets along. My mom and Spike got back together soon after and treated the whole thing like a big misunderstanding. Things got dicey when she turned up pregnant, but they smoothed it out. Gives new definition to the term unconventional family, huh?"

"Yeah." His eyes narrow. I worry he'll tell me my life's weird and say we shouldn't go out again, but he asks, "Is your mom part of the band?"

"Not directly. The guys call her their muse and want her to travel everywhere with them. It's great for her. She hates to stay in one place for long. I used to travel with them, until Lor asked me to move here."

"Let me get this straight." Now his face is full of awe. "You've been all over the world, touring with a rock band?"

"Only in the States. I never went on the international tours. I had a governess, like a nanny who's also a teacher, until I was sixteen. Her name was Vanessa, and she and I would stay at different FU estates or visit her family and sometimes, my grandparents."

"Thank you for trusting me." He brings my hand to his lips for a kiss and looks out the window at the red truck again. "I'd say they spared no expense."

"They never do."

"Excessiveness bothers you, doesn't it?"

"You can tell?" I appreciate his perceptiveness.

"I can tell. That's an amazing truck, though."

I take a small pack of tissues from my purse and hold it out for him. "In case you drool."

"Ha-ha."

The exterior house lights shine softly on his face. I lose myself in the curve of his lips. The line of his jaw. "How do you not have a girlfriend?" I wonder aloud. His grin fades. I must've touched a nerve. "I'm sorry," I say. "Never mind."

"It's okay." He shifts in his seat. "Uh, I was with someone last year. We split a few months ago, and not on good terms. Why don't you have a boyfriend?" He faces me. "You don't, right?"

"No. Never staying in one place makes it hard to get to know people. I haven't dated much, not in the traditional sense."

He studies me in the dim light. I wish I hadn't added the last part. I freeze, holding my breath, until he speaks again. "Eva, I hope you stay in Austin, and we can spend more time together."

I lean over the truck's console, toward him. "I want to get to know you better too."

Our lips brush, and he asks, "What are your plans this week?

When can I see you again?"

"Depends on what the Undertakers want to do with me while they're here."

"Sounds ominous." We laugh. "Maybe we can go out Thursday. I'll call you."

"You better."

He walks me to the door, kisses me one more time, and we wish each other goodnight.

In the guesthouse, I'm relieved Baxter's gone. Talina's not here, but there are fresh sheets on the bed. I doze off with Alex in my dreams.

Chapter Twenty-One
Alex

The next morning, I'm up and outside bright and early helping Dad. We have his truck backed up to the barn door, and we're unloading bags of cattle feed. I'm moving at twice Dad's speed.

"You're like the Energizer Bunny," he says. "I guess your date was a success."

"Yeah." I duck my head, grinning.

I'm still processing the things Eva told me. She wasn't exaggerating—her life *is* complicated, yet she's down to earth. And making out with her was the best. Oh, God, the sweet, sexy warm smell of her—like vanilla and sugar. I wanted more. A lot more.

"What's her name?" Dad asks.

"Eva. We met through her brother. He hired me for an errand."

"Oh, yeah? How's the side hustle going? Are you making any money?"

"Some. For next school year, I'll have to find a real job. Something with a steady paycheck." I wipe sweat from my forehead. "Rent at Cassidi's will cost more than the dorm."

"I'm proud of how responsible you're being with your money and schooling." He pats my shoulder with his gloved hand.

"Thanks, Dad," I say but turn my face away. I'm a fraud to accept his praise.

"I just hope Devin can straighten up and be more responsible." He shuts the tailgate. This is the first time he's mentioned Devin's predicament to me.

"How're things going with him?" I ask.

Dad shakes his head. "I won't sugarcoat it. He's brought shame on the family, and he'll have to deal with his choices. We bailed him out and helped him with an apartment deposit, but we told him we won't pay for a lawyer. That's on him."

His obvious disappointment in Devin makes me ever more thankful he's in the dark on my grades and what happened with Angie.

"We love your brother," Dad continues, "and he's part of the family, but we're not going to clean up his mess. We don't want him to be one of these kids who keeps moving back home. We've already got one child who needs our support for the rest of our lives." He grimaces, his eyes full of regret. "Shoot, if I sounded bitter, I didn't mean it that way. Alex, your sister is not a burden, and we love her very much."

"I know, Dad." And I do. My parents have never acted like having a child with special needs is a burden, but there's no escaping the reality of Lena's dependence upon them.

Once the bags of cattle feed are neatly stacked inside, Dad and I work on the dining table. Our plan is to have it ready by the end of the week. Despite Mom's darkened mood from Devin's problems, she's still having her annual summer dinner party for Saturday night. She's been fretting over having to use card tables for extra seating and will love the surprise.

I shower and remain in my room after lunch, replaying last night in my mind. I fall asleep and dream of kissing Eva. As it intensifies, I'm awakened by the ringing of my phone. Unknown number. It shouldn't be any of my customers. I switched to vacation status. The caller leaves a voicemail. Maybe I'm paranoid, but my gut says it's Angie. For some masochistic reason, I listen to the message and wonder if there'll be a clue as to why she had the nerve to call Devin.

"Alex," the recording of her makes my stomach lurch. "I have a surprise for you. Call me."

Fat chance. I delete the message and block the number. This needs to stop. I don't want her on my mind—ever. For sure not while I'm thinking of Eva.

Last night, I surprised myself, telling Eva about Angie. I didn't want Eva to think of me as the lame and inexperienced, lonely nerd I was before Angie. I've made great progress in getting past that image. The way I used to be was a big part of the reason I got sucked into Angie's web in the first place, but she's in the past.

Eva's the present.

Chapter Twenty-Two
Eva

My phone wakes me. Mom's name is on the screen. I snatch it up to answer so it won't disturb Talina, who crawled into bed a couple hours ago.

"Mom, what's wrong?" I whisper into the phone. She's never up this early.

"Nothing's wrong." The lightness of her voice eases my mind. "I'm doing my hair and makeup. Come keep me company. Word around here is you went on a date yesterday. Why am I the last to hear of it?"

"I looked for you yesterday. Where were you?"

"Sorry, there was a photo op downtown, but I'm here now."

"Okay, give me a few minutes."

I freshen up and cart my laptop over to the main house. If Mom's mood is as good as it sounded, maybe she'll help fill in some blanks in the digital family timeline I've started creating. After getting a croissant from the kitchen, I check in on Lor before going to see Mom. Jojo exits his room, closing the door.

My chest tightens with worry—and guilt over not spending much time with him since all these people arrived. "How's Lor doing?"

"He's great," Jojo assures me. "Darnell's helping him with a shower at the moment."

Relieved, I change direction and tap on the door of Mom and Spike's room.

"It's open." I find Mom sitting at the vanity, head tilted back and eyes wide with alarm as she studies herself in the mirror.

"Mom, are you okay?"

"I most certainly am *not*. I found a whisker. *On my chin!*" She shudders in revulsion.

"Say it isn't so!" I set my computer down and cover my mouth in mock horror.

"Don't you make fun of me." She swats playfully at my leg and points at the bedside table. "Bring me my phone."

"Who you gonna call, whisker busters?" I pick up the phone and hold it out of reach.

Her eyes dance as she edges toward me, and I back away with the phone behind my back. *"I'll get you, my pretty,"* she screeches, adding an evil laugh.

"How? By the hair of your chinny-chin-chin?" I burst into giggles, and she tackles me onto the bed.

We laugh and squeal like a couple of kids. She tries to snatch the phone, but I roll off the bed, escaping her manicured grip. She lunges at me with a hilarious battle cry.

"Help!" I say through my laughter.

Spike comes in, his brow furrowed, but the worry turns to mischief when he sees we're playing. He holds Mom, so I can tickle her.

Between laughs, she says, "Ike, where are you? I need your help!"

He rushes in. Mom escapes Spike's hold. Instead of coming after me, Mom and I exchange a conspiratorial look and lunge at Ike, tackling him to the floor. Ike yells for Spike's help. Spike easily pulls me away, and Ike flips Mom onto her back. He holds her hands above her head, and her face is radiant with joy. This spontaneity reminds me of past good times, but it's bittersweet. Mom and the guys will only be here for a few more days. I've missed them more than I realized.

The antics and laughter subside. Spike claps Ike on the back. "We gotta leave or we'll miss tee time."

Ike stands and gives Mom a hand off the floor. As he releases his grasp, his fingers brush the length of her arm, and her eyes flash with something more than friendly affection. What the hell? I pretend I didn't notice, telling myself I misread it.

Spike doesn't seem to have noticed any of it. He kisses Mom's cheek, and the guys leave.

Mom resumes her seat at the vanity, and I sit on the floor, with the computer on my lap. "What's that for?" she asks.

"I found this cool digital timeline software. I'm making one for our family and adding pictures of everyone. Grandma Covington sent me some of Spike and Ike when they were younger, but I need info on your childhood and teen years, like, before you had Lor."

Mom *was* smiling and nodding, showing interest, but now her face grows dim. She stares blankly into the mirror and starts brushing her hair again, even though she already styled it. "Eva, I don't like talking about my childhood."

"Can't you tell me *any*thing? Like, where did you live? Who were your parents?"

Her parents have always been a mystery to me, quite the opposite of my Covington grandparents in San Diego.

"Nothing in my life before eighteen matters," Mom says. "Not to me, and it shouldn't matter to you or anyone else."

"Is there…something you're embarrassed of?"

"I won't discuss this with you." It's pointless to press her further. She can put up a wall better than anyone. "Now, if you'll excuse me, I'd like some privacy."

I'm being dismissed. She also dismisses people better than anyone else.

"Fine." I close my computer and leave. We never even talked about my date with Alex, and now I don't want to tell her anything.

I avoid her the rest of the day, bingeing *World of Dance* and *Tiny House Nation* with Toby. Plus, I make plans for Alex to visit tomorrow, and I hope Mom won't be here.

Chapter Twenty-Three
Alex

When I arrive at Eva's, I'm shocked by who's at the house. Apparently, so is Eva.

It's her favorite band, California Nine.

One of the FU twins—Ike, I think, because he doesn't have a tattoo sleeve—tells Eva, "We heard your favorite band was in town for South by Southwest, so we arranged a private concert."

"Oh, my God." She hugs him and kisses Spike's cheek. "This is the best!"

Some guys bring instruments and equipment inside as the band chats with Spike and Ike.

"We were psyched when your manager called ours about doing this," the lead singer says. "We're big FU fans."

"And we love Austin." The drummer twirls a drumstick between two fingers. "Call us anytime."

Eva guides me into an alcove off the side of the living room. "I hope you didn't have plans for us this afternoon. The band was a total surprise."

"No set plans, and this'll be better than anything I might have arranged." More quietly, I say, "You look and smell amazing, Eva. Kiss me before I lose my mind from how much I've missed you."

Her lips curve in a sexy smile. With her hands behind my head, she guides my mouth to hers for a kiss I'll never forget.

I fight the urge to pull her against my hips, let her feel what she's doing to me, but I'm not sure how she'd react.

We're interrupted anyway, by the guys calling us into the living room.

We sit on one of the leather sofas, and California Nine plays their hit "Vigilante Heart." Other people in the house gather around. Pretty soon, the room is full.

Lor even joins the group, wheeled in by a guy in scrubs.

A woman walks in during the next song and sits beside Spike. As I get a better look at her, my eyes bug out—it's Sloane Silver, the supermodel. Spike throws an arm around her, and it hits me: she's Eva's mom. My mind's blown. Why hasn't Eva told me? I lean toward her, wanting to ask, but decide not to break the mood, especially in front of all these people.

California Nine plays a few requests from Eva. In a break between songs, the bass player laughs and makes an exploding head motion with both hands. "Man, I can't believe we're in the same room with FU *and* DeLorean. You guys should be playing with us."

Spike and Ike agree to play. Lor declines.

Eva goes for a bathroom break, and I wait in the hallway. When she comes out, I whisper, "Hey, by any chance is your mom Sloane Silver?"

She freezes for a beat, peers at me through lowered eyelashes. "Yes."

My mouth gapes open for a second. "Your mom is a *supermodel*," I say in disbelief. "Why haven't you mentioned this before?"

"Technically, she's a retired supermodel. And I figured you were overwhelmed enough, with everything else I've told you." She crosses her arms.

Shit, I'm acting like a starstruck idiot. "I'm sorry. I was shocked. I grew up seeing her on my mom's *Vogue* and *Cosmo* magazine covers, and here I am in the same room with her."

"*Ew*, Alex. Please tell me you didn't have one of those magazines under your pillow or something."

"No." I breathe out, hit with a thought. "Wait, your mom's a lot older than Spike, isn't she?"

"Yeah." She grimaces. "I try not to let the age difference bother me, but sometimes it does. I mean, Spike's only a few years older than Lor."

Now I really don't want Eva knowing about Angie. She's *fourteen* years older than me.

Eva frowns. "You think my family's weird, don't you?"

"What? No," I assure her. "It's not weird. It's…different, I guess."

"*Weirdly* different." She kisses my cheek and takes me by the hand back to the concert.

The bands do a couple FU songs together.

As things wrap up, and after a moment of hushed discussion, they play "Little Eva."

Eva has tears in her eyes by the end of the song. She hugs each musician. "This was fun, you guys, thank you."

California Nine's roadies pack up, and one of the FU twins says, "Let's go to The County Line for barbeque. Baxter, my man, round everyone up. Have the limos meet us in front in ten minutes."

Eva tugs my arm. "You can go with us, right?"

"I'd love to."

Before we can leave, she insists on freshening up, as if she needs to do anything to look beautiful.

I accompany her to the guesthouse. "There won't be any surprises in here like last time, will there?" I joke as we walk in.

"I don't think so." She laughs but looks around as if to check. "Nothing unexpected, other than the place being a mess, thanks to the drummer's kids. Have a seat while I change."

She disappears into her bedroom, and I sit at the kitchen table.

A few minutes later, she opens her bedroom door. "Alex, help me decide something." Her hair's pinned back, out of her face, and she gestures at a couple of wigs on her dresser.

"Why do you have—oh is this for the whole anonymous thing?"

"Yeah. I can't be seen in public with Mom and FU as myself. Should I wear red or brunette tonight?"

I point at the wavy red wig. The brunette one reminds me of Angie's long, dark hair.

"Good choice. This top goes well with the red." Eva adjusts the collar of her emerald shirt.

"And your eyes."

We smile at each other in the mirror. She raises her arms to position the wig, and her shirt rises. My eyes fall to the bare skin of her waist. I need a distraction, quick. With my eyes on her face again, I say, "I'd forgotten about FU's 'Little Eva' song. What's the story behind it?"

"When I learned where babies come from—" her eyebrows dance "—I was curious whether Ike or Spike was actually my biological father."

"Couldn't they have done paternity tests?"

"I wanted them to, but since they're identical twins, the results would've been inconclusive. Even before we knew that, they weren't willing to have the tests done."

"Why not?"

"They've each always thought of themselves as my dad and didn't want anything to change. They wrote 'Little Eva' to tell me it didn't matter which one of them was my biological father. I belonged to both."

"That's sweet." I brush a strand of the wig's auburn hair from her face.

"How do I look?" She adjusts the wig to cover all her blonde hair.

"Great, but like someone else. It's a little unnerving," I admit. She puts on glasses with dark green frames, and I say, "Very convincing disguise. It'll take some getting used to."

I take her into my arms for a kiss. She fits against me perfectly and kisses me back with the reassurance I need that she's the same girl—the one I'm falling harder for every day.

Chapter Twenty-Four
Eva

Alex and I climb into a limo with Mom, Spike, Ike, and Ingrid. I'm relieved Alex acts normal around Mom. She, on the other hand, ogles him and sends me a text.

> *Be safe riding your hottie cowboy. I'm not ready to be a grandma.*

> *Mothers are NOT supposed to say that kind of thing.*

She winks, and I shake my head in exasperation, putting my phone away.

At the restaurant, we're ushered through a back entrance to a semi-secluded dining area. Austin's SXSW music festival is in full swing, so the place is packed. Celebrity reporters are on the prowl. I face away from other people as much as possible. Since we're with Mom, FU, *and* California Nine, our group gets *lots* of attention.

Alex's eyes flit around nervously. This is his first taste of what my life can be like. His eyes are a bit wide in wonder. "I get why you disguise yourself. Maybe I should've borrowed your other wig."

I laugh at the mental picture and kiss his cheek, glad the overcrowded table offers me an excuse to sit really close to him.

During dinner, he asks Spike and Ike, "What's the story with your band name?"

"Our parents have a funeral home business," Spike begins. "We grew up around coffins, going to graveyards. As the only Covington kids, we were being groomed to run the business someday, but *music* was our thing."

Ike takes over. "We once staged a music video in the funeral home. With a smoke machine and special lighting. Us jumping out of coffins. The works. It was epic. Totally worth the trouble we got into afterwards." He high-fives Spike, and everyone laughs. "When we got serious about forming a band, Spike came up with the idea to call ourselves The Fabulous Undertakers."

"It's a great name," Alex says. "How'd your parents feel about the whole thing?"

"Not happy at first. After we cut our first album, they started to accept it."

Talina squeezes over to me and shouts over the hubbub: "Toby and I are going clubbing. You and your boyfriend should come with us."

"You wanna go?" I ask Alex, hoping he does. I'd love a chance to dance with him.

"Sure, if you want to." After Talina walks away, he asks, "Who's Toby?"

"Her brother, across from Johnny down there." I nod in Toby's direction.

After we've finished eating, Rob has one of his security guys help us slip outside.

Talina and Toby sit opposite Alex and me in the limo. Loud music pumps from the speakers. I lower the volume and introduce Alex to my friends.

"Nice boots," Toby tells him and nudges my foot with his. "You got a fake ID?"

"No, do you?" I ask, and he takes out his wallet, showing me an Illinois driver's license with his picture. It looks real but shows his name as Justin Case.

"Get it?" He laughs. "I have it, just in case I need it."

"And you think you'll pass for twenty-one?" I ask with a laugh.

"If I don't, I can always have Twyla Drummond buy me drinks." He points at Talina who flicks him on the back of the head.

Since I'm not with Mom or FU now, I take the wig off and brush my hair out.

Alex twirls a strand between his fingers. "Much better."

"And it'll be cooler."

The limo drops us off at a club on Austin's famed Sixth Street. We wander the sidewalk from club to club, greeters calling out drink specials. The doorman at the place Talina leads us to checks our IDs. He doesn't question Toby and Talina's fakes. Alex and I receive an X on the backs of our hands.

Inside, the place is packed and loud. The yeasty smell of beer mixes with an occasional waft of sweat from the gyrating bodies on the dance floor.

"There they are!" Talina waves at someone and steers Toby toward the back.

Within seconds, they disappear into the crowd. Alex raises an eyebrow. I laugh and shrug. We order sodas at the bar, and I have *déjà vu* from the previous year when I was in a club like this. I was staying in San Diego for a month visiting my grandparents and met a guy named David. He held my hand and we danced, but his eyes followed every hot girl who walked by. Titling my head to watch Alex, I'm glad to see he isn't looking at anyone but me.

Talina and Toby circle back. They've met up with some guys they hung out with at The Oasis a couple nights ago. "Hey, we're headed for another club," Talina shouts.

"Have fun," I say.

Alex waves goodbye to them and asks me, "You didn't want to go?"

"No, the music's good here. I'm ready to dance." I set my empty glass on the bar and lead him by the hand onto the dance floor.

"Okay, but fair warning: the Two-Step is pretty much all I know. I don't think country dancing's gonna work here."

We join the mass of dancers. I move with the music. He mimics me—awkwardly. We laugh, and he says, "Told you."

"I don't care. I like a guy who can laugh at himself."

The music changes to something a bit slower, more rhythmic. I slide my arms around his neck and close the space between us. At first, he doesn't do more than sway with his hands on my hips. As I dance against him—a brush here, a nudge there—he loosens up and mirrors my movements.

There's nothing awkward about his dancing now. Placing his hands on my lower back, he slips a thigh between my legs. I cling to his shoulders and indulge in a little grinding. It wouldn't take much of this amazing friction to get me off, but we're in public.

I spin around, with my back against his chest and bring his hands to my shoulders. He drags them down, palms skimming the sides of my breasts, fingers sliding to my ribs and stomach. Our bodies mesh in perfect synch. Drunk on his touch, his spicy cologne, and the heavy bass reverberating through me, I grind my hips and press into the unmistakable firmness of his arousal.

He tightens his grip on my hips and lowers his mouth to my ear.

"Eva." My name escapes his lips, a growl full of longing. He turns me around and kisses me before whispering in my ear again. "Do you wanna get outta here?"

"Mm-hmm," I murmur, kissing him until I'm dizzy.

We make our way outside. At the curb, he positions himself behind me, arms around my waist as we scan the street for a cab. "Using me as cover," I tease and nudge my backside on the front of his jeans.

Still hard, he nuzzles my neck and lets out a little laugh. "Busted."

A limo stops almost in front of us.

Spike swings a rear door open, and he and Mom emerge.

I step aside, planning to ignore and avoid whatever attention they'll draw. Unfortunately, Mom exclaims, "Oh, it's you, baby girl." She throws her arms around my neck in a sloppy hug, and her breath reeks of liquor. I panic and pry her arms away, needing to escape.

People on both sides of us already have their phones aimed our way.

All at once, yet in what feels like slo-mo, Alex throws an arm across my shoulders and Spike leads Mom away.

Rob jumps out of the limo and steers Alex and me toward it.

I duck into the backseat, followed by Alex, and Rob closes the door.

Spots blur my vision for a moment. My breathing's shallow, and my fingers tingle. I clench my fists, trying to convince myself this isn't happening.

"Are you okay?" Alex asks, looking me over.

"Yeah, but I did *not* see that coming. Sorry you got caught in it."

"I'm fine. Eva, people took pictures. I'm sorry I didn't act faster." He puts an arm around me. I scoot closer to him, shaken.

The limo starts moving, taking us away from the madness.

Alex places a hand on mine, making me aware of how frantically I've been rubbing at the scar on my left hand. Damn, I need to kick this habit.

"Maybe nobody got a clear shot of me," I mumble. "It'll…be okay. It'll have to be." I'm not sure how much I believe my own words.

I hear the sound of the intercom, and the driver says, "Rob asked me to drive you to Mr. Jenson's. Will you need me to make any stops on the way?"

"No, thank you," I tell him, and he disconnects.

Once my breathing slows, I snuggle into Alex's embrace, wanting to regain some of the magic we shared at the club. Anything to replace the idea of my face on gossip websites.

He strokes my arm soothingly. The fingers of his other hand

entwine with mine.

I breathe in his comforting scent. "Safe to say my mom killed the mood, huh?" My ear is to his chest, and I feel his quiet laugh.

"It's okay." He kisses the top of my head. "It's getting late. I've got a long drive back to Florence and need to be up early in the morning."

"Well, we have the ride back to Casa Lor." I nuzzle his neck. "Have you ever made out in a limo?"

"I've never even *been* in a limo before today. Have *you* made out in one before? No—don't answer that." He pulls me closer. "I don't want to know."

"I haven't, but there's a first time for everything." I graze his lips with mine.

He cradles my face with his hand. The intensity from earlier is gone, but his sweet kisses make everything else fade away.

Chapter Twenty-Five
Alex

Saturday morning, I help Dad put the finishing touches on the dining table, and it's a big hit with Mom. She keeps running her hands across it, laughing, and hugging Dad.

He beams with pride. "Couldn't have done it without Alex."

She hugs me next. "Thank you. Oh, and now there's room for one more at tonight's dinner. Alex, why don't you invite Eva?"

"Um…okay. I'll ask her, but it's kinda last minute."

I call Eva, who says she'd love to come. My mind spins after we hang up.

Eva's coming *here.*

What will she think of my family? What will they think of her? How much of herself is she willing to share? Are we girlfriend and boyfriend? Why do I feel *fifteen* again?

Later, Mom's friends from the middle school arrive, followed by a couple who are long-time family friends. I wait on the front porch for Eva. She drives up in her truck, clad in a dress modest enough to be Mom-approved yet hot as hell. Everything about her makes my pulse race. I leave the porch and pull her into my arms, not caring who sees the long kiss we enjoy before heading inside.

As I introduce Eva, Lena enters the room. She's extra loud and boisterous, excited about having guests. My gaze shoots over to watch Eva's reaction. In my book, the way a girl treats my sister is a test of her character.

Eva chats with Lena like she doesn't even notice she's different. She takes it in stride when Lena grabs her hand to *ooh* and *aah* at her bracelet.

"Oh, God. Where's your finger?" she asks loudly, drawing everyone's attention. I hold my breath.

Eva shows only a flicker of embarrassment before dazzling everyone with her smile. "I lost it in a hotel door accident."

"What do you mean?" Lena's face clouds with horror. "It got cut off? Eww!"

"Lena," I warn at the same time Mom makes her own quiet reprimand.

"It's no big deal," Eva says. "You'd be amazed how well you can manage without a finger. I love your nails. What color is this?"

They discuss nail polish, with Eva unaware she's earned a place in my heart that no other girl has ever claimed. I'm now positive I want Eva to be my girlfriend. Now I just need to figure out how to ask her.

Dad's friend Martin is the last to arrive.

"Eva?" Martin's eyebrows lift in surprise.

Her pupils grow large. "Martin!" She laughs and hugs him.

"How do you know each other?" Dad asks, which is what I'm wondering as well.

"I have family in the music business," Eva says. "Martin was their sound engineer."

"Yeah, my wife and I have known Eva since she was a little girl," Martin adds.

"Where *is* Rosy?" Eva asks. "I'd love to see her."

It blows my mind she knows Martin *and* his wife.

He frowns. "She couldn't make it. Her arthritis is really bad right now."

"Oh, I'm sorry." She squeezes his arm. "Tell her I said hi."

"Visit our place in Georgetown sometime. She'd love to see you."

Dinner at my house is much quieter than the rowdy crowd partying with Eva's family last night. I'm worried she'll feel out of place, or even bored, but she makes easy conversation and laughs a lot.

Cassidi arrives, dressed in her waitress uniform, as everyone's clearing the table.

"Hey, I didn't know you'd be here," I say, carrying a stack of plates to the kitchen.

She follows with a handful of dishes. "Yeah, your parents asked if Lena could stay with me tonight."

We both shudder and share a laugh. Lena sometimes spends the night with Cassidi, an arrangement my parents devised under the guise of giving Lena time away from home. Cassidi and I know it's more about

Mom and Dad having the house to themselves.

Several of us wander to the front porch with its wooden rockers and porch swing.

Martin and I lean against the railing, facing Eva who takes a seat on the swing.

"Eva, how do you know the Marshalls?" Martin asks.

"We ran into each other a couple weeks ago." She motions for Lena and Cassidi to join her on the swing, and I love how comfortable she seems with my family. "How do *you* know the Marshalls?"

"Alex's dad, Ed, is my insurance guy. We've gotten to know each other through our building projects."

"What are you building?" Eva asks.

"Here lately, a tiny house for a friend of Rosy's."

Eva's face grows even brighter. "Cool. I met a lady recently who has a tiny house." She opens a picture on her phone and shows him. "Her name is Sue, and she's traveling with it right now. She'll eventually park it on her brother's property and live there. I'd love to see the one you're building."

Lena asks to see the picture and without hesitation, Eva hands her the phone. Lena swipes through more pictures. I'm about to tell her she shouldn't look through the phone without asking when she exclaims, "Turtles! They're big!"

Eva glances over. "Oh, yeah, giant tortoises. My mom took those photos when she visited the Seychelles. Keep scrolling to see the beaches. They're incredible. Do you like beaches, Lena?"

"I love beaches, but I never saw one like this."

"I haven't either." Eva chuckles. "I told my mom she better take me with her next time."

Cassidi leans in to look at the pictures. Her eyebrows rise, and she gives Eva a critical eye. Shit. I doubt the Seychelles is a typical vacation destination. I bet Cassidi's judging Eva, like she's one of the snobby restaurant patrons. If Cassidi learns the truth of Eva and her family, I suspect I'll never hear the end of it.

"Whose King Ranch Ford?" Martin asks, pointing at Eva's truck.

"Mine," she says. "It's an early birthday present." She adds, "From my dad and uncle," under her breath and shares a knowing look with Martin

"Eva, that's one heck of a truck," Martin says. "Speaking of tiny houses, you could easily haul one with that."

Her face gets a faraway expression, as she stares at the truck. The others keep talking. I stretch my foot out and nudge hers. She glances at me. *You all right?* I mouth.

She reassures me with her smile.

Later, once the guests have left, Mom and Dad join us on the porch.

"How did you meet Alex?" Cassidi asks Eva.

Eva hesitates for a second. "Um, a few weeks ago, he delivered something to my house."

"Her brother hired me for an errand." I take Eva's hand and tell her, "I want to show you around town before dark."

"Can I go?" Lena asks.

"Lena," Mom says. "Let's have some pie before you leave to spend the night with Cassidi."

I'm thankful Lena likes the idea of pie better because I want to be alone with Eva.

Lena goes into the house, calling over her shoulder, "Glad I got to meet Alex's girlfriend."

My sister doesn't know better, but I wish she hadn't said that. Eva's looking at her phone and acts like she didn't hear it. Dad stifles a laugh.

On her way inside, Mom squeezes Eva's shoulder. "Bye Eva, thanks for joining us."

"Pleasure to meet you." Dad nods and waves as he follows Mom.

"You, too. Thank you for inviting me, and dinner was great." She holds the truck's key fob out to me. "You wanna drive the big honking truck?"

"I thought you'd never ask."

We wave goodbye to Cassidi, who's still on the porch.

In the truck, I breathe in the new car smell, mixed with Eva's sweet perfume, and nearly drool at the spotless leather interior and leading-edge technology.

I take one last look at Cassidi as I drive from the house. In my mind, an imaginary thought bubble appears above her head considering how rich Eva must be. Her smug smirk dampens my spirits, but only a little.

"I'd like to apologize for my family," I tell Eva.

"Why? They're nice and normal. Where was your brother tonight?"

Her question catches me off guard. "He, uh…" I release a breath through my pursed lips. "I guess he couldn't make it." But I wonder—did Mom even invite him? *Ouch.*

Eva interrupts my thoughts. "You look good driving this truck."

I sit up straighter and beam at her. "Thanks. What's gonna

happen to your Prius?"

"Spike said he'll have someone bring it to the house after the repairs are done."

"You'll have a car and a truck?"

"Yeah, but I've considered returning the truck."

"Don't. You'll break my heart." I clutch my chest dramatically. She smirks and swats my arm. "No, I'm kidding," I say. "You should do what you want."

"Yeah. Hey, where're we going? You said you want to show me around town."

"Which will take all of *five* minutes, but I wanted to rescue you from my family asking so many personal questions."

"Thanks." She takes my hand.

Is now a good time for the boyfriend-girlfriend conversation?

She eyes me. "You look like there's something else you want to say."

"I was thinking of—" I lose my nerve "—how you acted with Lena, and I wanted to thank you for not treating her like she's different. A lot of people are uncomfortable around her."

"I think she's incredible."

"She is."

I show her a few places and landmarks as I drive around and then pull into the parking lot of the high school. "And now you've pretty much seen Florence. What did you think?"

"You weren't joking, it is small. But your tour showed me something I missed out on growing up. I've never been to a high school football field. Could we, like, maybe sit in the bleachers?"

"Sure, if the gate isn't locked." I drive to the lot by the field and park.

We test the gate. It opens, and we let ourselves in and choose a spot at the top of the bleachers.

There's a slight chill, and it's breezy. I scoot closer to her. "Are you cold?"

"Only a little." She snuggles against me. "You can keep me warm."

We look out at the dark field, and I ask, "Were you embarrassed at Lena calling you my girlfriend?"

"No, were you?"

"It was awkward since we haven't talked about it. Listen, I'm sure I can't compare to the guys you've been around. Rock stars and celebrities—"

"Nobody like you, though." In the moonlight, her beautiful

green eyes peer into mine. "I like you a lot, Alex."

My breath catches, and here goes nothing. "Eva, will you be my girlfriend?"

"Yes." A smile takes over her face, and she throws her arms around me.

I slip my hand to the back of her neck, under her hair. She shivers and tilts her head toward mine. I press my lips to hers, desperate to taste her, touch her—experience her. She thrusts her tongue into my mouth, kissing me with such eagerness, it's hard to keep myself in check. Even harder as I flash back on how we danced last night. Her soft moan as I kiss her neck fills my mind with thoughts of other sounds I'd love to inspire.

We both startle at a flashlight suddenly shining brightly at us.

"You kids shouldn't be there," someone says. "Wait—Alex Marshall?"

"Yes sir," I answer, unable to tell who it is down below.

"Hey, man." He redirects the beam of light, and now Pete's face is visible. He's in his police uniform. "Sorry, I expected to find a couple high schoolers. Who's with you?"

"My girlfriend, Eva." It feels good to say. "Eva, this is Pete."

"Hi, Pete. Are we in trouble for being here?"

"Nah, no worries. I was patrolling the area and saw a truck in the lot. Figured I'd better check. Sometimes kids drink here and leave their bottles lying around." He gives us a nod. "Y'all enjoy your evening. Tell your folks hi, Alex. Nice to meet you, Eva."

I'm hoping Eva and I can return to what we were doing, but she jumps to her feet, ready to go, and I follow.

"How'd you like your first time in the bleachers?" I ask.

"Loved it. It's where I got my first boyfriend."

This gives me a thrill. I've never been anyone's first. I hope I don't screw this up.

On the drive back to my house, I say, "It's cool you know my parents' friend, Martin, and y'all got to talk tiny houses."

"Yeah. He got me thinking more about them. It's weird. I've spent a lot of time on tour buses and kinda miss…the closeness. I think of doing what Sue's doing, but I have no idea how. I'm too chicken."

She sounds sad and lost, and I can't believe she thinks she's chicken. To me, she's nothing like that, but I can almost understand where she's coming from. Being along for the ride—even in the shadows—of multiple celebrities must have created limitations I can't imagine. Her face looks anxious, and she leans her head against the passenger-side door.

We've arrived at my house, and I park her truck beside mine but put my hand out to stop her from opening the door yet. I want her to be comfortable telling me what she's thinking.

"Hey." I squeeze her hand. "You can talk to me about anything."

Her eyes search mine. "Thanks. I'm fine. Sorry I got kinda moody on you." She gets out and comes around to the driver's side.

I'm relieved the worry on her face has faded. I descend from the cab and caress her upper arm. "I'll be back in Austin tomorrow. Can I see you again?"

"Sure. I think Mom and the band are leaving in the morning."

"Oh, I'm sorry. I've taken you away from spending time with them on their last night."

"No big deal. They had other plans. I wanted to be here with you."

She hugs me and feels amazing in my arms. I don't want to let go.

I give her one last kiss and watch as the taillights move down the driveway, turn, and disappear. I miss her already.

Chapter Twenty-Six
Eva

At home, I want to talk with Lor and hope he's awake. The main house is eerily quiet. Everyone must still be out partying. Upstairs, Lor's TV and bedside lamp are on. He's propped in bed, but asleep. So's Darnell, on the couch. Easing the remote from Lor's hand, I switch the TV off.

He stirs and opens his eyes. "Oh, hey. What's up?" He yawns. "Didn't you go out with the rest of them tonight?"

"No." I can't stop grinning. "I was visiting my boyfriend and his family."

His eyebrows shoot up. "Alex?"

"He's nice. And funny. And *normal*." I'm practically gushing, and my cheeks heat.

He laughs quietly. "You have me to thank for introducing you two."

"Yeah, thanks." I squeeze his hand. "I'm glad I came to live here. Thanks for that too."

Lor lays his head back against the pillow propped behind him.

"Sorry I woke you," I say.

"It's okay." He yawns again. "Goodnight, sis."

My stomach growls. I wish I'd eaten some of the pie at Alex's earlier. I rummage in the main house kitchen for something simple and settle for cereal. I'm crunching on Lucky Charms when Talina and Toby enter, laughing and talking loudly.

"Eva!" Talina squeals. "Check out my tattoo. It's a unicorn." Lifting her skirt, she shows me the red, angry skin on her inner thigh where there is, indeed, a unicorn. The horn, pointing toward her crotch, looks less like a horn and more like something else.

"Um, Talina, did you know the horn was going to look like...*that?*" I ask.

"Yes! Why do you think I wanted it right *there?*" She laughs, and I wonder if she'll think her permanent decision was such a great one in the morning.

"What about you, Toby?" I ask. "Did you get a tattoo?"

"No, but guess what, Eva." He claps his hands together. "I talked to my dad about L.A. He's okay with me going and didn't even give me much shit for wanting dance lessons."

"Toby, how exciting," I say. "You'll like L.A."

"The catch is—" Talina slaps him on the arm "—he has to take me with him."

He rolls his eyes. "Yeah, Dad says I have to keep an eye on her. How's that for the younger kid taking care of the older one?"

"I feel ya," I murmur, thinking of myself and Lor.

Toby and Talina bid me goodnight and head to the guesthouse. I remain in the kitchen to finish my cereal and hear a light, muffled laugh. It sounds like Mom. I swing the kitchen door open a little, peering into the dim living room.

Off to the side, in the shadows of the alcove, Mom and Spike are making out.

I cover my mouth in a silent laugh and resist calling out, "Don't y'all have a room?" Instead, I decide not to interrupt them and take a step back but wait a minute... I crack the door open again.

That isn't Spike kissing Mom. It's *Ike*. I can tell by his un-tattooed left arm.

A wave of nausea threatens to make me hurl the undigested cereal, yet I can't look away.

Am I really seeing this?

"Ike," Mom coos. "Before I marry Spike, we need one more night, for old time's sake?"

What the...

"We can't." Ike sounds tortured. His arms drop from around her. "I swore this wouldn't happen anymore."

Anymore?

Mom hums. "You've sworn that a *few* times." She wraps a leg around his hips.

My skin crawls as his hand lingers on Mom's bare thigh where her dress rides up.

"We can't," he says again. This time, he gently pushes her off.

"I've got Ingrid upstairs waiting for me. Spike's up there, waiting for you. Sloane, you should accept his proposal. And this *can't* happen between us again." He moves toward the stairs.

I back up, hoping to retreat to the safety of the kitchen, but my elbow bumps the swinging door, and both their heads turn my way. Ike stops halfway up the stairs and looks in my direction. His face fills with regret. "Shit. Eva, I'm sorry."

"Yeah, me too," my voice squeaks. For some reason, it isn't *him* I'm most upset with.

He hangs his head and climbs the rest of the way up.

Mom scowls at me. "Were you spying on us?"

"No! Mom, what the hell? You and *Ike*—"

"This is none of your business," she practically barks.

I recoil, struck with another wave of nausea. She approaches me, softening her expression.

"Eva." Her voice also softens. "Sorry you saw…our little indiscretion. Let's forget it. It's nothing." She taps my nose, an endearing gesture of hers, but she's never done it to placate me, and I back away.

"Mom don't—don't tell me it's nothing. It didn't look like nothing to me. What's going on with you and Ike?"

"We have a complicated history. You know that."

"I had no idea you and Ike… How could you—"

"*What?* Live my life the way *I* want to? Don't judge me." She starts to walk away, but our conversation is nowhere near finished.

"Of course not," I call after her, anger bubbling. "I wouldn't dare." My sarcasm drips so heavily Stella will need to mop it up. "I guess this is another example of how you live by a different set of rules than us mere mortals."

Mom pauses at the bottom of the stairs, one bejeweled hand on the rail. "What is that supposed to mean?"

"It means… I think you're wrong." My throat constricts.

"Your idea of wrong is the real problem. I'm not hurting anyone."

"Yes, you are! You're hurting Spike—cheating on him with his *brother*." I ball my fist at my chest, needing Mom to understand my world's no longer what I thought. I've never thought her capable of such betrayal. "You shouldn't get to do whatever you want just because you're Sloane Silver and you're beautiful and rich and famous." I hurl the words at her, hoping they'll make her *care*.

She makes a disgusted face and snorts. I've never seen her…ugly before and it's jarring. "Eva, what *I* do shouldn't matter to anyone but me. It's a shame you've gotten yourself upset, but I must be off to bed now."

She's more than halfway up when I dare to ask, "Does Spike know?"

Without missing a step or turning to look at me, she continues to ascend. "Spike knows what I *want* him to. Like I said, this is none of your business." There's more than a hint of warning in her tone.

She disappears from the landing, behind her closed door.

I'm alone, digging my thumbnail into the scar on my left hand to the point of pain. I press harder. Somehow, it keeps me from drowning.

Numb, I return to the guesthouse. Toby's asleep on the pull-out sofa bed. I peek into my room. Talina's fast asleep. It's for the best. This isn't something I'd be comfortable talking to them about. I don't think there's *anyone* I can tell of this. It's a dirty secret I picture burying deep inside me as I lay next to Talina without even changing clothes.

Sleep is impossible. I alternate between disgust, confusion, and worry.

As the first rays of sunlight bleed through the curtains, I rise, desperate to disappear before Mom and FU's big send-off today. I grab my purse, phone, and keys, and hurry to my truck.

Curtis is the only one out here. He's loading the tour bus trailer. So much for a clean getaway. "Did you see your new license plates?" he asks. The truck's personalized plates say LIL EVA. "The guys asked me to put them on for you. What do you think?"

I force a smile. "They're great, Curtis. Thank you. Sorry, I've gotta go."

I need to run away until all of you leave.

"Okay, we're leaving right after lunch. Hopefully, I'll see you again to tell you goodbye."

"I'll be here," I lie, unable to meet his eyes.

Chapter Twenty-Seven
Alex

It's Sunday morning, and I'm glad my roommate hasn't returned to the dorm yet. I'm taking my time unpacking when Eva calls.

"I was just thinking of you." My face heats with embarrassment at how excited I sound, but I can't help it; I'm crazy for this girl.

"Alex...I need your help. I'm lost." Her voice is distant, sad.

My chest tightens. "Where are you?"

"At a parking garage. I'm trying to figure out how to find you."

"You're on campus?"

"I think so, but after driving around for a place to park, I'm turned around. You live in Jester, right?"

"Describe where you are, and I'll find you." She gives me the name of the parking garage. "You're close. I'm on my way."

I leave the residence hall and jog in her direction.

We meet, and she throws her arms around me. I hold her close, ecstatic she came looking for me, but concerned that she's still wearing the dress she wore last night, and her eyes are watery.

"What's wrong?" I smooth her hair away from her face.

"I needed to get away from Casa Lor, and I wanted to be with you." She takes an unsteady breath.

"Okay, do you want to go to my residence hall?"

"Yes." She drags a hand through her hair. "Sorry I'm a basket case. I must look terrible."

"You aren't a basket case, and you're beautiful." I kiss her cheek.

"You *have* to say that. You're my boyfriend."

"But it's true," I insist. "You *are* beautiful."

We enter Jester West Hall, and her eyes pop. "This is where you live? It's huge. Can we go somewhere...smaller?"

"How about my dorm room? My roommate isn't back from spring break yet." I steer her toward the elevator, and we ride to my floor.

As we enter my room, Graham approaches his own door and gawks at us. "Man, spring break was good to you, huh, Alex?"

"Shut up," I mutter and close my door behind me.

Eva's posture relaxes. She even cracks a smile. It becomes a frown when her phone vibrates. She checks the screen, clicks ignore, and sets the phone on my desk.

"Here, have a seat." I pull out my desk chair for her, and I sit on my bed.

She stays standing and glances around the small, cluttered room. "What's your roommate like?"

"He's pretty much an asshat." This makes her laugh.

Her phone vibrates on the desk. Ignoring it, she sits with me on the bed. Our shoulders brush. Legs touch. Her beautiful green eyes peer into mine.

"Kiss me," she whispers, and I brush my lips against hers. She responds with a heated urgency, her tongue sliding past my lips. I wrap my arms around her and hold her close.

Her mouth never leaves mine as she presses me onto my back and lies on top of me. I can't hide she's given me a massive boner. She must not mind. She rocks her hips, grinding.

"Oh, God, yes, Eva." I thrust between her legs.

She's a dream come true. I did, in fact, dream of this exact thing last night. I groan at the sweet warmth of her fingers slipping under my shirt. They brush lower, down my abs, to the top of my jeans, but her face looks troubled, like her mind's elsewhere. All at once, what felt so right feels totally wrong, and her damn phone won't stop vibrating on the desk.

Finally, I say, "Maybe you should answer—"

"Dammit." She rears back, raises up, and bumps her head on the top bunk. She cries out in pain and slides off the bed, jumping to her feet.

I quickly stand. "Are you okay?"

"This is embarrassing." Her eyes are watery again.

"What's wrong?" I tuck her hair behind her ear. "Talk to me."

Her eyes squeeze shut. "I can't—I don't want to talk about it. I don't even want to *think* about it. My family's...crazy." She brushes her fingers over my T-shirt where her tears have made it wet. "I'm sorry."

"I don't mind, but I think I'll change it." I take the shirt off, and her eyes widen. She touches my tattoo but freezes, startled as the door swings open.

Sean walks in. "Whoa." He sets his bag on the floor and eyes Eva like a piece of meat.

"Get the hell out, Sean," I growl.

"Didn't mean to interrupt. I'm dropping my bag off and leaving. Catch ya later."

The door closes, and I apologize to Eva for the interruption.

"Was he the asshat?"

"Yep." I use my thumb to wipe a tear from her cheek.

She closes her eyes, takes a deep breath, and looks calmer. "I think I'm... I guess having so many people at the house for a week has been too much for me."

"Are they still leaving today?"

She nods.

"You don't want to be there?"

She shakes her head.

I want to know what the problem is, but if I push her to talk, she might leave. And I really, *really* don't want her to leave.

"I don't have plans today," I say. "I'm all yours. What would you like to do?"

She glances at my bed, and her cheeks blush.

Chapter Twenty-Eight
Eva

My gaze flits back and forth from Alex to his bed a couple times. I'd like to be back in it with him, especially now that he's taken off his shirt. His sexy, bare chest is inviting as hell. He's chiseled and smooth, and there's an irresistible vertical line of fine hair starting below his navel. It disappears beneath the waist of his jeans.

Heat floods my face—and other places—at the reality of where it leads, and I force my eyes back up. He's more shredded than I knew. The biggest surprise is the tattoo on his left pectoral.

I'm not sure why I never pictured him as having any ink, but I like it. Actually, I love it. The head of a longhorn is at the center, surrounded by concentric rings of intricate patterns of stars and barbed wire. It's burnt orange, detailed and unique.

I trace one of the horns with my fingertip. At my touch, he inhales sharply and covers my hand with his. His heart beats fast like mine, and I whisper, "This is beautiful."

"Thanks. It was to celebrate getting into UT." He steps to a closet and puts on another shirt. "Are you hungry?"

I'm disappointed he's fully dressed again, but I'm also starving and should pull the reins on ravishing him while I'm so unstable. "Yes. Food. Good idea."

We order pizza slices and sodas from the dining hall. I power my phone off and focus on being here with Alex, in his element. I soak everything in.

He takes me to a library. "This is cool," I say. "I haven't been in many libraries. And never a university one. Libraries aren't the kind of place my family goes out of their way to visit." I roll my eyes. "Now, if we're talking Hard Rock Cafés, that's a different story. I've been to dozens. Also theme parks."

"I've only ever been to one theme park—Six Flags in San Antonio."

"Do you like rollercoasters?" I ask.

"As long as they're not too crazy."

I wonder if he's starting to see my life, with all these ups and downs, as one of those crazy coasters, and my stomach sinks.

He doesn't notice and instead, spreads his arms, gesturing at the rows and rows of tall bookshelves. "What do you think?"

"Wow," I whisper, happy for the reprieve. The smell of old books makes me feel like I'm *inside* of a book.

We wander around, and I'm mesmerized by the thousands of volumes.

Soon, I've lost sight of Alex. As I round a corner, we almost collide. He has a mischievous look on his face, like he's been waiting for me. He leads me to a more secluded spot, kissing me.

I kiss him back. We make out, right here in the library. It's like we're alone, in our own little world, our bodies desperately smashed together for a few blissful moments.

Once we cool off, I ask, "Was it a fantasy of yours, to do this here?"

The spark in his eyes is my answer, and I say, "I'm glad we made it happen."

"So am I." He kisses me one more time and takes my hand. "Let's go. There's another place I want to show you."

After an uphill walk, we enter another building, the Harry Ransom Center. "Your choice," he says. "Do you want to visit a photography exhibit or something on Shakespeare? Fair warning, if you choose Shakespeare, we might have to break up."

"Lead the way to the photography exhibit. I'm not a fan of The Bard either."

"I knew there's a reason I like you so much."

"Only one?"

"There might be *one* other reason. If I can think of it, I'll fill you in."

I laugh and hug him. "Thanks for spending the day with me."

Next, we visit the famous UT Tower, then some buildings where he has classes, the student union, and lots of places in between.

He snaps photos of me, including a few selfies of us together. "I promise I won't put them on social media or anything."

"Thanks. Send some to me. I love the one at the fountain."

"Here, let's take a break." He points to a bench in the shade.

We've walked a lot, and it's nice to sit. He leans his head back, eyes closed.

I power my phone back on to check the time. I've missed several calls and messages. A few texts were from Toby, Talina, and Lor. Most were from Spike, and my stomach twists in a guilty knot. Running off the way I did without telling at least him goodbye was wrong, but I can't do anything about it now.

There are no messages from Mom or Ike. No surprise.

Last night's indignation has faded some, but it stings to think of how wrong I've been all my life. Mom wasn't only with Ike the one time that might have resulted in my conception. I thought I knew my family better than this. Again, I wonder if Spike knows about Mom and Ike? Have he and his brother made a sharing arrangement?

Gross! I shudder. What is wrong with these people?

Alex places a hand on mine. I was scraping my thumb against my scar again.

"Everything okay?" he asks.

I clench my jaw and nod. It's a silent lie. All day, I've considered telling him what's going on, but it's too bizarre and embarrassing.

"I should probably get home," I say. "Will you help me find my way back to the big honking truck?" My attempt at a laugh sounds hollow and sad.

He puts an arm around me, making me feel protected and safe, and walks me to the parking garage. After he kisses me goodbye, I head for Casa Lor, relieved Mom, FU, and their entourage will be gone.

It's like a ghost town. No tour buses or limos.

I enter, going straight upstairs to Lor's room. He's the perfect person to talk with about Mom.

He sees me in the doorway, frowns, and holds out a hand to me. "Eva, where've you been? Everyone was looking for you."

"I'm sorry." I enter and take his hand, squeezing. "I had to…be away from here until they were all gone."

Scooting over, he makes room for me to sit on the bed with him and puts an arm around me. "What's wrong?"

"Last night, I saw…Mom and Ike. They were…" I stammer. What should I call it? Tears sting my eyes. I let them fall, unable to keep everything bottled up anymore.

Lor hugs me to his chest and rests his chin on top of my head. "I'm sorry you found out about them like that, Eva."

"What?" I sniffle. "You knew?"

"Yeah, sis. I knew."

I pull away enough to look him in the face. "Why didn't you ever say anything?"

He sighs. "I knew it would upset you, but I'm glad you know now. It's time you stop living in the bubble she's put you in your whole life."

"Does Spike know?" I squeeze my eyes shut.

"He pretends not to. Mom and Ike have never been open about it. I know because I walked in on them once, several years ago."

"Oh, and a couple nights ago—" I sit up "—Mom hugged me. In public. I wasn't wearing a disguise, and she was drunk. Didn't realize what she was doing." The scene, which I'd sort of forgotten with everything else going on, rushes back, and I shudder.

"Damn," Lor mutters. "Can't believe she was so careless."

We sit quietly for a moment, until he says, "Eva, I need you to do me a favor. There's a bottle of rare, single malt Macallan. It's *somewhere* downstairs."

My heart sinks with disappointment. "What makes you think it's down there?"

"FU's roadie, Baxter." He scratches at his stubbly cheek. "He texted me after they were gone and said it got left behind by accident."

"And let me guess. The bottle's been calling your name ever since."

"More like screaming it." He rests his head on the pillow propped behind him.

"I won't bring it to you." I stand beside the bed, arms crossed.

"I'm not asking you to. Find it and take it out of the house, along with any other alcohol you find. Get rid of it. I don't...trust myself. I've been sitting here thinking how I could have Darnell take me downstairs in the wheelchair. I planned it all in my head. I'd tell Jojo and everyone else to take the day off so I could look for it." He breaks down in front of me like I've never seen him do before. "I'd have probably drunk myself unconscious."

I squeeze his hand, relieved. "The important thing is you *didn't* do any of those things. I'm proud of you."

He clears his throat. "I promised you, and... I've told myself if I ever break that promise again, I'll put myself in rehab. But rehab's not the publicity I've ever wanted."

"I'll find the bottle and any others. Get some rest. You look tired."

"Yes ma'am." He quickly wipes tears from his eyes.

Chapter Twenty-Nine
Alex

When I return to my room, Graham's here with Sean.

"Have you seen this thing on SLY?" Graham shows me his phone. The screen's open to a video thumbnail for SLY's celebrity gossip website.

Angie was a gossip hound and watched stuff on SLY all the time. I hated her weird fascination with the private lives of people in the public eye.

I don't want to see whatever Graham's trying to show me, but he shoves it in front of my face and asks, "Isn't this the girl you were with earlier?"

My breath hitches as Sean taps the screen and celebrity gossip reporter Carla Kinsey, says, "Does this mystery girl look too much like supermodel Sloane Silver for her to *just* be an acquaintance or friend? What *is* their connection?" A couple of photos appear on the screen. They're from the other night downtown. A drunken Sloane is hugging Eva, undisguised. Whoever took the photos caught the horror of the moment on Eva's face.

I rake a hand through my hair. Damn. This is the kind of thing Eva was afraid of. I'm twisted up inside, wondering if this is what was wrong with her earlier.

No…she would have told me. I'd like to think so, anyway.

"It's her, right, the girl you were with?" Graham asks.

"Alex, you gotta give us details," Sean says. "Who is she?"

Not saying a word, I leave and drive to Casa Lor. Eva needs to know of this, and I don't want to tell her on the phone.

The guardhouse at the security gate is unmanned again, and the old code doesn't work anymore. Makes sense they'd have changed it. I call Eva.

"Hey, boyfriend." She sounds happy and sexy as hell. "What's up?"

It's gonna be a shame to dampen her upbeat mood. "I'm actually here, at Casa Lor. Can you let me in?"

"Oh...sure." She tells me the code, and she's waiting on the porch as I drive up and exit my truck. "Is everything okay?" she asks.

"Eva, there's something you need to see. I'm sorry to have to show you this. It's a celebrity gossip thing." I take my phone from my pocket.

She frowns as she beckons me inside.

Chapter Thirty
Eva

Alex and I sit on the main house living room sofa, and I brace myself for what he wants to show me on his phone.

Oh crap!

It's photos.

Of Mom.

With me.

As myself.

Undisguised.

I stare and wait for the tightening of my throat.

The prickle of my skin.

The panic I've always imagined would follow when the inevitable happened.

All I feel is…numbing exhaustion.

Alex scrolls to a video clip, and there's Crazy Carla, Mom's number one stalker, saying, "Does this mystery girl look too much like supermodel Sloane Silver for her to *just* be an acquaintance or friend? What *is* their connection?" Carla, with her full, round face and big eyes, talks about me like I'm a national secret she's on a mission to uncover.

"Well…*damn*." I'm at a loss for what else to say. Or think.

Alex sets his phone on the coffee table and rubs my shoulder. "At least they don't have your name. Or know your connection to Sloane."

This may be the saving grace. People will grow bored with the reporter's weak speculation.

Won't they?

I slump back against the sofa and think of escaping this absurdity. I could get a tiny house or have one built. Hit the road and never look back.

But who am I kidding? I don't have the guts. Nor do I want to abandon Lor.

Alex shifts on the couch beside me, and I study his profile. The way his hair falls onto his forehead. Those full lips. Strong jawline.

No, there's no escape for me. I've grown particularly attached to him. He's so much fun and gets me on a level nobody else ever has. With him, I can be myself. I don't want to lose that.

He's writing on a notepad from the coffee table. I look closer. He's drawing, not writing. And wow, he's talented. He's drawn a woman, somewhat cartoonish, with a big head like one of those popular 1980s dolls. She's holding a microphone to her wide mouth. He draws a box around her, like she's on a TV screen, and adds "Cabbage Patch Carla" at the bottom.

I laugh. "That's what she reminds me of, but I couldn't remember what those dolls were called. I didn't know you were an artist."

"Oh, I'm not." He turns the paper over and begins sketching again.

I'm mesmerized as he moves the pen across the paper, drawing another woman. This one has softer features. Long, flowing hair and an hourglass figure. He finishes it by drawing her smile. It lights up her face. He writes "Mystery Girl" above it. And, maybe in case I don't realize it's me, he adds my name in tiny print below it.

"Is this how you see me?" Warmth blooms in my chest, into my neck.

"If you were two-dimensional. Lucky for me, I get the real you." He kisses me.

I nod in appreciation, thinking he was generous with the way he drew my chest, but it's flattering. The most remarkable thing is the woman's posture. She appears striking, with her shoulders back and her hands on her hips. If only I could *feel* that confident.

Leaning on Alex's shoulder, I close my eyes and shut everything out.

Next thing I know, he's whispering, "Eva, wake up."

"Huh…" I rub my eyes. "Oh, did I fall asleep?"

"Yeah, sorry to wake you." He kisses my cheek. "I gotta go. I have class in the morning."

~ * ~

The next day, Mom sends me a picture of her *ginormous* engagement ring. Doesn't she remember what went down between us? I don't respond, and later she sends a message.

Quit sulking. Be happy for ME.

Everything's always about *her*. I can't bring herself to reply. I'd rather not spend any time thinking of Mom or FU. I'm not even going to bother asking if she's heard the two of us are in the gossip news.

My ACR shift isn't for another few hours, and I'm restless. It's been a while since Stella cleaned in here, so I go to the main house and find her in the kitchen.

"Where do you keep the cleaning supplies?" I ask.

"Why?" She stops chewing her gum and eyes me with skepticism over the top of her magazine.

"Because the guesthouse needs to be cleaned." It's also time I start doing these chores for myself.

Stella shrugs and shows me where the supplies are. I set to work, scrubbing my first toilet, mopping my first floor, and even vacuuming my first carpet. By the time I'm finished, I've worked up a good sweat. A little manual labor is surprisingly therapeutic.

When I leave for ACR, there's a white car on the opposite side of the security gate, parked off the driveway. I wish FU's security was still here. I drive through, making sure the gate closes behind me, and open my window. The car's driver's side window is halfway down, and I call out, "This is private property. You need to leave. Please."

A woman opens the door, gets out and approaches me. "Is this the residence of DeLorean Jenson, son on Sloane Silver? I'm with SLY and have a few questions if you have a moment."

Another woman gets out of the passenger seat and snaps pictures of me.

Panicking, I drive away, rolling the window back up. What was I thinking, talking to them? I can't believe it didn't occur to me they could be vulturous reporters.

My hands tremble on the wheel as I turn onto the road at the end of the driveway. My eyes keep going to the rearview mirror, worried the white car's following me. So far, I don't see it. I'm afraid to drive further until I've stopped shaking.

After a few deep breaths, I call Lor. "I just left, and there's a reporter at the gate."

"Shit. It happens sometimes. Did they say what they wanted?"

"She asked if it was your residence and mentioned you being Sloane Silver's son."

"Huh…that's no secret. If she didn't ask about you, I wouldn't worry."

We hang up, and I grip the wheel, wishing it were as easy to not worry as he made it sound. I pull back onto the road and drive to ACR. Nadine's in the lot between the buildings and watches me park. Her eyes grow big and round. This is the first time I've driven here in this truck.

As I climb out of it, she says, "Nice truck, but where's your Prius?"

"Um, someone backed into it, and it's in the shop. The truck's an early birthday present from...my family."

"Wow. Okay." She gapes at me and then the truck. I weigh, for a moment, sharing everything with this kindhearted woman who's the total opposite of Mom, but I don't want Mom casting a shadow on ACR. I rub my hands together and ask Nadine, "What did I miss last week?"

"Something exciting." She links her arm through mine as we enter the showroom. "We found out ACR's eligible for a grant. It would step things up around here. Blair, Hank's daughter, emailed the info. We need to compile some records, including photos, and complete the application."

"Great. I can't wait to meet Blair. Where does she go to college?"

"Santa Barbara, where Hank's ex lives. Blair finished high school here in Austin, and she keeps in touch with local non-profits. It's how she heard of the grant."

"Tell me how I can help."

114

Chapter Thirty-One
Alex

I got my fill of trashy celebrity gossip during my time with Angie, but I've been compelled to check what's online about Eva in the last several days. And I'm pretty sure I'll vomit if I hear SLY's motto of: "We'll Share your Secrets, but We *Still Love You*" one more time.

Fortunately, Cabbage Patch Carla hasn't reported anything else on the "mystery girl."

Even so, Eva's reluctant to be spotted in public, and I don't blame her. We decide it's best to hang out at Casa Lor. She invites me for dinner.

I drive to the house, and she's on the porch wearing shorts and a tank top. The sight of her does my heart good. She runs to me as soon as I leave my truck. I pick her up and love the way she wraps her arms and legs around me.

I laugh. "What's got you in such a good mood?"

"You're here." Her bare legs squeeze my hips, and she kisses me. I could become real used to this, with her breasts mashed against my chest and my hands cupped under her butt.

"Come on." She slides down my body—oh *damn*, that was hot—and takes my hand. "Hector's teaching me to cook. We're making salmon with roasted red pepper pesto."

In the kitchen, Hector's setting out ingredients and cookware. "Hello, Alex. Eva wants to learn to cook. Any idea what that's about?"

"No idea." I grin, appreciating the Wonder Woman apron Eva's putting on.

"You like it?" She strikes a pose.

"I love it." I pull her to me and kiss her, long and hard.

Hector clears his throat—loudly. "Are we cooking here, or what?"

"Sorry, Boss." Eva laughs, and I move to the other side of the bar.

A pen and notepad call to me, begging me to draw the scene. In my sketch, I nickname Hector "Honcho," as in head honcho. I draw Eva in a Wonder Woman costume. She and Hector put the salmon in the oven, and she heads over to sit down by me at the bar when he orders her to the sink. "These dishes aren't washing themselves."

"Sir, yes sir!" She salutes him. "Show me what to do."

He explains what needs to be washed by hand and what can be put in the dishwasher, like it's the first time she's done this. How strange and different from me. I've been washing dishes since I was five years old. Mom had me stand on a chair to reach the sink.

Hector throws together a rice and vegetable side dish.

Once everything's ready, Eva and I carry our plates to the theater room.

"Have you watched *Buffy the Vampire Slayer*?" she asks.

"Yeah, it's good. Cassidi and I watched the whole series a few years ago."

"I'm up to the ninth episode."

By the end of the show, we've finished eating and share the after-dinner mints she brought from the kitchen. She shuts off the lights. We get comfy in the oversized theater seats and play the next episode. It's about nightmares coming true in an alternate reality. One of them involves a character being chased by a scary clown.

Eva switches the lights back on and shudders. "I hate clowns."

"I'm sorry, I forgot that part of this episode. We can skip it if you want."

"No, I wanna see the end, but can I sit on your lap?" She laughs. "Wow, how cheesy."

"I like cheese," I joke. And of course, she's welcome to sit on my lap anytime she wants.

She leans against my chest, and I put my arms around her. She smells delicious. It's the usual vanilla but with a hint of something else. Peaches?

The rest of the show is lost on me. I concentrate on having her close.

As the episode ends, she nestles her head between my neck and shoulder and our fingers entwine. Can she hear how fast she makes my heart race?

I press my nose to the top of her head. "You smell like peaches and cream."

She looks up at me with those beautiful green eyes. "Is that a good thing?"

"It's a very good thing." I kiss her, and she shifts on my lap, pushing the button to recline my seat back. Soon, she's lying on top of me.

Chapter Thirty-Two
Eva

My body settles on Alex's. I'm heady from his spicy cologne and rugged guy smell, but as much as I want to see where this could lead—especially as he slides his hand up the back of my shirt—I'm not sure if I'm ready for more.

Shifting to the side a little, I'm not right on top of him now, and rest my head on his chest. His heart's beating fast. We stay like this for a few minutes, catching our breath.

He sighs and lazily runs his fingers through my hair. "Was that the Prius I saw when I drove up?"

"It was delivered today. Repaired, like new."

"But the truck is growing on you, isn't it?"

"Yeah, it is. Oh, and Nadine was psyched. She talked of trailers and towing capacity and asked if we can use it to haul stuff for ACR."

"Are you okay with that?"

"Absolutely, but you know what's been increasingly on my mind about the truck?"

"A tiny house."

I lift my head. "Am I such an open book?"

"I notice things."

"Is that right, Mr. Observant? What's my favorite color?"

"Red. Not royal red. More like ruby red. The color of your truck."

"Okay, show off. What's my favorite number?"

"Nine." He grazes his fingertips down my side. It tickles, and my squirming encourages him to do it again. My giggles seem to give him great satisfaction.

"Oh, my gosh!" I laugh and squeal. "Animal."

"I'm not an animal. You're the one who was climbing all over *me* a minute ago."

I swat his shoulder playfully. "No, I meant what's my favorite animal?"

"Tell me." His strong arms pull me back on top of him, and he tucks my hair behind my ears.

"Giraffe. When I was a kid, there was a noise, like a whistling sound, I used to hear on the tour bus, and I asked…Govern'Essa…what it was. Hmmm." I close my eyes, lost in the warmth of his lips on my neck. My body quivers on top of his.

"Go on." He nips my earlobe between his teeth. "What did Govern'Essa say?"

"Um, she called it a draft, and I thought she said, 'It's a giraffe.' I imagined there must be a miniature giraffe somewhere on the bus, like a band pet or something. A *secret* giraffe. Nobody else ever—*oh, Alex*." I'm breathless from the kisses he trails from the side of my neck to the base of my throat.

"You have the sexiest collarbones," he murmurs.

His lips skim one, then the other. The light grazing of his teeth across my skin has me tingling. He slides his hands to my butt. I moan, aroused by how hard he is, pressing right between my legs. I imagine ripping his clothes off. Touching him. Him touching me.

Wait. Think, Eva.

I shouldn't let this happen. What if he thinks I'm a tease? My whole life, I've seen people treat sex like such a casual, selfish thing. It gets cheapened and can have painful consequences, emotionally and physically. I should stop this, but my brain struggles to send the signals to keep my body from responding to Alex's. My hips grind in synch with his, guided by his hands.

He groans, and my brain kicks in.

"Alex, wait. We should—I'm not sure…" I can't find the right words. He must understand. He stops and stills his hands.

His eyes open, full of remorse. "I'm sorry, Eva." He helps me move off him, back to the seat I started in. He apologizes again and sits up, rubbing his face.

"It's okay." I fan myself, and an embarrassing laugh escapes me. I can't stop worrying about what happens after sex. Sure, everything's hot and heavy now, but after…what then?

Stories I've heard from Talina and other people swirl in my head. Things get weird after sex. Feelings change. People act different. And then, it's on to the next person. I don't want to mess up what we have. Or lose him. And the fact I can't say any of this to him right now—I figure it means I'm not ready.

After an awkward moment, he clears his throat. "So…a giraffe, huh?"

"Yeah." I take in a calming breath. Exhale slowly. "What's your favorite animal?"

"I guess I don't have one. But my favorite color is green, like your eyes, and I've always been partial to the number two. Lots of good things are in pairs. What's your favorite food?"

"Hmm, I love pizza with Canadian bacon and pineapple, Hawaiian-style. And my favorite dessert is cake. Hey, isn't your birthday soon?"

He gives me an appreciative smile for remembering. "Next Wednesday."

"Any plans?"

"Not until Saturday. I'll spend that day with my parents."

"Can I take you to dinner next Wednesday?"

"Sounds fun."

We take our dinner dishes to the kitchen. Instead of depositing them in the sink like I usually would, I rinse them and load them in the dishwasher like Hector showed me earlier.

Alex jumps right in to help, like this is natural to him, and it's refreshingly "normal" to stand there at the sink with my boyfriend, sharing an everyday chore.

Chapter Thirty-Three
Alex

Friday night, I'm awakened by Sean entering the room with a giggling girl.

"Hey, trying to sleep here," I grumble.

They ignore me and don't even bother going to his bunk. She's perched on the edge of his desk, and their clothes start flying off faster than I can jump up and put mine on.

There's the unmistakable crinkle of a condom wrapper being torn open. I grab the bag I've already packed for spending tomorrow night in Florence. Might as well head there now.

For a hot minute, as I drive off campus, I consider going to Eva's. I miss her like crazy, but *I'm* to blame for not seeing her in several days. I've made the excuses of a hectic schedule, errand running, needing to keep school in check. The deeper truth is I've needed time away from Eva. Not because I don't want to be with her. It's because of how much I *do* want her. My last—and only—physical relationship didn't require any holding back. I can't be that free with Eva, not after she put on the brakes the other night. But, man, I'm sure tempted to show up at Casa Lor, tell her how much I want her, scoop her into my arms, and carry her to bed.

At my parents' house, I let myself in, figuring they're asleep. The lights are off, but muffled noises filter in from the dining room. As I take a peek, I get an eyeful of Dad—or rather his ass. Buck naked, illuminated by a stream of light from the kitchen.

Oh, shit.

My parents are doing it on the table! No wonder Dad wanted to build it "hella" sturdy.

I back away, covering my face, and silently begging for eye bleach. Jeez, I hope Lena isn't here. Surely, she's spending the night with Cassidi, or my parents wouldn't be getting busy in the open like this.

What now?

If I spend the night in my room, my parents will suspect I saw them or at least heard them. That could lead to a conversation I do *not* want to have. I leave and drive around, trying to clear my mind.

There's a Honda at the high school stadium, and I recognize it as Jessica's, my friend from high school. I wonder what she's doing here in the middle of the night and hesitate to peer into her dark car—don't relish witnessing a third couple having sex. Although it would provide me with an embarrassing story on Jessica as she has on me. My gut clenches from the memory of our conversation outside the dance hall, that night she asked about me being with an older woman.

Nobody's in Jessica's car.

The sound of bottles clanking draws my attention to the football field. She's sitting there in the moonlight. Alone. A six-pack of beer at her side.

I pass through the open gate and walk toward her. "Jessica? What are you doing?"

She gasps. "Alex, you scared me!" Her face is red, splotchy, and streaked with tears.

"What's wrong?" I sit beside her, and she collapses against my shoulder.

"My grandmother had a stroke, and my dumbass boyfriend broke up with me. He's such a jerk. And I'm failing two classes." She hiccups. "My life's a freakin' mess."

"I'm sorry. Is your grandmother going to be okay?"

"They think so, but she'll need to be in a nursing home now." She wipes her face on her sleeve. "Hey, why are you here? In Florence, I mean. But also, here."

"My dorm room turned into the set of a porno. Damn roommate and his latest conquest. I got the hell out of there and drove home since I'm spending tomorrow with my family—"

"Oh, your birthday's next week, isn't it? Happy Birthday."

"Yeah, thanks, but I couldn't stay at the house, either."

"Why not?"

"Walked in on my parents. Having sex. In the kitchen." I cringe.

She laughs. "Woo-hoo, Mr. and Mrs. Marshall! Still going strong."

We spend the next few hours talking and laughing. And drinking the rest of the six-pack.

Lightheaded, I lay back on the grass. "I shouldn't drive. And you for sure shouldn't."

~ * ~

I awake in the morning with a dull headache. Sunlight warms my face, and I keep my eyes shut, trying to remember where I am. My arm's asleep, under Jessica's head. I try pulling it from under her without waking her up and have the strange sensation of being watched.

"Hey, mister," a kid's voice pierces my ears. "Why are y'all sleeping on the field?"

My eyes pop open. A bunch of kids in soccer uniforms stare down at me, giggling and pointing. As their coach herds them away, shooting me a nasty look, I nudge Jessica.

She yawns and brushes my hand away.

I whisper with urgency, "Get up. We gotta go."

Her eyes pop open, and she bolts upright. "Crap."

We race to the parking lot and wave to each other as we drive away separately.

I spend the rest of the weekend with my family. My parents show no indication of knowing I was in Florence Friday night, but Brady sends a text on Monday.

WTF, Alex?

Next, he sends a photo of Jessica and me asleep on the field.

I call him right away. "Dude, where'd you get the picture?"

"Garrett."

"Your little brother? Oh, hell, he was one of those soccer kids? Look, Brady, it was nothing." I explain what happened with Jessica, and Brady laughs his ass off.

I hope it's the last mention of it, but Mom calls the next afternoon.

"Alex, there's something I need to discuss with you." *She* isn't laughing. "One of my students passed around a photo on his phone today."

Turns out, Garrett's in one of her classes at the middle school.

"Mom, let me explain." I give her the main details but don't mention I ended up at the football field because of her and Dad doing the deed on the damn dining table.

"The photo sure seemed…intimate," she says, and I imagine her cheeks are red. "The boys made the most inappropriate remarks about you *scoring* with a *total babe*."

"God, Mom, stop." Now *my* cheeks burn. "We were fully clothed! Nothing happened."

"This is a small town, son. People talk. Please be more mindful about what you do."

I'm kicking myself for causing her embarrassment and worry how bad it'd be if word gets around about Angie. It puts me in a foul mood for a couple of days. I'd hate for Eva to find out and misconstrue the situation. She's taking me to dinner for my birthday tonight, and I need to snap out of my funk ASAP. We're supposed to meet at a parking lot near my dorm.

I walk there, and she must see me. She steps down from her truck in boots and a mid-thigh length dress, giving my mood a lift. We haven't seen each other in eight days, and damn, what've I been thinking?

She's too hot for words. I pick her up and spin her around.

She laughs. "Happy Birthday."

"You look amazing." I set her down and kiss her, like *really* kiss her, holding her body close to mine. When I break the kiss, her eyes are dazed, and her cheeks flushed.

"You wanna drive?" she asks, breathless. "I'm not sure I can now."

I bend and hook my arm under her knees, picking her up. An image of carrying her to bed flashes through my mind.

We buckle up in the truck, and I see she has the GPS taking us to Jacoby's on Cesar Chavez. "Jacoby's is pricey. Are you sure—"

"I've got it covered, birthday boy."

"Okay, if you insist." I drive out of the parking lot. "How's Lor doing?"

"Good. Cooperating with physical therapy. We've been watching *Buffy* together. It's funny how many one-liners he knows by heart. How have you been?"

"Relieved," I say. "My grades have improved enough I'll be off academic probation after this semester. Oh, and I got a job. You're looking at the newest UT Tower tour guide. I start the week after school gets out."

"Congratulations! Tour guide, huh? You'll be a great one."

At the restaurant, a waiter serves our drinks in mason jars, and Eva glances around the dining room. "I hope nobody recognizes me. Maybe I should have worn a disguise."

"I'd be surprised. There haven't been any more gossip reports about you."

"True, but the other day when I was leaving Casa Lor, a reporter was at the security gate. She was asking if Lor, son of Sloane Silver, lived there. The fact he's her kid has always been public. Why's someone asking about it now?"

"Who knows?" It sounds like someone's digging deeper into Eva's connection to the family, but I don't want to worry her by saying so.

The waiter returns and takes our orders.

Eva hands me the gift bag she brought in with her. I take out a sketchbook and box of art pencils.

"You say you aren't an artist, but I disagree," she says. "And I wondered if you've ever considered adding color."

"I have, especially when I draw you. Now I'll be able to make those beautiful green eyes of yours stand out. Thank you, Eva, this is awesome." I take her hand and feel like I've won the lottery.

"Tell me about your weekend," she says during dinner.

For a second, I worry she knows about Jessica and the damn picture of us, but that's stupid. How would she have heard?

When I don't answer, Eva asks, "What did you and your family do for your birthday?"

"Oh yeah. My mom makes a big deal of birthdays. She gets sentimental. We went to the farmer's market for old times' sake. It's our tradition because she can never wrangle my dad or brother and sister into going. I'm always the sucker who goes along to carry stuff for her."

"That's sweet." There's a hint of teasing in her voice.

I pretend to be defensive. "Are you making fun of me?"

"I'm not! I *do* think it's sweet. Go on, what else did you do?"

"We ate a picnic lunch at the park and went canoeing with the whole family, except for my brother."

"Where was your brother?"

"Working." At least that's what he claimed, and I was glad he wasn't there.

"Canoeing, huh? Sounds fun."

"Yeah, have you ever canoed?" I ask, and she says no. "I'll take you sometime. We also went to see a country band at a dance hall. I helped Lena practice two-stepping. She wants me to take her to prom."

"How sweet. I did online school. Didn't have a prom." Eva looks a little sad. I wish I could help her experience the stuff she missed, then I think of a way I *can* introduce her to more of UT.

"There's a star party on campus tonight," I say. At her confused expression, I add, "It's an astronomy thing, to look at the stars. Wanna go?"

"I'd love to."

After dinner, I drive us back to campus, and we stroll to Robert Lee Moore Hall, where we join a dozen or so other people on the building's roof.

"Are you having a good time?" I ask her as we wait in line for the telescope.

"Yeah, it's like a field trip would've been, if I'd gone to school."

Her sweet attitude makes me want to kiss her, but we have an audience. I settle for circling my arms around her waist as we wait.

She goes first at the telescope and then I take my turn.

I'm not big on astronomy but viewing the stars through the high-powered telescope is mind-blowing. I've been listening to the speaker describe different constellations and hadn't noticed how still and quiet Eva has become. Her earlier sense of awe is gone, replaced by distress, and her face is a little pale.

"Are you all right?" I whisper.

Her shoulders rise in a shrug. "Is there such a thing as the *opposite* of claustrophobia?"

"Is it the feeling you have when you want to be in a smaller space because everything feels too big?"

"Exactly. The universe is…huge. Sorry I'm such a freak." She tries to laugh it off.

"You're not a freak. You're fine." We head to her truck, and I say, "I wish we could go to my room, but there's likely to be an asshat or two hanging around."

Her lips curve upward. "We could always make out in my truck."

I squeeze her hand, and we walk faster, like we can't get there soon enough.

In the truck, she's behind the wheel and I'm in the passenger seat. I lean toward her, telling myself this *can't* lead to anything other than kissing. But, damn, it's easy to want more once her sweet mouth is on mine. Our tongues touching, warm and wet. Hands exploring. She runs her fingers down my shoulders, around to my back. As she kisses my neck, I slide a hand from her knee to the hem of her dress. Her bare skin's soft and smooth. I want to lose all control.

~ * ~

The next time Eva invites me over, she's wearing her Wonder Woman apron again, helping Hector cook dinner. For the hundredth time, I'm blown away by how beautiful and fun she is. A playlist I made for her is playing in surround sound.

"What is this?" Hector asks. "Have you gone country, Eva?"

She winks and turns it up.

Once the food is in the oven, she walks over and looks at my drawings.

"Ooh, these are great, Alex." She flips through my sketchbook.

I don't know where Hector went. Eva and I are alone. I gather her hair to the side and kiss her neck.

She tilts her head and sighs. As I trail kisses from beneath her ear to her shoulder, I feel her muscles relaxing.

Her hands reach around to untie the apron at the small of her back. I stop her. "Let me," I murmur and remove it. I fight the impulse to continue undressing her. My lips are back on the sweet skin of her neck, and her pulse is strong and fast under my lips.

"Kiss me lower," she whispers.

My lips move deep into the V-neck of her shirt where the swells of her breasts strain against the top of her bra. As if *this* wasn't enough to drive me wild, she slides her hand up my thigh and brushes her fingertips across the bulge in my jeans. I'm not sure if the touch was intentional until she does it again, this time with added pressure. I'm a breath away from suggesting we forget dinner and go to the guesthouse.

She suddenly backs away.

"What's wrong?" I ask, aching for her touch again.

"Sorry," she whispers, smoothing her hair and clothes down. "Hector's coming."

I spin around and face the bar as Hector walks in. I have no idea how Eva knew he was about to walk in, but I'm glad she did, and I quickly compose myself as well.

~ * ~

Later, Eva and I are almost done eating when my phone rings. No name appears with the number, but it could be an errand services customer.

"Sorry, I need to take this," I tell Eva.

"Go ahead."

"Hello, this is Alex," I say into the phone.

"Alex, don't hang up—"

I reflexively yank the phone away from my ear, as if Angie could reach through it and get to me. The phone falls from my hand, clattering to the floor.

"Shit," I mutter and scramble to retrieve it. I disconnect and block yet another number.

"Everything okay?" Eva asks.

"Um, wrong number." I shrug and don't meet her eyes.

My phone rings again. A different number, same area code. What the hell? Angie's going to great lengths. Does she have a lifetime supply of burner phones or something?

"I'm gonna step out for a minute," I tell Eva and step out to the back patio to answer.

"Alex, are you there?" Angie asks. "Why won't you talk to me?"

"Why do you think?" My teeth grind.

"When will you stop being mad at me? I thought we had something—"

"You lied to me. About everything. Leave me alone."

"I've tried, but my life sucks without you. I think I'm... Oh, Alex." Her voice wavers and fills with pleading. "I don't want to talk on the phone. I need to *see* you."

"You are the *last* person I want to see. Ever again."

There's dead air for a moment.

"You *will* talk to me." Her voice has turned cold. "I'll find a way. And if you keep refusing, I might *accidentally* tell people—"

"Don't." An alarm goes off in my head, but I have to believe she's bluffing. "Look, Angie, you have to stop calling me."

I end the call and put my phone in Do Not Disturb mode, but it's too little, too late. Angie has ruined my mood. My appetite. My evening.

Back inside, I rub my temples a couple of times, and Eva asks, "Is something wrong?"

"Killer headache." It isn't a lie, and I end up telling her I need to leave sooner than I'd have liked.

"Oh...okay." Her face fills with disappointment, and she sets our plates beside the sink.

"I'm sorry."

She kisses me goodbye at the door and, and I can't believe I'm walking away from her right now, but I can't shake this black cloud hanging over me.

It's dark as I pass through the security gate. I always make sure it closes behind me, so I'm watching in the rearview mirror when a small flash of light catches my eye. I blink and look again. Nothing. Shit, this headache's making me see things. Or maybe not. After I leave Lor's driveway, I catch a glimpse of a white sedan making the same turn and lagging in the distance behind me. A few miles later, it's gone.

Alone in my dorm room—thank God Sean's gone—I feel better and more in control. The best thing I can do right now is keep ignoring Angie and not let her ruin any more of my life. Or my time with Eva, like I did tonight.

I call Eva before falling asleep. "How are you?" she asks, her voice sleepy.

"Headache's mostly gone. I wanted to tell you again I'm sorry for skipping the rest of our evening."

"Hmm, it's okay. I'm glad you're better."

I hear what sounds like a yawn. "I'll let you sleep, but I wanted to tell you when I left, I could swear there was a camera flash. And I think there was a car following me as I drove away."

"Damn. What color was the car?" she asks with a whimper.

"White, I think. Why?"

"The car I told you about after the first SLY story was also white."

"Should Lor hire security like FU had?"

"Maybe. I'll talk to him. I don't like the idea of someone hanging around there, not during the day, and especially not at night. Super creepy."

~ * ~

Lena and I order pizza and watch TV Friday night. I'm staying with her while our parents are out of town at an insurance convention for Dad's job.

"Have you got your tuxedo and my corsage yet?" Lena asks.

"What do I need a tuxedo for?" I tease.

"For prom tomorrow! Alex, don't you remember?" She gawks at me, wringing her hands.

"Yes, I'm sorry. I was kidding. I'll pick up my tux tomorrow. Along with your corsage and my boutonniere. You wanted something hot pink, right?"

This time she knows I'm joking and gives my arm a light shove. "No pink. Yuck. My dress is blue. The flowers need to be ivory."

"It's a good thing I got a purple tie. Those colors go good together, right?"

"Oh Alex, you're killing me. I better show you my dress, so you'll know what color you're supposed to have." She goes to her room and returns with a semi-formal gown.

"Beautiful dress. You'll look great in it." I reassure her my tux will match.

She switches to asking about makeup—a subject on which I'm clueless.

"Let Mom help you when she gets back, okay?"

Worry still creases her brow, but she agrees and takes her dress to her room. Several minutes later, she hasn't returned, so I check on her.

She's stressing over various cosmetics spread across her dresser and appears to have attempted applying some blue eye shadow. It's gotten all over the place because she's crying and rubbing at it.

Once she gets an idea in her head, she's hard to dissuade, and this is one of those times. She insists she has to figure her makeup out tonight.

"If you'll calm down, I'll help you with a trial run," I offer. Only

I have no idea what I'm doing. I call Eva. "If you aren't busy, I need a favor."

"What's up?"

I explain my predicament, and she tells me she'll be on her way as soon as she showers.

I've missed her more than I realized. She's all I can think of as Lena and I wait for her arrival.

She arrives carrying a box and an insulated cooler. I enjoy how she takes charge of the situation. She removes a carton of ice cream from the cooler and hands it to me. "Freezer, stat."

I do as I'm told, and she sets up a makeup mirror on the kitchen table and removes cosmetics from the box, chatting with Lena the whole time.

"You should go away," Lena tells me.

"What, and miss this?" I sit and watch Eva explain the mysterious process of skin care and makeup techniques for a "natural look."

I soak in everything about her. It's sinking in how much I like her and what she's become to me. She catches me gazing at her like a lovesick schoolboy. With an impish grin, she swivels around in her chair and faces me, one leg crossed over the other. Her sandaled foot is in front of me, and I tap the heel of her shoe with my foot. Her sandal sails onto the floor several feet away.

"You lost your shoe," I say with a straight face.

"For that, you have to scoop the ice cream. Lena, do you like mint chocolate chip?"

"Yes! Alex, scoop."

"You heard the girl." Eva shoves me out of my chair. I happily scoop the ice cream into three bowls. Eva gets a couple more items from the cosmetics box and tells Lena the importance of proper makeup removal.

"Who is Allison Sever?" Lena asks. "And why did she send you this box?"

"Oh, it's a pretend name my mom uses sometimes when she orders things for me. Her real name's Sloane Silver."

I'm surprised Eva gave this away.

And mortified as Lena blurts, "Alex, didn't you have a poster of Sloane—"

"Hey, Lena, here's your ice cream," I interrupt, handing her a bowl.

"Poster, huh?" Eva asks in a flat voice. "Alex, I thought you said—"

"No, I didn't. You asked if I had a magazine under my pillow. A poster's not the same."

Her eyes narrow at me. "I'll deal with you later."

"Can't wait," I say.

She smirks and catches a drip of ice cream on the side of her bowl. Her perfect, pink tongue licks the bowl's rim. My blood rushes south, leaving me momentarily brain dead.

"Thanks for helping me, Eva," Lena says, reminding me Eva and I aren't alone.

Eva hugs her. "You're welcome."

"I'm glad you're Alex's first girlfriend."

I cringe.

Confusion creeps into Eva's face, but she graciously changes the subject. "Are y'all going to the prom in a limo?"

Lena's face lights up. "Alex, let's get a limo!"

"Uhhh, are you forgetting I'm a poor college student?"

"I could arrange for it," Eva offers.

"What? You don't have to," I protest. Lena claps her hands, begging. "Let me talk to Eva about it later, all right?" I tell her. "Why don't you eat your ice cream and change clothes for bed?"

Sorry, Eva mouths at me.

"No problem." I'm not upset with her about the limo, but I *am* distracted, worrying what she'll ask once we're alone, like why does my sister think I've never had a girlfriend before?

Chapter Thirty-Four
Eva

I wait in the kitchen while Alex sees Lena off to bed.

He had a poster of Mom in his room! And he said he'd been in a relationship before, so why did Lena say *I'm* his first girlfriend?

As I close the cosmetics box, Alex returns the kitchen.

"I'll leave the makeup here. Sorry for the limo comment," I say, unsure how to broach what I really want to know. "I should've—"

"Eva." He wraps his arms around me. "A limo's fine."

I'm relieved I didn't cross a line. "I was trying to live vicariously through her. Her prom should be special."

"It will be. Thank you for being here tonight." His lips cover mine, and the passion he pours into the kiss takes my breath away. "Let's go to my room." His low, sexy voice makes me forget everything else.

Almost.

"Um, it depends." I take a step back. "Is there a poster of my mom in there? There's no way around it—that'll kill the mood."

"The poster is long gone. I can't believe Lena said that in front of you."

"*Please* tell me you didn't, like, fantasize about my mom...no—never mind. I don't want to know."

He laughs and leads me to his room. I hold in a breath of nervous anticipation, but in the illumination from a bedside lamp, the only thing hanging on any walls is an outdated calendar beside the desk.

I sit on the full-size mattress for a better look at photos on the headboard's built-in shelf.

"Was this your senior year?" I point at a framed snapshot of him with girl in prom attire.

"Yeah, that's Jessica. We grew up together. I asked her to prom as a friend." He turns some music on low—California Nine—and sits beside me on the bed.

I study the photo again. The way they're standing beside each other without touching looks more friendly than romantic.

I face him. "Why does Lena think I'm your first girlfriend?"

He rubs the back of his neck. "She doesn't know about Angie. None of my family does."

It's the first time I've heard his ex's name. I don't like how it makes her more real.

"Hey." I touch Alex's shoulder. "I'm sorry for being nosy, but why was Angie a secret?"

"I didn't want my parents knowing of her. Being with her was…a mistake." He stares at the floor, shoulders hunched. I've stirred up bad memories and hate Angie for whatever she did to hurt him.

Trailing my hand from his shoulder, I massage his neck, wishing it would erase his pain the way it seems to ease his tension. He relaxes into my touch, and I start using both hands.

"You're the first girl to ever be on this bed," he murmurs.

"Other than those few minutes in your dorm room, I've never been in a guy's bed before." I lie down and tug his arm for him to lay beside me. He brushes my hair behind my shoulder.

His eyes close when I kiss him, and we melt into each other. My fingers inch up his shirt.

"Do you mind?" I whisper and pull up the hem of his shirt, ready to have it out of my way.

He sits up, takes it off, and lies right back beside me, hurrying to draw me close again, like those few seconds apart were more than he could stand.

Smothering his chest with kisses, I'm drunk on his scent and taste. His skin's like a drug, and I'm an addict. My lips graze his tattoo and downward to his nipple. He shivers, dancing his fingers across my waist where my shirt has ridden up.

He kisses his way over my ribs, onto my stomach. I moan with need for more and ask, "Is there a lock on your bedroom door?"

"Yes…I locked it. Is that okay?"

I sit up and take my shirt off. Then my bra. I stretch beside him, emboldened by his adoring gaze.

"Eva," he murmurs and gathers me to him. "You're perfect."

He kisses me, and I revel in the warmth of his bare skin on mine. The gentle touch of his hands on my breasts. His lips and tongue tugging my nipples into his mouth. Heat builds in me, deep and low, like there's a direct connection between the most sensitive points of my body. He isn't even touching me *there*, but I swear an orgasm's building.

As if he can read my mind—or maybe my body—he shifts his weight and lies between my legs. His arousal presses against me in the best way.

We move together, hips tilting, rocking. I moan from the sweet friction.

He kisses my neck, and I close my eyes. Give into the rising sensation. It climbs...and climbs. And feels so damn amazing. I cling to him, my body shuddering as I ride out the intensity in waves. My body trembles as he slows his hips.

"Oh. My. God." The words escape in gasps as I try to catch my breath.

He kisses my neck. "That was hot. I love how sensitive you are." Lifting his hips, he reaches for the button on his jeans. "Is this okay?" The zipper pull is between his fingers. Words fail me, but I put my hand on his and guide him to unzip. I touch him over his underwear. My fingers trace the thick, warm length of him.

He groans and closes his eyes. "I want you, Eva."

I want him too.

I think.

He unbuttons my shorts. I don't stop him, but I'm flooded with a fear of things being ruined between us once we do this incredibly intimate thing.

Will he change? Will I?

I can't get a deep breath. Is this normal?

It's embarrassing I don't even know what *normal* is in these situations.

Why am I shaking?

"Alex." My voice cracks.

His eyes open, and his face fills with worry. "Eva, what's wrong?" He shifts, lying beside me, and touches my face.

"I'm nervous. I'm sorry." I'm also so embarrassed I can't look at him.

He cradles my face in his hand. "It's all right. We don't have to...I mean, I wasn't expecting...well, I was *hoping*, but—"

"Have you had sex before?" I blurt out.

His eyes widen. "Yes."

"How many times?" I've lost my filter and can't keep thoughts from spewing. "I'm making a fool of myself asking you this stuff, but you seem *really* experienced. I'm guessing you've done it more than once." I clamp a hand on my mouth.

He carefully pries my fingers away. "You can ask me these things. I've only ever been with one person."

"Angie?"

"Yeah. We were together six months, so…"

In other words, more times than he can count.

"What would you want with a virgin like me?" I ask in wonder, and oh, jeez, somebody, please, tape my mouth shut already.

He takes his time answering. I worry he might decide he doesn't want *anything* to do with someone who pushes for information he's obviously uncomfortable giving.

Finally, he says, "Eva, I want a lot of things with you, not just sex. I won't deny I want you so much I can't think straight half the time. I want to be your first. But more than anything, I want you to be *one hundred percent* sure it's what *you* want." He touches my cheek. "And I can tell you're not sure, which is fine with me. I promise. I'm not in any hurry."

Relief washes over me. "I think you're right," I whisper. "I'm okay with fooling around like we just did, but I'm…not ready to have sex."

"Okay, but can we talk about it? What is it you're worried about? I'm not asking to try and convince you or anything. I want us to be comfortable discussing this, okay?"

I swallow hard. "Being around people my while life who've treated sex like it's nothing—no big deal—has made it a *bigger* deal to me. I've seen how it ends up…messing with people's lives in ways they never imagined."

"I get what you're saying, Eva, and I'm in no hurry. We'll wait as long as you want."

I'm thankful he's such a gentleman.

Chapter Thirty-Five

Alex

Eva and I are half naked in bed, and it's both heaven and agony. I ache to be inside her, but what we have, relationship-wise, is about more than the physical stuff. I'd never forgive myself if we do something she isn't ready for. No way will I jeopardize our relationship over sex.

I give her a kiss on the forehead. "Are you okay?"

"Yes." She smiles, sheepish. "But you made me feel like I've never felt before, and I didn't even return the—"

"Shhh." I put a finger on her lips. "Eva, I like making you feel good. I'm not looking for anything in return. Don't worry, okay?"

She snuggles against me.

We lie here until I wonder if she's fallen asleep, but then she rolls away and sits up, putting her bra back on. I'm sad to see her beautiful breasts covered again. "I should head back to Casa Lor. Are you sure you aren't upset we didn't…"

"I'm positive."

She puts her shirt on and stands. "Will your mom be here to help Lena tomorrow night?"

I drag myself off the bed. "Yeah, and Lena will be ecstatic you're leaving the makeup behind for her. Thank you."

I walk her out and kiss her goodbye.

My phone buzzes on the nightstand as I'm dozing off. It's Eva.

"You okay?" I ask.

"I'm fine, and maybe it's paranoia, but I think a white car was tailing me after I turned off your parents' driveway. By the time I left Florence, I didn't see it anymore, but—"

"How?" I sit up, no longer sleepy. "If it was the same person I saw leaving your place, how'd they know where my parents live? Did they follow you here?"

"I have no idea. I mean, I never noticed anyone behind me all the way to Florence."

"Shit. There was a camera flash in the dark that night. My head hurt so bad, I thought I was seeing things, but what if the person took a picture of my license plate? I use my parents' address as a permanent address." I pace my room, skin crawling at the idea of someone lurking around here, of all places.

"You still there?" Eva asks after I remain silent for a minute.

"Yeah. I'm here." I sit on the edge of my bed.

"I apologize if those stupid reporters start hassling you."

"Eva, it isn't your fault. Let's try not to worry."

"Okay. Don't forget to let me know how Lena's prom goes."

We hang up, and when I do finally fall asleep, instead of dreaming of Eva in my bed, I have nightmares of reporters chasing us. They wield their microphones like weapons, and the cameras won't stop flashing.

~ * ~

The next night, I call Eva from the limo on the way home after prom. "We had a great time. Thanks for your help."

"Yay! Can I talk to Lena?"

I glance over at my sister. "She fell asleep a few minutes ago."

"Oh, bummer."

The disappointment in her voice tugs at my heart, and I tell her, "I'll have her call you tomorrow."

"Okay, well, I'm glad she had fun. Did you?"

"Yeah." I stretch my legs out. "It would have been better if you'd been there."

"You're so sweet. What are your plans tomorrow?"

"It's Mother's Day. My dad, sister, and I are taking my mom to lunch or dinner. How about you?" I feel bad, knowing her mother isn't around.

"Martin and Rosy invited me to their place in Georgetown. I'm gonna ask Martin's advice on building a tiny house."

I hope whatever tiny house she builds won't be on wheels. It would take her away from me, but I don't tell her I'm thinking this. "Have fun," I say with my fingers crossed.

"Goodnight, Alex."

Eva's scent is on the pillow and sheets. I can't stop thinking of her in this bed with me last night, half-naked, so turned on by my mouth on her breasts that she came beneath me. I'm rock hard at the memory and about to take things into my own hands for release when my phone buzzes.

Unknown number.

Dread douses my steamy thoughts of Eva as a text pops up.

Hope you'll have a change of heart. Maybe this will help.

A picture of Angie and me follows, and I break into a cold sweat. We're in her bed. I'm on my back, shirtless and asleep. She has her arm outstretched, taking the selfie, and her lips curve up wickedly.

Delete. Block. Resist the need to vomit. Damn, will she ever quit?

Chapter Thirty-Six
Eva

Before leaving to visit Martin and Rosy, I pop into Lor's room and check on him.

"I called Mom for Mother's Day," he says. "Left a message. You gonna call her?"

"I guess."

Not.

Silent, he settles his gaze on the bookshelf where several photos are displayed, including an old portrait of his dad, Franklin Jenson. Or maybe his focus is aimed at Mom's picture on the cover of *Vogue* in the height of her career. The sadness on his face makes him look older.

"What are you thinking about?" I ask softly.

His gaze moves back to me. "A lot of things."

For a second, I think he'll say more, but Darnell enters with his lunch.

"I'll be back later." I head for my truck.

When I arrive at Martin and Rosy's, there's a southern meal of fried chicken, mashed potatoes, and green beans on the table in their quaint country home. We eat and visit for a while, catching up.

"This is such a nice place," I say. "I see why you wanted to retire here, Martin."

Rosy laughs. "It's not *really* retirement. He keeps plenty busy. Eva, why don't you both go to the workshop and let him show you what he's working on?"

This is all the prompting Martin needs.

He and I step outside toward his...well "workshop" isn't an

accurate term. It's huge! Two-stories and bigger than their house.

"Let's talk tiny," I say.

"I'll start by showing you."

Behind the workshop, right there, on a trailer, is a tiny house. It's similar in size to Sue's but with a more rustic exterior.

"This is awesome." I love the design. "Is it finished?"

"Almost. There's still a little work to be done on the inside. Come have a look."

"I love the stairs. It's better than a ladder." I admire the extra built-in storage under them.

"The buyer has arthritis in her hands. A ladder wasn't a good idea."

He continues the tour; we discuss plumbing, lighting, and appliances. He's surprised, as am I, at how much I've learned from my research. Granted, I'm lost on some of the technical jargon, but for the most part, we're speaking the same language.

We return to his workshop, and he shows me the original plans, describing changes made along the way.

"So, I'm curious." He takes a seat on a stool. "You're the daughter of Sloane Silver, sister of Lor Jenson, and heir to FU. Also, your Covington grandparents have quite an empire in the funeral home business, and you're their only grandchild. In other words, you're inexplicably set for life. I can't fathom what makes someone with your lifestyle want to live tiny."

"I'm not a fan of extravagance. I may not go 'all in' on living tiny, but I can't stand being in Lor's mansion for very long. It's like the opposite of claustrophobia; I'm more comfortable in smaller places."

He chuckles. "Makes sense. You mostly grew up in the confines of tour buses. But a tiny house would be an extreme reaction to your phobia."

"Maybe, but I love how every square foot is used intentionally. I've been volunteering at Austin Creative Repurposing, and there's a whole network of people to tap into for building with reclaimed materials."

"I can tell you've put a lot of thought into this." He holds up a finger. "But there's something you should be aware of. It might not make a bit of difference to you, but you may catch some flak from the diehards who turn up their noses at people going tiny for the wrong reasons."

"What do they consider the wrong reasons?"

"Rich people jumping on the bandwagon to be part of the fad instead of embracing the hardcore minimalist mindset. A lot of folks think wealthy people are wasteful and have the houses built, tire of them quickly, and treat them like throwaways. *I* don't think that's what you're doing. Not with your interest in using reclaimed materials."

"I hate wastefulness, but I'm also not willing to be hardcore minimalist," I admit.

"Which is fine. It's a free country. I was only telling you what the community buzz is. So, do you want to do this?"

"I do." I'm excited to have a plan, and I can't wait to tell Alex.

Chapter Thirty-Seven
Alex

I'm finishing a hamburger in the dining hall when Graham and Sean take the empty seats on each side of me.

"Hey, Alex." Graham angles his phone toward me. "Your girlfriend is on SLY again."

Shit. I mentally kick myself for not checking the gossip news lately. What did I miss?

Sean grins. "Dude, she may be the sister of the guitarist in Polly's Poison. His mom's Sloane Silver. She's probably your girlfriend's mom too. Why are you holding out on us?"

They show me snapshots of Eva leaving Lor's estate. Plus, Carla Kinsey has found photos of Sloane with a little blonde girl. I've never seen pictures of Eva as a child, but I'm betting it's her. My eyes zero in on Carla's questions in bold: "Is this Sloane Silver's long, lost daughter? Where has she been all these years, and where is she now?"

"Why didn't you tell us you're hooking up with a celebrity?" Graham asks.

"Mind your own damn business." I stand, gather my trash, and leave, calling Cassidi on the way to my room. She answers, and I ask, "Can I move in sooner than planned?"

"Sure. Why? Did something happen at your dorm?"

"Yeah, but I'd rather not talk about it."

"Okay, what were your plans for furniture? The room's empty."

"I'll sleep on the couch until I can find furniture."

Several hours later, I've moved my stuff from the dorm, eaten dinner, and showered again when Eva calls.

"Hey, I can't wait to tell you about my day with Martin and Rosy." Her voice is bubbly.

I lie on the couch, taking in her words like a parched man in the desert. It doesn't sound like she knows of the latest SLY report, and I'm not ready to drop it on her. "Are you going to hire Martin to build you a tiny house?"

"We have a lot of details to decide on, and I'm not in any hurry. But yes, I want to do this."

"I can tell you're excited. I'm happy for you."

"Thanks. What's up with you? How was your day?"

"I've moved into Cassidi's apartment earlier than planned."

"Oh…why?" Her voice loses its excitement.

"Couldn't tolerate my roommate anymore. He and the guy across the hall got ahold of a new report by Cabbage Patch Carla. It was like asshats on parade. I couldn't take it anymore."

"What was Carla saying this time?" she asks with hesitation.

"There are pictures of you as a little girl with your mom. Here, give me a sec, I'll send you a link." I take the phone away from my ear and forward the SLY link to her.

"Did you get it?" I ask, putting the phone back to my ear.

"Yeah. Hang on."

The silence on her end worries me. "Are you all right?"

"I'm okay…I don't remember these pictures. How old would I have been, and where were we?"

"Could you ask your mom?" I still wonder what the deal is with her and her mom.

After another quiet moment, Eva finally says, "I don't think so."

Her evasive manner breaks me up inside. Something bad went down between her and her mom. I don't like how she's keeping me at arm's length.

Chapter Thirty-Eight
Eva

Focusing on tiny house planning is a good distraction from worrying about the stupid SLY reports. I'm at ACR telling Hank and Nadine my building plans when a green VW bug pulls into the parking lot. Nadine touches Hank's arm. "Hon, is that Blair?"

His eyes widen. "I'll be damned, it is! She's a few weeks early."

He and Nadine have mentioned Blair a lot, and I'm excited to finally meet her.

A brunette gets out of the car and runs to Hank. "Daddy!"

"Blair!" He hugs her. "Good to have you home. I didn't expect you this soon."

Nadine hugs her next. "Is everything okay?"

Blair adjusts a daisy headband on her long wavy hair. "I didn't finish the semester."

"What?" Hank frowns. "Hold on a minute. Why didn't I know this?"

"Don't worry. I'm not quitting." She breezes over to me, her skirt swishing. "You must be Eva! I've been looking forward to meeting you." Her bangle-laden arms embrace me in a hug.

"Nice to meet you." I can't help being affected by her spirited personality. She's even more vibrant than Hank described.

"It'll be great having someone here closer to my age than these old folks," Blair teases.

Hank and Nadine ask Blair and me to sort donations in the warehouse.

"How's college?" I ask her. "What's your major?"

"Environmental science with a focus on sustainability. It's fun, but I took some time off to work with a group on a housing project. When I return, I'll have a better idea of how I want to finish my degree. Do you have college plans?"

"I haven't decided yet," I say. The conversation leads to me describing the tiny house I want to build.

She's about to bust her hippie chick seams as she tells me more about the housing project. "And guess what we used? Repurposed building supplies. You and I are two peas in a pod!"

At home, I rush to Lor's room and excitedly tell him about Blair.

"I'm glad you're making friends, and as much as I worried ACR would turn you into a tree-hugger, I can tell it's been good for you." We start a game of cards, and he asks with a sheepish expression, "How're things with Alex? Is he treating you right?"

My eyes widen, and I reply in a southern drawl, "Well, I reckon so, big brother. Alex Marshall's a fine fellow. A gentleman and a scholar."

Lor's face reddens a little, but he plays along. "Do I need to have a talk with him about his intentions?"

In his own way, he's trying to say he cares for me, and it's touching.

~ * ~

Alex asks me to stop by his apartment and surprises me with a gift. It's a framed, poster-sized storyboard with his own comic-strip drawings, each one starring me.

"Alex, it's incredible." I rave at each of the scenes.

There's the private concert with California Nine and the two of us dancing at the club downtown, plus one of me driving the truck. In another, I'm in front of ACR, wearing a cape with the recycling symbol on it.

I laugh and kiss him. "You're brilliant."

"You like it?"

"I love it!" Throwing my arms around his neck, I smother him in more kisses.

He shows me his room, which doesn't have much in it besides a full-size bed, dresser, and desk. "You'll be happy to know, except for the mattress, all the furniture's used, not new."

He sits on the bed, and I join him.

We lie back, facing each other but not touching. I wonder if he'll act different, because of that night in his room at his parents' house.

Will we fool around again?

I prop my head on my hand. "How's the tour guide job going?"

"Great. When they start letting me do my own tours, I want you to check me out."

"I bet you're the sexiest one. Do girls throw themselves at you?"

"You've got nothing to worry about." He gives me a soft, sweet kiss. "I'm all yours."

"I like the sound of that. Oh! I want to tell you about yesterday. Blair and I went to a house scheduled for demolition. We salvaged some materials. Guess what that's called."

"Mining."

My heart swells in happy surprise. "*Someone's* done their reclaimed materials homework."

"Yep. Tell me what you found on your mining expedition." He scoots closer to me.

I nuzzle his neck, breathing in his spicy scent. "There were nine things we hauled away."

"And what were they?" He trails his fingers up my bare leg, giving me goosebumps.

"We got a door and five windows, one of which is stained glass. It's beautiful."

"What else?"

"There was a bathroom skylight Blair said I shouldn't pass on, even if it doesn't turn out to work for the tiny house."

"You've only listed seven things." He playfully swats my butt. "Keep going."

"Some wood and a crossbeam."

He groans in exaggerated ecstasy. "Say crossbeam again, baby."

"*Crossbeam.*"

"You're so sexy." He nibbles at my neck, his breath warm and tantalizing on my skin. "I want to give you nine of something," he whispers.

"Are you saying you have a nine inch—" I clap a hand over my mouth.

His eyes spark. He takes my hand and strokes his thumb across my bottom lip. "Glad to know where your mind's at, but *I* was talking of giving you nine orgasms."

I gasp. "I think I'd drop dead, or at least fall into a coma."

"You wouldn't, I promise. For now, how about nine kisses?" He brushes his lips across my forehead and cheek. "That's one and two and here's three and four."

My lips, top and bottom. He nips at my earlobe. "Five."

Grazing my bare shoulder, he lowers the spaghetti strap of my blouse with his teeth. "Six."

He pushes the bottom of my shirt up and nuzzles my stomach. "Seven."

A lingering touch of his lips on my bare inner thigh is number eight. It sends such a rush of heat and longing through me. Could he really give me *nine* orgasms?

The next kiss is on my ankle.

"You missed a few other places," I say, breathless as he lies back beside me.

He laughs. "I'm not going to kiss your feet."

"Ha. Not what I meant." I nudge his hand higher on my thigh.

"Hmm." He slides his fingers under my shorts, along the edge of my underwear—lacy red ones I wore just for him.

An insistent knock on the door makes us jump.

"Alex, I need to talk to you. Right now," Cassidi calls out.

Alex's face clouds with frustration.

She knocks again, and he gets up.

Chapter Thirty-Nine
Alex

I swing my bedroom door open, ready to chew Cassidi out for bad roommate etiquette, but I freeze when she shoves her phone in my face.

It's the picture of me asleep with Jessica on the football field.

Cassidi scowls. "This made the rounds with the boys at your mom's school."

Eva's beside me now. She sees the photo, and her face pales.

"It isn't what it looks like," I insist.

She shrinks away from me. "When was that picture from?"

"A couple weeks ago," Cassidi *un*helpfully offers.

Eva hurries to put her sandals back on and grab her purse. "I can't believe this is happening."

I break into a sweat. "Eva don't leave."

Cassidi has conveniently disappeared, leaving the doorway wide open.

Eva walks right out. I chase after her, all the way to her truck.

"You have to let me explain," I plead.

"I can't stand cheaters, Alex." Her voice shakes as she swings the driver's door open.

"It isn't what you're thinking. I didn't cheat on you. Please, don't go."

Tears glisten in her eyes, but her feet stay on the ground. She isn't getting in her truck.

My heart swells with hope. "Eva, I know it looked bad, but there's a good explanation."

"I thought you were just friends with Jessica." A tear starts to fall, and she swipes at it.

"I *am*. That picture was from the weekend before my birthday, I wasn't gonna leave for Florence until Saturday morning, but my roommate had a girl in the room Friday night. I drove home, only to walk in on my parents having sex, and I left." I ramble on, wanting so badly to ease the skepticism that's all over Eva's face. "Then I drove around with nowhere to go and came across Jessica at the school, but nothing happened. She'd just heard her grandmother died. We ended up falling asleep because we drank too much to drive."

"All you did was sleep?" Eva's brow creases.

"Yes. That's all, and I talked about *you* practically the whole time." I reach for her hand.

"You promise nothing happened?"

"I promise it was platonic. Trust me. Please."

She accepts my hand.

I'm flooded with relief. "Do you want to come back up and stay a while? We could order dinner."

Sadness flickers in her eyes. "No, I better go." She gives me a quick kiss, releases my hand, and climbs into her truck.

I wave goodbye and return to the apartment, ready to ream Cassidi out, but she's holed up in her room with music blaring.

~ * ~

A few days later, Cassidi tells me her co-workers were talking about a SLY report. I expect it to be the one I've already seen, until she shows me. It's new. There's another photo of Eva as a little girl. Her left hand's visible, index finger missing. Carla's fans have sent her some recent pictures of Eva with Sloane. In these shots, Eva's wearing a wig, and her left hand is visible, sans index finger. Despite the wig, it's clearly Eva.

According to Carla, this confirms the mystery *child* and the mystery *girl* are the same person. In a video clip, Carla vows to her fans she'll uncover the significance of the missing finger.

"Is Eva really the daughter of a supermodel?" Cassidi asks. I look away, trying to think of how not to break my promise to Eva. "Oh my God, Alex, seriously?" Cassidi flops onto the couch and covers her face.

"Cass, I don't know why you're being this dramatic."

"*You* don't understand because *you* don't appreciate what I went through when your fling with Angie blew up in your face. *I* was the one who was there for you when your shit fell apart, and I hated watching you get hurt." She moves to the edge of her seat on the couch and gestures wildly with her hands. "But more than that, I've had to keep those secrets from your family—my family! Do you know how hard it's been?"

"No—"

"Alex, your parents are like parents to me too. I hate hiding things from them, and here you are with another woman with more secrets."

Stunned by her tirade, I sink down beside her on the couch. "I knew asking you to keep quiet about Angie was a lot to ask, but I had no idea you've felt like this. I'm sorry."

"Face it, Eva's world is different from yours. She's one of *those* people. Being with her is going to bite you in the ass. She's in the public eye. Do you want to be there with her?"

"Don't be ridiculous. I won't be. This SLY stuff will blow over. It will."

"You're living in a dream world, but whatever. Go ahead and have your fun. Just please don't ask me to keep secrets from your parents about *her* or anything else, okay?"

"I won't, I promise, but give Eva a chance. If you get to know her, you'll see she isn't what you think."

"Fine." She huffs. "But I see right through those people."

"She's not one of *those* people," I insist and walk away before I add something I'll regret.

In my room, I call Eva and say, "Sorry I'm always the bearer of bad news. Cabbage Patch Carla has struck again." It feels like *déjà vu* as I send her the link and wait.

"Damn." She breathes out deeply. "The picture of me in the wig is from the day I went shopping with my mom."

"Cassidi could tell it's you. She's who showed me."

"I bet she feels lied to and doesn't much like me," Eva grumbles.

I search for a way to discuss this without revealing anything about Angie and decide to stick with Cassidi's prejudice. "It's not that she dislikes *you* as much as the world you come from." I run a hand through my hair. "Her mom is—well, I'll put it this way: my dad calls her a flake, and my mom calls her a floozy. When Cassidi was fourteen, her mom abandoned her to follow this stupid wannabe actor to Hollywood. He promised her a rich and famous lifestyle."

"Let me guess. It didn't work out," Eva says.

"Of course not, but she's still in L.A. looking for the next celebrity to latch onto. And ironically, Cassidi works in a fancy downtown hotel restaurant popular with celebrities. She's always complaining about how stuck-up and extravagant they are."

"How convenient. She lumps me in with the stereotype without knowing me."

"Once she spends more time around you, she'll see you're not like that."

"What do you suggest?"

"She and I are both off work tomorrow. Let's spend the day with her. I'll invite Brady too. I'm dying for him to meet you."

"Can Blair join us? She's been asking if my hot boyfriend has any single friends."

"You have a hot boyfriend? You better warn him I'm gonna kick his ass."

"Don't hurt yourself."

I love the sound of her giggle. The fact she can laugh about all this makes it easier to believe what I told Cassidi. This will blow over. It has to.

Chapter Forty
Eva

Lor's propped up in bed, watching TV after his physical therapy. It's some annoying reality show, and he thankfully lowers the volume as I enter.

I drag a chair close and set my computer on the overbed table. "The SLY reporter discovered I'm missing a finger."

"Yeah. And that you're my sister. How are you handling it?"

"I don't like it, but what can I do?" Surprisingly, it doesn't bother me as much as I always worried it might. Maybe because my focus is on other things, between volunteering, spending time with Alex, and tiny house research.

"I told you it wasn't such a big deal," Lor says. "Just live your life, okay?"

"I'm trying." Tapping the picture of myself as a little girl, I ask, "Any idea when or where this was taken?"

"I don't remember. I bet Mom's pretty pissed you're stealing some of her spotlight."

I scowl at his glib tone. "If anything, she'd be worried about the invasion of my privacy."

He cuts his eyes at me. "Eva, the anonymity crap is to make sure *she* gets the attention instead of you. That's all it's ever been."

Our eyes lock. There's a dropping sensation in my stomach as my mind trips over his words. So, not only is Mom a cheater, but another part of my life has been a lie. I break the stare with Lor and find myself doing something I haven't in days—pressing my thumb to the scar on my left hand.

"But staying anonymous *protects* me," I say, regurgitating Mom's rationale for lack of anything else in the moment. "I don't have to deal with the expectation that everything in my life should have entertainment value."

He draws in a deep breath. "Right, but there's truth in what I said."

"What, that Mom has her own reasons? Sure, got it." I turn my computer toward him, wanting to change the subject. "This part of my timeline is on you. It's missing a few details."

He uses the touchpad to expand the section labeled with his name and slowly warms to helping me fill in some blanks regarding his early life. He picks up his phone and emails me a picture from his camera roll. It's of his dad, Franklin Jenson.

"My part of your timeline wouldn't be complete without it," he says.

I save the photo and study it. Franklin looked like a stuffy businessman.

"Did you know him very well? I always got the impression you didn't."

"Sort of." He shrugs. "I lived with him in Michigan until he died from a heart attack when I was thirteen."

"Did Mom live with y'all?"

"She came and went. Her modeling career was in full swing. It wouldn't do for a supermodel to be seen with a little kid you know?" His words hold an undercurrent of bitterness.

"At least you had your dad growing up."

"We weren't close. I had a nanny and practically lived in the nursery." He sighs. "But he *was* the reason I got interested in music."

"Did he teach you guitar?"

"I didn't learn to play until after he died, but I guess you could say he's responsible for it indirectly. I inherited his estate, since he didn't have any other kids and never married—"

"Why didn't he marry Mom?"

His head tilts in a thoughtful way. "I don't think he ever forgave her. She got pregnant with me on purpose. Everything she did was for money."

The skin on the back of my neck prickles.

"She was eighteen and worked for a cleaning company," Lor continues. "The maids wore sexy outfits and cleaned the homes of *well-to-do* bachelors. Classy, huh?"

"How do you know this stuff?"

"My dad told me. Plus, he wrote down a lot of stuff Mom told him."

I stare at the laptop screen, debating whether I want to hear this bit of history.

"Mom worked at Franklin's house," Lor says. "She became his regular maid, and they…got involved. It caused *quite* the scandal in his family when she came up pregnant."

I visualize the scene as if it's an old movie. Maudlin. Overdramatic. "Did he love her?"

"He cared for her. Helped her break into modeling." His eyes are dull, his mind lost in memories. "If not for him, she might not have risen above the poor, homeless girl she was."

"Wait…what? Homeless?" I wipe my sweaty palms on the chair's cushion.

He rubs his face and grimaces. "Eva, there's family history Mom will never tell you, but I think you should know. Mom ran away from home when she was sixteen. She was the oldest of six kids in a dirt-poor immigrant family."

My heart plummets. "Immigrants from where?"

"Hungary. Her parents came here from Budapest and lived in New York. During a riot, her dad—our grandfather—got arrested for looting and starting a fire. Someone died in the blaze. While her dad was on trial, Mom ran away from home."

"This is crazy." I'm dizzy and try to shake it off. "Why would she run away?"

"Her mom was sick, like all the time, and couldn't work. Mom knew if her dad went to prison, she was the only one who could work and take care of those kids."

This sounds like the shows he watches to fill his endless hours of tedious boredom.

I drag the edge of my thumbnail over my scar.

Hard.

Harder.

I need it to hurt.

The pressure keeps the crack in the dam from widening.

"I don't believe you." My voice is weak. I flash back to Mom's face when I told the boutique lady I was from Budapest.

"Come on, Eva. Haven't you wondered why you only have one set of grandparents and why Mom won't discuss her past? You like to think Mom is—"

"I don't want to discuss her anymore."

"Okay…what do you want to talk about? Ask me anything."

My gaze falls to his dad's picture. "Why was Franklin the reason you got into music?"

"He was a major blues fan. He *sometimes* let me look at his vinyl collection but never for long. After he died, his stuff became mine." His eyes are sad. "Anyway, I poured myself into it—his albums and his books about the bands. I fell in love with the blues too. What sucks is, when he was alive, all I wanted was for him to let me share that world *with* him. But he kept me at a distance. He's been on my mind a lot lately. He was such a...cold man."

"I'm sorry." I hold his hand. It's my turn to distract him from unwanted thoughts. "If you liked the blues, why'd you pursue hard rock?"

He shrugs. "I love music but didn't want to play the kind he loved." Releasing my hand, he's quiet for a minute. I fiddle with the hem of my shorts and wait. "I always wanted to please my dad," he says in a softer voice. "But I don't know *why*. He didn't care... Why did I give a damn what he thought?"

"He must've cared, or he would've left his estate to some other relative."

"It doesn't matter. It was only money. What I wanted was..." He sniffles. "I'm sorry, Eva. I can't do this right now. My head hurts. Can we talk later?"

"Of course." I stand. "Do you need anything?"

"No, turn the light off. I think I'll try to nap."

I do as he asks and retreat to the guesthouse. The stuff he said about Mom feels unreal, and I push it down. Instead, I consider the one thing he left unsaid: what was it he always wanted from his dad?

Chapter Forty-One
Alex

At the restaurant, Eva and Blair are in the ladies' room when Brady and Cassidi arrive.

"Where's your girlfriend?" Brady asks, glancing around as he takes the seat next to me, across from Cassidi.

"She'll be right back." I'm excited to finally introduce them.

"Is her friend here?" Brady looks toward the restrooms, and his eyes widen as Eva and Blair emerge "Dude." He elbows me. "There's the mystery girl SLY's been reporting on. She's hot. I wonder what she's doing here."

"Wait." I narrow my eyes at him. "You know about that stuff? Why didn't you say anything?"

"Uh, why would I?"

Cassidi chuckles.

"You'll see." I rise and put my arm around Eva as I make introductions.

Brady recovers from his shock, and now he's checking out Blair.

She smiles at him above her menu. "What do you guys recommend?"

"They have the *best* crawfish," he says. "They're boiled with potatoes, corn on the cob, and Cajun spices."

"Sounds good." She nudges Eva. "I've never eaten crawfish, have you?"

"No, but there's a first time for everything."

After we place our orders, Eva asks Cassidi about her college classes.

She answers, but she's a bit aloof, probably watching for signs to confirm the rich girl stereotype she's used to. No way is that gonna happen. Eva's the most genuine person I know.

A waiter spreads butcher paper on the center of the table and pours steaming buckets of crawfish on it.

"Oh." Eva laughs. "They serve 'em with the shells still on."

Blair rubs her hands together, laughing. "Cool. Show us what to do."

"You pinch the tail and suck the head," Brady demonstrates. He and Blair laugh together, either from the innuendo or the juices dripping down his chin.

"Go ahead, give it a try," Cassidi challenges with a pointed look at Eva.

Eva and Blair each pick up a crawfish and copy Brady.

Blair does it in a rush, swallows with a gulp, and laughs into her napkin. Eva takes her time chewing, smiles, and takes another, her eyes on Cassidi the whole time. Cassidi won't meet my eyes, but I can tell from the arch of her eyebrows that she's impressed.

Our plans to canoe at Lady Bird Lake are nixed because of rain, and we end up at a bowling alley.

After each of our first turns, it's clear, except for Brady, we're terrible bowlers.

"Astounding," Eva teases after my ball hits the gutter.

I take a bow, and she's next. We laugh together when her ball enters the gutter even sooner than mine. Blair does a granny roll and *almost* hits a pin. Cassidi manages to knock a couple pins over. Eva high-fives her, and Cassidi even looks like she's having fun.

As Brady coaches Blair on her turn, a firm hand claps me on the back of my shoulder, startling me. "Hey, little bro. What're you up to?" Devin's voice booms in my ear.

Stunned, I feel like the wind's been knocked out of me. I can't speak for a moment, watching in disbelief as he takes the empty seat to my right. What the hell is *he* doing there?

"Ain't you gonna introduce me to your friend?" Devin asks.

The sleazy way he leans forward and gazes at Eva snaps me to attention. I take Eva's hand and clear my throat. "This is Eva. Eva, my brother Devin."

"Hello." Eva's gaze darts from me to Devin and back. The slightest rise of her eyebrows tells me she understands how on edge I suddenly am.

"Hey, cuz," Devin nods at Cassidi.

"Hi, Devin. How long have you been working here?"

And now it dawns on me. Devin's wearing a Larry's Lucky Lanes shirt and nametag.

"Started last week," Devin says. Of all the places we could've gone today...

Brady and Blair return to the seating area, and Devin chats them up, acting like he's the life of the party.

Eva whispers, "You okay?"

"Yeah, but I wasn't expecting him to be here." I sigh. "Your turn."

I stay near her, not wanting to leave her side with Devin around. She rolls another gutter ball, as do I, but it isn't funny anymore. It's like Devin cast a dark cloud over our day. He points and teases me about my poor bowling skills.

"Don't you have work to do?" I ask him, wondering what it'll take for him to leave us alone.

"Nah, man, my shift is done. Thought I'd hang out. Catch up with my little brother. What better way to get to know your friends, especially your girlfriend?"

"How about *not*," I mutter.

"Chill. What's got you sour?" Devin switches to the seat Blair vacated on Eva's left. "You sure are familiar." He studies Eva's face. "But I can't think of why."

"I'm new to Austin." She leans away, nestling against me.

"Oh, yeah, whereabouts are you from?"

"I was in San Diego before here," she answers. She flashes an uneasy look as Devin's attention is drawn away by cheers from the others.

Blair finally manages a decent roll. Eva applauds and steps away from Devin and me.

Devin gets up, right on her heels. "You're nothing like Alex's last girlfriend. I mean, she was a babe too—still is, which I know because I saw her recently." His eyes flick to me. My blood freezes in my veins. "But she and Alex wouldn't have worked," he continues. "Angie's a lot—"

I'm on him in an instant, yanking the front of his shirt. "What the hell are you doing?"

He laughs. "Having a little fun."

Eva places a hand on my arm. "Let's go. The game's over. Brady won."

"Aww." Devin smirks. "Leaving already?"

I release him with a shove and slide my hand into Eva's. As he smooths down the front of his shirt, he looks at our entwined hands. A spark of recognition flashes across his ugly mug. The instinct to whisk Eva away from here is strong, but Devin's already figured out who she is. His eyes are fixed right where Eva's left index finger should be.

I rearrange my fingers to cover her lack of one and face the others. "Time to leave."

"We're with you, man," Brady says.

The group has already started changing out of their rental shoes.

"Fine." Devin has a shit-eating grin. "Maybe next time. Y'all have a good day." He stalks off.

I apologize to Eva while tying my shoelaces with shaky hands.

"It's okay." She squeezes my arm.

I glance over at Devin and catch him aiming his phone at us, taking a picture. He winks at me and pockets his phone, escaping through a door marked Employees Only.

We head to the car. The rain has stopped, and the sun peeks out from behind the clouds with false cheer. All is *not* right with the world. My brain's scrambled.

Eva murmurs something to Blair I can't hear.

Blair points across the parking lot. "Let's get ice cream." She links arms with Brady, leading the way, and Cassidi follows. Eva and I trail behind.

Before we catch up with the others, she stops and circles her arms around my neck. "Your brother's a jerk. I see why you never talk about him."

I rest my hands on her hips.

"Do you want to go home?" she asks.

"No, I'm sorry. I'm trying not to be angry, but he wanted to embarrass me in front of you."

"Why does he have it out for you so bad?"

"That's how he is. Always has been. I'm sorry you had to meet him." I touch my forehead to hers and will the tension from my body.

She rises on her tiptoes and kisses me, her lips pleading with mine for a response. My arms tighten around her waist. Our bodies feel right together, and the wall I've erected from the run-in with Devin crumbles.

We're totally caught up in each other, forgetting the rest of the world exists until, from inside the ice cream shop, Brady knocks on the window.

Eva and I enter, and Blair greets us with: "Let's go dancing tonight!"

~ * ~

Eva's the hottest girl in the dance hall. It gives me a high to lead her around the floor, one song after another. I've shut Devin out of my mind.

Eventually, Brady cuts in, and I switch to Blair. It gives me the chance to watch Eva from a distance. The way her legs look in her dress and those boots—*damn*, she's fine.

"Have you told her yet?" Blair asks as we two-step.

I tear my gaze away from Eva, confused. "Told her what?"

"That you love her." She beams with the pride of discovery.

"Um, what makes you think that?" I stammer, my face heating. "I've only known Eva for a few months."

"You're not fooling anyone but yourself. Trust me. I can tell." She trades places with Eva again, and I wonder if she was right.

I thought I loved Angie. In the end, my feelings for her didn't run that deep. The way I feel for Eva is way different. I respect her and love being with her. She met my family and has accepted them, especially Lena, which Angie never would've done, and she believed me about nothing happening with Jessica despite the photograph of us.

Eva's truly a keeper.

Chapter Forty-Two
Eva

The next day, I'm playing cards with Lor when out of nowhere, he mentions, "Mom and Spike got married in Paris yesterday."

A breath whooshes out of me like I've been punched. I can't think of a thing to say. My mind spins in so many directions. I guess I didn't believe she'd follow through with it.

My heart aches that she didn't even try to invite me to the wedding. Hell, maybe she did try. I've ignored her messages.

"Eva let's talk." Lor sets the cards aside. "There's more I need you to know about Mom."

Sucking in a deep breath, I nod. "Fine, but you have to answer a question of mine first. I'll be right back." I run downstairs and grab the framed Budapest postcard.

Back in his room, I hand it to him. "Will you tell me what this is about?"

He gestures for me to keep it. "Open the frame."

With trembling fingers, I remove the back and take the postcard out. It's addressed to Sarika Szabo in big loopy writing. "Mom's real name," Lor says, and it looks extra foreign to me. How can Mom be anyone to me besides Sloane Silver?

"She kept her initials," I murmur and rub the goosebumps on my arm.

Lor takes the postcard from me and holds it in both hands like it's a fragile bird that might fly away. "This was sent to Mom from our great-grandparents in Hungary."

"When? How long ago?" I can't read anything on the card.

"No idea. Mom threw it away. Luckily, my dad saved it, and I kept it from his estate."

"Mom lets you keep this on display like you do?" My eyes widen. "Why?"

He scowls. "She didn't *let* me. I'm a *grown-ass* man, and this is my house."

I hunch my shoulders. "Of course. Sorry." I'm an adult and should stop thinking in terms of Mom having any say over what I do either.

"It's okay. I understand why you asked," he says.

"Do you...know anything about them? Her family in Hungary, I mean?"

"No. For years I wanted to connect with that side of the family, but she threatened to disown me."

"Is she hiding something? I can't believe she changed her name."

"I have no idea." He hands the postcard back to me. "I used to think she was protecting some big, dark family secret. I've decided it's just her being selfish and trying to protect her reputation. She's worked hard to transform into the sophisticated model Sloane Silver and pretend Sarika never existed. It's all in the journal my dad kept. Want to see it? It's in a box in my closet."

"No." I feel like he's rushing me. I'm suffocating from the weight of all this new information.

Do I know *anything* about Mom? "It can't be true. Maybe your dad made it up because he was bitter at Mom for getting pregnant. She wouldn't have kept this from me *my whole life.*"

The bones of my chest feel like they're caving in. Breaking. Crushing my heart.

Lor's gaze bores into me. "It's time to take the blinders off, Eva."

"Why are you doing this?" Hot tears stream down my cheeks. "Do you hate her or something?"

"I don't hate her. You're not listening to me." His tone hardens. "What I hate is how you stick your head in the sand. Can't you see what a selfish bitch she is? She's created a world that revolves around *her*. She gets away with whatever she wants. She was nothing but a groupie when she got pregnant with you, sleeping with guys from FU *and* Polly's Poison—"

"Shut up." I cover my ears.

He pulls one of my hands down. "And there's something else. I'm the only one who knows this. Mom made up the bullshit on you almost getting kidnapped as a little kid."

My arms fall to my sides. "Why would she do something like that?"

"Because when you got old enough to resist going along with the anonymous crap, she needed something to convince you."

It's all too much! I run from the room, bursting into tears.

In the guesthouse, I throw myself on the bed and cry until I can't breathe. I curl into a ball, aching for the comforting arms of a mom—not *my* mom, but a mom who didn't build a life of lies. One who didn't abandon her parents and siblings. Didn't sleep around.

Oh my God! I bolt upright and clutch my stomach.

If Mom was a groupie when she got pregnant with me... I might not even be a Covington. My dad may be some stranger Mom hooked up with one night. This sends me straight to the bathroom.

I barely make it to the toilet before I lose the contents of my stomach.

My phone rings from my bed. Weak, I ignore it and lean against the tub.

The phone dings. Whoever called left a message. I pull myself to standing and take a look.

Grandma Covington. Spike and Ike's mom. *Is* she my grandmother? I cradle my head in my hands.

My paternity was already questionable, but this is unthinkable.

I run back to the main house and to Lor's room with a new sense of urgency.

Darnell's helping Lor into his wheelchair.

"Hey," I say, my voice flat.

"Good, you're back," Lor says. "Darnell, could you give us a minute?"

"Yes, sir."

I wait until he's gone. "Is it possible Spike or Ike may not even be my dad?"

"Ah, jeez, no. I'm sorry if that's what you thought." His shoulders slump. "Eva, you're definitely a Covington. Mom had paternity tests done on them."

"*What?* I thought they didn't want to do paternity tests."

"She did it without them knowing. The results were overwhelmingly conclusive. *One* of them is your dad, but we'll never be sure which. Now, push me to the closet."

Relief soaks in, relaxing my tense muscles. I'm not sure why it matters to me. I guess with all the lies, it's one truth to which I can cling.

I wheel Lor into his walk-in closet, and he takes a small journal from a box on a shelf near the floor.

"It's yours now." He hands it to me. The cover, a dark brown leather with worn edges and scratches like scars, is cold in my hand.

He has me wheel him back to his bed and ask Darnell to return.

I'm carrying the journal to the guesthouse when Alex calls. "Have you heard?" he asks.

"What? Oh no, SLY again?"

"Yeah."

I sigh. "I'm in the middle of something. Can you send me a link, and I'll call you back later?"

"Sure." He sends the link as soon as we hang up, and the words swim on the screen.

"SLY Reveals: Secret Daughter of Sloane Silver is Fabulous Undertakers' 'Little Eva.'"

Chapter Forty-Three
Alex

Eva said we'd talk again, but that was three hours ago. I have no idea how she's dealing with the SLY reveal on the FU twins.

I call Eva, and she doesn't answer. In desperation, I call Lor's number and ask if he has any idea of her whereabouts.

"Not exactly."

"What does that mean?"

"She's probably fine, but there's...stuff, like family stuff, that upset her. She left a while ago and didn't say where she was going."

Shit. I flop onto my bed.

"There's a new SLY report on Eva," Lor says. "Have you seen it?"

"Yes." Dammit, why'd I send her the link *after* hanging up with her?

"Look, Alex, I'll call you if I hear from her. And if you hear, let me know."

Restless, I get in my truck and drive. Before I know it, I'm headed for the comfort of Florence. My phone vibrates as I hit the outskirts. Finally. Eva. It's a text. I pull over and read it.

> *Sorry I didn't call you back, but I'm not ready to*
> *talk. Dealing with too many things right now. I'm*
> *on my way to visit a friend in Louisiana.*

"What the hell?" I reread it and want to throw up. *Who* is she going to see in Louisiana? It could be some other guy. I should've told her I love her. My finger hovers above her number, but I shouldn't call her. She said she's not ready to talk. Instead, I send a text.

I'm worried about you. Please let me know what's going on.

Since she's driving, I don't expect an answer, but I sit here wishing for a reply anyway. In the rearview mirror, I see a blue car has stopped behind me on the narrow shoulder of this two-lane road. I stick my arm out the window, waving for it pass. It slowly returns to the lane of travel and passes. The windows were tinted, but I think someone waved. Maybe they thought I was having engine trouble.

Next, I send Lor a message.

I've heard from Eva. She's going to visit a friend in Louisiana. Any idea who?

Not a clue.

His answer is zero help, and there's a hollowed-out feeling in my chest. I drive around on the familiar backroads of my childhood, trying to clear my head and spot a red sportscar on the side of the road with its hood up. I'm not in the mood to stop and offer help, but it's in my country boy bones. I park behind it.

When I step out of my truck and see who's in front of the car, I wish I'd kept driving.

Angie. *Un-freakin'-believable.*

A knot forms in the pit of my stomach.

She's leaning over under the hood in a sheer low-cut blouse and tight jean shorts. Her long, dark hair blows across her face as she looks up.

"Alex, oh God, what a sight for these sore eyes you are." Her eyes widen, like she's shocked I'm here, and she has the audacity to try to hug me.

I step aside, shoving my hands in my pockets. "What are you doing here, Angie?"

"If you'd take my calls, you'd know. I'm back at the ranch. Sonny and I split."

"Huh. What makes you think I care?"

"Alex, I can't stop thinking of you. Don't you ever think of me?" She rubs her fingers on my chest, flattening her palm where my tattoo is. I brush her hand away. She bites her lip, looking hurt. "Okay, could you give me a lift to my place?"

"Isn't there someone you can call?"

"I've tried. Nobody can help me way out here, but *you're* here." She bats her eyelashes. "All I'm asking for is a ride. You were already going my way."

"Fine." I kick at a rock and walk to my truck. "Let's go."

She shuts the hood of the car and gets into my passenger seat.

We head toward her ranch, where we spent a lot of time *in flagrante*, as she called it. I liked working the ranch, even alongside Devin. Once he quit, that left just her and me—then, less of her clothes and more of her finding every excuse to put her hands on me.

At the time, having this beautiful older woman seduce me was hot. Now she's next to me, the smell of her designer perfume and hair products filling my nostrils, yet she might as well be a stranger passing through town. I feel nothing for her. I'm a different person. Yeah, she's drop-dead gorgeous, but everything else about her is the opposite of the things I love about Eva.

"What's the matter, Alex?" Angie asks. She's been talking nonstop. I haven't heard a word. "You don't act like yourself. Talk to me." She trails her hand up my thigh.

I grip it and move it away. We're almost to her ranch. I only need to endure this a little longer.

I drive up in front of her house and stop, wait for her to get out.

She scoots closer to me. "Baby don't fight it," she coos. "Remember how good we are together?"

At the touch of her hand, higher on my thigh, I hurry out of the truck. She slides out, right behind me.

Cat-like, she maneuvers to pin me against the truck. "I love you, Alex. It's what I've wanted to tell you, but you wouldn't talk to me."

Her arms circle my neck. She does a little hop and wraps her legs around my hips. I flashback to that stormy night, carrying her like this into her bedroom. My stomach lurches and suddenly, her lips are on mine. Her hands are all over me, tugging my hair and groping at my chest and shoulders. She's well-versed in what gets me going. I turn my head and walk to the porch with her body clamped onto mine, kissing my neck.

"Stop Angie." I jerk away. "Where's your key?"

"Oh, damn. It's in my purse. I left it in the truck." She peels herself off me. "Hurry, Alex, get it. I need you."

I jog to my truck, glad for the distance from her.

A blue car has turned into the driveway. The driver's window is partway down. I can't see their face or anything.

Where did this car come from, and how did we not notice him pull up?

Oh shit. My mouth goes dry. It's the car I waved around me on the road earlier. It followed me here. "Angie who the hell is that?" I point at the car.

"How should I know?" She yells, "Hey, off my property!" to the driver and calls out to me, "Forget him. Get my purse, and let's go inside."

I pluck her purse off my truck seat and take it as far as the porch steps.

This is bullshit.

"I can't…Angie, you don't love anyone but yourself." I toss her purse onto the porch. "If you did, you wouldn't have lied to me. Or let me be humiliated the way you did. You wouldn't have stood by and done *nothing* when your husband threatened me."

"I know that now, but you're all I think of." Her face crumples.

"You disgust me. I'm with someone else now."

She moves as if to jump on me again. I hurry to my truck and slide behind the wheel. The blue car peels out ahead of me. I curse myself for not getting the license plate. I'm not sure what I'd do with it, though. My skin still crawls from Angie pawing at me. I feel guilty for letting her touch me, but she was like an animal. God, what if someone in the blue car took photos of us?

I wipe sweat from my forehead and try to convince myself I'd have seen a camera.

With my heartrate slowing, I'm more certain than ever I love Eva.

Whatever's going on with her, I'll wait, no matter how long it takes. She's worth it.

I pull over and text her.

> *Thank you for telling me where you're going. Hope you'll let me know what's going on. Be safe. I'm here if you need me. I miss you already.*

I almost add, "I love you," but I want to wait and tell her in person.

Chapter Forty-Four
Eva

After the things Lor told me and reading the latest SLY headline, I called Vanessa, my former governess. She said I could visit, no matter what time of night. Her invitation felt like a lifeline, and I told her I was on my way. The more miles I put between myself and Austin, the easier I can breathe.

I arrive around two o'clock in the morning and find her house, a cute little red brick one-story on a suburban cul-de-sac. Carrying an overnight bag, I walk up the driveway.

The door swings open before I even knock. "Eva!" Vanessa hugs me tight. It's been a few years since we've seen each other, and the sight and scent of her bring back my best childhood memories. When we pull away, we both have tears in our eyes, but I think this is what they call happy tears.

Her red hair is shorter. Otherwise, she looks like she did years ago. She has the slight, slender frame of a dancer. And freckles, *tons* of freckles. I loved them as a child, and I love seeing them now.

I follow her down a hall, past a half-open door. A nightlight illuminates her little girl, curled up on a bed with a teddy bear. Envy sweeps through me. How different would my life have been if I'd grown up in a house like this, with a mom like Vanessa?

Taking my hand, she leads me to the end of the hallway. We enter a room with a desk and small couch. She closes the door behind us and motions for me to sit. "James has to work in the morning, even though it's Memorial Day, and I don't want to wake him. We can talk in here. Do you need anything? Something to eat or drink?"

"No. Thanks for letting me visit. I'm such a disaster. It's embarrassing."

"Eva don't be embarrassed. I'm glad you called." Her words help drain more of my stress. "Tell me everything."

"I made it to the ripe old age of twenty, flying under the radar, undetected."

"Almost twenty-one. You've got a birthday soon."

"But now the gossip vultures have sunk their talons into me." I lean back on the couch. "The world knows who my mom is and that I'm the daughter of *one* of the Fabulous Undertakers."

"Yeah. I looked at the links you forwarded. I'm sorry. This'll die down. The reporter will lose interest and chase after the next hot story. You know how it works."

"I do, but I'm most upset about stuff Lor's been telling me about Mom."

Vanessa's expression clouds, and I ask her something I've always wondered. "Why did you quit being my governess?"

"I wasn't qualified to be your teacher anymore." She picks at a piece of lint on the couch.

"Is that what Mom said? Did she chase you off?"

She purses her lips. "Pretty much. Sloane didn't make things easy, for sure. I felt like I was being watched constantly, and she never missed a chance to criticize everything I did with you and for you."

"I'm sorry I had no idea—"

"Shhh. It's in the past. What did Lor tell you about her...if you don't mind sharing"

I give her the basics of Mom's hidden background. She doesn't show surprise or disgust.

"Did you know?" I ask.

"Nothing specific, but I always suspected she had lots of baggage. Maybe all the men and the moving around were her way of trying to distract herself."

"Like a coping mechanism. You're so wise." What would my life be like now if she'd stayed in it?

We're quiet for a moment, until she breaks the silence. "What's it like in Austin?"

I tell her about ACR, the people I've met there, and my tiny house plans. She remembers Martin and Rosy and says she's glad they're in my life again. Then I tell her about Alex.

"Oh Vanessa, he's cute, and he's *genuine*, like 'what you see is what you get.' I trust him, and he understands me and figures out things that are important to me without me having to say anything. But I've been trying to hide this stuff about my mom from him."

"Why?"

"It's humiliating. He knows *who* Mom is. They've met, but he doesn't know the stuff Lor's been telling me. I took off without saying why and sent him a text, of all things, instead of calling. I'm a horrible person." I cry again, and she hands me a box of tissues.

"Do you love him?"

"I think I might, but how can you tell for sure if you love someone? How did you know you loved James?"

Her eyes turn dreamy. "When I realized life wouldn't be worth living without him."

My mind jumps to thoughts of life without Alex, and it feels like my chest is being scooped out. Is this what Vanessa means?

We talk until the first rays of sunshine sneak through the window beside us.

I awaken later beneath a blanket she must have used to cover me after I fell asleep on the couch. I stretch and walk into the kitchen yawning.

Vanessa's at the sink. "Good afternoon. How are you?"

"Better," I murmur, taking in the adorable sight of her three-year-old daughter at the table in a blue princess gown. "Hi, Serena, I'm Eva. I like your dress."

"Thank you." She swipes her hand over the costume fabric. It's the same color of Alex's blue eyes.

I ache for him again. What if, in my hurry to escape, I messed things up for us? I meant to call him after talking with Vanessa last night—or rather this morning—but fell asleep.

I excuse myself and retreat to her home office where I left my phone. The battery's almost dead, and I forgot to bring a wall charger. Hopefully there's enough power left for one call to Alex.

His voicemail answers. Maybe he's at work right now. "Hi," I say, leaving a message. "I wanted to tell you I'm okay. I miss you and—" I pause and bite my lip. I'm pretty sure I love him, if the ache in my chest is any indication, but it isn't something I want to say for the first time in a message. I end with, "I'll call you later, okay? Bye."

Hanging up, I see a message from Blair.

> *Hey, girl, what's up? Nadine says you're taking a few days off from ACR. Everything okay?*

> *Sure. I'm out of town, but I'll let you know when I return.*

I don't have the impression Blair's tuned into celebrity gossip news, but if she's heard about me, I hope she isn't resentful I didn't tell her more about myself. Hank and Nadine too.

Back in the kitchen, Vanessa's putting plates with grilled cheese sandwiches on the table, where there are already steaming bowls of tomato soup. She remembers my favorite comfort foods. "You hungry?" she asks.

"Starving." My mouth waters. I sit across from Serena, marveling at this little clone of Vanessa. Her red hair is lighter than her mom's.

She climbs down from her chair and dances around, singing the chorus of "Little Eva."

Unlike me, she can sing on key. She takes my hand. "Dance with me."

I do, and soon, I'm laughing instead of crying. It's such a relief. I'm tempted to stay longer, but there's a guy back in Austin who's probably worried sick about me. And I won't abandon Lor.

Before I leave, Vanessa hugs me one last time, and I climb behind the wheel of my truck.

Rolling down the window, I say, "Thanks for everything. I appreciate you letting me stay the night."

"Anytime." She leans closer. We're eye to eye. "Don't hate your mom. She isn't who you thought she was, but she's your mom, and she loves you. I'm sure she never did anything to hurt you on purpose. Try to accept her for who she is. It'll take less energy and do less damage to *you* than hating her will." She reaches in and squeezes my shoulder, and I nod but that'll be easier said than done.

We wave goodbye, and I plug my phone in to charge. I drive away with determination to not let Mom's past define me. The resolve sinks into the cracks left by Lor's revelations.

Near the Texas border, I receive a call from Mom. I don't answer, and she tries again.

After her third attempt, *Spike* calls. I give in and accept his call.

"Eva! Oh my God, are you there?" Mom's voice blasts on the truck's speakers. I almost swerve out of my lane from the shock.

"Answer me!" she demands.

"I'm here! Stop yelling."

She heaves a sigh, and I can hear her tell someone else, "She answered."

Spike and Ike are in the background asking questions as Mom says, "Eva, what the hell are you doing in Louisiana?"

I grip the wheel tighter. "How did you—"

"Not important. I'm trying to tell you're in the damn gossip news."

"I know."

"You do? And it didn't occur to you to tell me?" Her voice rises to a fevered pitch again.

"I've been busy," I say, keeping *my* voice cool.

"I *never* should've let you live with Lor. He doesn't protect you like I do—"

Maniacal laughter escapes me. "Mom, it's *your* fault! You were drunk off your ass and caused a scene with me in public!" I pull off the highway, shaking like a leaf.

"Eva, listen." Her volume drops a notch. "You need to leave Austin. We can still do things to keep you from the public eye."

"No!" I yell, my resolve kicking in. "Me staying anonymous was only ever about *you*."

"Excuse me?" She's not used to me talking back like this.

"You lied about the attempted kidnapping. I'm not leaving Austin," I say as firmly as possible. "I'm done letting you tell me what to do."

"Be careful, Eva." Her tone is hateful. "Everything you have is thanks to *me* and I can take it away, just like *that*."

I feel like I've been hit in the chest and can't breathe. Not because she threatened to cut me off, but that she did it the *second* I dared to defy her.

"Fine. Go right ahead." I don't even sound like myself, my voice is flat. Hollow.

"You little—"

"Whoa, whoa, whoa! Sloane give me the phone," says someone in the background.

There's scuffling and raised voices and the noise fades.

"Hello?" I say tentatively.

"Baby girl, this is Spike. I went to another room. Listen, we want to make sure you're okay. Is there anything you need?"

"Not from her," I scoff.

"I'll talk to her. We love you. Stay safe."

"I will."

We hang up, and I call Lor. He answers with, "Eva, please come home."

"I'll be back tonight. I'm sorry I kind of ran off." My eyes sting from oncoming tears. I clear my throat. "How are you doing?"

"Fan-freakin'-tastic, now I know you're okay."

"I needed time to think things through. I visited Vanessa."

"In Louisiana?"

My eyes widen. "How did you know I went to Louisiana?"

"Alex told me. It's what you told him."

"Oh…and you told Mom?"

"No. I haven't talked to her. Why?"

I look around with the sense of being watched. "She somehow knew. I don't know how. Do you think there's a tracker on this truck?"

"Wouldn't surprise me."

"Okay, I gotta go."

My next call is to Alex. He hasn't replied to the voicemail message I left for him earlier, and I'm worried he's upset with me.

Chapter Forty-Five
Alex

Eva calls late Tuesday afternoon and says, "I'm on my way home."

"Oh, thank God." I release a sigh, like I've held my breath the whole time she's been gone. "I've been worried."

"I'm sorry." She sounds sincere.

"Thank you. How are you?"

"Better. I visited Vanessa, my governess. Remember me telling you about her?"

"Of course, I remember," I say.

"It helped. I'll be back in Austin late, but can I come see you tomorrow?"

"You better," I say, relieved she's returning.

I drop into bed early and have the most incredible dream of Eva, here in bed with me. I tell her, "I love you," and take my time undressing her. Kissing her. Touching her. Delaying my own gratification until I've pleased her.

The dream stays with me all day at work. I'm going crazy from missing her. It's a good thing her truck's already in the parking lot at my apartment when I arrive home. She opens the door and jumps out. A breeze blows her hair. It shines in the sun, making her radiant. The way she carries herself is different. She glows with a new confidence.

I step out of my truck, grinning a mile wide, and take her in my arms in a much-needed hug.

"You sure are a sight for sore eyes," I say.

She laughs. "You saw me two days ago."

"But then you were *gone*. You left." Can she tell how much that messed me up?

"I'm sorry. I'm here now." She runs her fingers through the hair at the back of my head, and I inhale her sweet vanilla scent. "Let's do something fun Alex. Like visit the theme park in San Antonio."

I brush my lips against hers. "Absolutely. When do you want to go?"

"Now. As soon as possible." She kisses me back.

"I have to work tomorrow, but I could try to switch shifts with someone."

"Are you sure? I'd hoped we'd be gone for a couple of days and told Nadine I wouldn't be available to volunteer this week. I already packed a bag, but maybe we should wait until you have some time off?"

"I'm sure."

She *packed a bag*. I'll move heaven and earth to make this happen.

We enter the apartment. Cassidi's on the couch watching TV.

On the way to my room, I mention that Eva and I will be heading to San Antonio for a couple of days.

"Oh...okay," Cassidi says.

Eva stops at the bathroom. "I'll be there in a minute."

I call my boss and put my phone on speaker as I stuff some clothes into a duffle bag. "Hey, Carlos. This is Alex. Something has come up. Is there any way I can have the next two days off?"

"Aww, man. This is super short notice."

"I'm sorry, but if it's at all possible to switch me with someone else, I'll take their weekend shifts."

"Hang on."

On hold, I retrieve a pack of condoms from the back of a dresser drawer and because it's been a while, I check the expiration date. Satisfied. I toss the pack into my bag.

I'm antsy for Carlos's answer. What if he can't cover my shifts?

A couple of minutes later, he'd back on the line. "I can cover tomorrow's shift for you and Brittney will do the next day. You owe us, man."

"Thank you *so much* and tell her thanks for me."

My door's half open, and after I hang up, Cassidi enters. "Are you really doing this?"

"What? Were you eavesdropping?"

"You're making a big mistake, jeopardizing your job to run off with that girl."

"*That girl* has a name. It's Eva, and she's my girlfriend." I throw the strap of my bag over my shoulder.

"You trust people too much, too soon, and you learn the hard way they aren't who you think they are. Did you learn nothing from being with Angie?"

I shut my door, hoping Eva didn't hear her. "This isn't for you to worry about, Cass. And don't you understand yet Eva's not the rich, spoiled brat you make her out to be?"

"Who's paying for this trip? She shows up and says jump, and you say how high."

"You've got it all wrong."

There's a knock on my door. Eva opens it. "I can hear everything y'all are saying. Alex, I appreciate you defending me, but I'd like to speak for myself."

She enters and faces Cassidi. "Please don't judge me when you barely know me. I'm not one of those snobby people you wait tables for. I don't sit around letting other people do everything for me. I mean, yes, my brother has a cook and a housekeeper, but I'm doing those things for myself now."

I'm impressed with how Eva's keeping her cool and standing up for herself like this.

"I don't plan on a life of extravagance," she continues. "I hate wastefulness."

Cassidi's lips form a straight, disapproving line.

Eva and I leave. In the parking lot, she questions if I'm sure about the trip.

"Positive."

I'm about to put my bag in her truck, but she stops me, saying, "No, let's take your truck. These license plates are an announcement of who I am."

"Good point."

"Plus, I think this thing has a tracker on it or in it, and I don't want anyone knowing where I am."

Oh no. Is she running away again?

"Eva...did you tell your brother or anyone at Casa Lor you're leaving?"

"Yes." She places her palms on my chest and rises on her toes and looks me as much in the eyes as she can. "I told Lor. Don't worry. It's not another vanishing act, okay?"

With my heart about to burst from my chest, I give her a hug and kiss. "Okay, we'll take my truck. Grab your stuff."

She gets a bag from the back seat, along with a champagne bottle.

I laugh. "What are you doing with the champagne?"

"Bringing it with us. FU left it behind. Do you still have the cooler in your truck?"

"Yeah."

"*Déjà vu*, huh?"

Chapter Forty-Six
Eva

I doze off for a while on the drive to San Antonio and awake energized.

"I can't wait to ride the rollercoasters." I squeeze Alex's hand.

He laughs and squeezes back. "I'm getting you there as fast as I can."

I find the park's website on my phone. "Damn. They closed an hour ago. Why so early? Oh, their summer hours start *next* week."

"There's always tomorrow. What time do they open in the morning?"

"Ten thirty."

"We'll be in San Antonio in a couple of miles. What's the new plan?"

"Let's decide where we're going to stay the night. I'll search for a hotel."

The air in the cab of the truck fills with the unspoken question: Will we *share* a room? I'm hoping we will. Hope it's also what he wants.

"There's a decent-looking one called The Henley." I tap the screen and view the information. "It's near the park. Should we check it out now? Or is there, like, something else you want to do first? I mean, it's up to you. You're driving. Go wherever you'd like." Jeez, I should stop talking. I'm making myself more nervous.

"Now's good." He drums his fingers on the wheel. "How do we get there?"

We arrive at The Henley a few minutes later, its parking lot packed.

"I wonder if they'll have any rooms open," I ponder. Alex finally spots a place to park.

Shutting the engine off, he runs his finger down my arm. "Let's find out."

Inside the lobby, there's a sign directing attendees of a Journalism of the Future Conference to turn left.

"Explains why they're so busy." He takes my hand, and we proceed to the check-in desk.

The guy behind the desk seems out of place, like he belongs on a beach, surfboard in hand. He's got a killer tan, windblown hair, and his hotel uniform shirt stretches around bulky biceps as he leans forward on his elbows, talking to a woman who's in her mid-forties. She's in ripped jeans and a Metallica concert T-shirt, smacking a wad of gum.

They're both focused on the phone she's holding.

I clear my throat. "Excuse me. Are there any rooms available?"

"Oh. Sorry, didn't see you." The guy moves to the computer, and his fingers fly across the keyboard. "As you may have noticed, there's a conference going on right now, but you're in luck. We have one room left with two queen beds. Would you like me to book it for you?"

"Yes, please," I say. "Two nights?"

The guy takes my ID and credit card, and his eyes linger on my left hand. There's a spark of recognition as he exchanges a quick look with the Metallica-shirt-wearing woman. Dammit. But what can I do? This is my life now, and I'll do what I want, whether people know who I am or not.

The guy passes the key cards to us for the room. "Enjoy your stay and let us know if there's anything you need." A normal thing to say, but there's a scheming glint in his eyes. I wish we'd put the room under Alex's name instead.

We return to the truck. I figure we'll retrieve our bags and go to the room.

Alex pauses. "I'm hungry. Are you hungry? I mean, maybe we should have dinner somewhere."

"Oh, yeah, good idea." My cheeks warm a little.

At a nearby fondue restaurant, the host seats us at a booth in a cozy, dimly lit section of the dining area.

We have salads first, followed by a cheese main course, taking our time with the cheese-dipped chunks of bread and crunchy veggies.

"This is so good." I skewer a bread chunk and dip it in the fondue pot.

"*So* good, but save room for chocolate."

"Oh, I will. Especially if there are strawberries for dipping."

There are, of course, strawberries, along with pineapple, marshmallows, and bite-sized brownies. Dipped in creamy chocolate, it's sinfully yummy.

I tell Alex about Vanessa and her family and avoid mention of Mom. This isn't the time or place. As far as Alex knows, I ran off because I was upset about media attention.

"Should we...go back to the hotel now?" he finally suggests.

"Yeah." I stand too fast, feel lightheaded, and almost knock over my water glass.

"Are you all right?" He takes my hand. His touch both calms my nerves *and* accelerates my heart rate.

"I'm good." I bite my bottom lip as we leave, hand in hand.

Back at the hotel, we take our bags and the bottle of champagne to the room. The place is nothing fancy, but it's nice and comfortable. I open the bottle, pouring some for each of us in the little glass tumblers next to the ice bucket.

"Cheers," I say, and we clink glasses. Taking a sip, I power up the TV and flip through the channels and stop on a sitcom episode.

"Leave it there," Alex says. "This show's funny."

He sits on one of the beds, champagne in hand, with his back against the wall. I do the same, settling in next to him. We watch what's left of the show, laughing together, and refilling our glasses. The bubbly, sweet champagne, mixed with anticipation for what tonight could bring, has me more than a little buzzed in no time.

Alex shuts off the TV. "Let's play a game."

"Okay, how about... Never, Have I Ever?" I giggle. "You start."

"I've never watched... *Lord of the Rings*."

"I don't like that kind of thing." I don't have to take a drink. "I've never been to a rodeo."

"Aww, not fair. I've been to the rodeo almost every year since I was four." He laughs and takes a drink. "My turn. I can play dirty too. I've never been backstage at a rock concert."

I take a drink. "I've never had a sister."

"What? No fair. It's like me saying I've never been a girl."

"Fine, we'll throw it out. Here's one: I've never been six feet tall."

"You're not playing right." We're lying on our stomachs on one of the beds, and he reaches back and pinches my butt. I squirm and spill a little champagne.

He jumps up for a towel and refills our glasses.

"Don't forget," I say. "You have to take a drink because *you're* six feet tall."

Handing over my glass, he takes a gulp from his own. "I've never broken a bone."

She shrugs, not drinking. "Me neither. Hmm. I've never swam in a lake."

"Never?" He laughs and takes a drink. "You've swam in the ocean, though, right)?"

"Of course. Is that your turn?"

"No. Here's my turn: I've never been to California."

I roll my eyes as I sip. "I've never gone to college."

Another gulp. "I've never had a pedicure."

"You've got me there. Mani-pedis are Mom's favorite mother-daughter activity after shopping." I drink and shove away thoughts of Mom. "I've never lived in an apartment."

He throws back the remains of his champagne and refills the glass, studying me for a moment. "I've never been homeschooled."

"You're killing me. We need less obvious things, like..." Thinking, I lie on my back, my head over the edge to let my hair hang almost to the floor. "I've never sang karaoke."

Lying next to me, he says, "I had the chance to do karaoke once but chickened out. Here's a less obvious one for you: I've never been kicked out of a bar."

I sit up and bring the glass to my lips. "For the record, it wasn't my fault." I take the drink and counter with, "Never, have I ever...gone hunting."

After his sip, there's a long pause, during which his eyes sparkle, full of mischief.

"Uh, oh." My eyes widen, and I'm lightheaded. "Go on, gimme your best shot."

He sits up with me. "I've never gone skinny-dipping."

I toss back what's left in my glass, and he gapes at me. Laughing, I flop onto my back and roll away from him, right off the bed.

"Are you okay?" He jumps to his feet and helps me up.

"I'm fine." I wink and set my empty glass down.

He wraps his arms around me, bringing his lips to mine.

Chapter Forty-Seven
Alex

Not wanting to rush anything, I give Eva gentle, hesitant kisses. She kisses me back with such insistence, melding her body to mine, that I'm hard in an instant.

Her hands slide up my shirt. "Take it off," she whispers.

Together, we pull it over my head. She smothers my bare chest with warm, wet kisses. When her mouth's back on mine, I slide a hand up the front of her shirt. I cup her breast. My fingers slip into her bra, teasing her nipple. She arches her back and moans. I love the uninhibited noises she makes, and I ache to touch her everywhere. And for her to touch me.

She fumbles with the button on my jeans. I groan and guide her hand to press against me through my jeans. I've never wanted her more, but the sweetness of the champagne on our tongues reminds me neither of us are thinking straight.

Damn.

I call on every ounce of willpower I can and cover her hand with mine and stop her from unzipping my jeans.

She makes a noise of frustration and pulls away, swaying a little. I steady her, and we sit on the bed, both breathing fast.

"Why'd we stop?" she asks. "What's wrong?"

"Eva, I don't *want* to stop. I want you more than you can imagine, but I…" I pause and run my hands through my hair. *My* first time was after Angie plied me with a few beers. I reposition and face Eva. "I don't want our first time—*your* first time to be after we've been drinking. I love you too much to let it happen like this."

She looks into my eyes. Hers are full of surprise. "Did you…um, did you say you—"

"Yes, Eva, I love you." I entwine my fingers with hers.

"I love you too." Her beaming expression takes my breath away as much as her words. "I was planning to tell you tonight. You beat me to it." She brushes her lips on mine.

I kiss her back, slower than before. There's less urgency. What we've said to each other sinks in, and I focus on that instead of what I want to do with her.

We lie on the bed, face-to-face.

"Tell me again," she whispers.

"I love you, Eva." I touch my forehead to hers.

She smiles. "I love you, Alex. And you're right. Our first time should be when we we're sober, but will you sleep with me, like in the same bed, if we keep our clothes on?"

"I'd love to."

She rolls over, her back to me and says, ever so sweetly, "Then come on and spoon with me, cowboy."

I rest my arm across her waist but avoid direct contact of my body to hers. She's asking more of me than she knows. Once she's breathing evenly, fast asleep, I get up and take a cold shower.

In the morning, I awake with Eva's warm body snuggled against me. I sink my face into her hair. Peaches and cream. Heaven.

Her eyes flutter open. They widen, and she covers her mouth with her fingers.

"Good morning," she whispers from behind them.

I laugh. "What are you doing?"

"I went to sleep without brushing my teeth." She laughs and gets up.

I watch her cute butt sashay all the way to the bathroom. She shuts the door and runs the shower, and I can hear her singing. This is killing me! Not her singing, because, while it's as awful as mine, I think it's adorable. It's knowing she's in there naked.

A few minutes later, the water shuts off. She emerges, clad in only a towel.

"Hmm," I murmur, eyebrow raised. "They may not let you in the park like that."

She chuckles and carries her bag into the bathroom, closing the door again. When she reopens it, she's wearing shorts and a red tank top. The shirt showcases its contents with perfection.

"Keep me company as I finish getting ready."

I accept the invitation and perch on the side of the tub.

As she blows her hair dry, brushing it in long strokes, her movements are graceful. Almost sensual. She puts her hair in a ponytail and applies a little makeup before spraying perfume on her wrists. I breathe in deeply and exhale slowly.

She gives me a curious look. "You okay?"

"I'm hungry. Let's have some breakfast," I say instead of giving voice to the lascivious thoughts running through my head. Her stomach growls, as if on cue. Even that's sexy, and I have a feeling the day's gonna be one long, hot—agonizing—foreplay session for me.

Chapter Forty-Eight
Eva

After breakfast, Alex and I exit the hotel, only to be rushed by Carla Kinsey, who appears out of nowhere, waving a microphone. "Eva Covington, may I have a moment of your time?"

I ignore her, and she shoves the mic in Alex's direction and asks, "Sir, what's your relationship with Eva? Are you romantically involved?"

His face blank, he keeps quiet as we speed-walk to his truck.

Another lady, who's with Carla, has a camera aimed at us the whole time.

Alex guides me into the passenger seat, then gets in on the other side. Carla waves as we drive away, a smirk on her round face.

"How the hell did she find you *here*?" Alex asks.

"I think the guy at the front desk last night recognized me. He must've tipped her off."

"What the—isn't that illegal?" Wide-eyed, he grips the steering wheel with both hands.

I tuck my own hands under my legs and hope he won't notice how shaky I am. "It's a fine line," I say, somehow keeping the panic from my voice. "At least Carla wasn't aggressive. It could have been worse. Let's try not to worry. I don't want her to ruin our time together."

He sighs and nods. "Me neither." We're quiet for most of the drive until he exclaims, "She looked even more like a Cabbage Patch Kid in person."

I join him in laughter. "Yeah, I wish she'd go *back* to her cabbage patch and leave me alone."

At the park, we stop at a park bench outside the main entrance to apply sunscreen.

His breathing speeds up as he rubs the lotion onto my back and shoulders with firm, thorough fingers.

Everything around us fades away until I can't resist turning around to kiss him. I don't care if other people see us. The park isn't busy yet.

Alex trails a finger along my jaw and onto my neck, giving me a delicious chill in the morning sun.

"I have a question for you," he whispers.

I'm so turned on and sure he'll ask if we can have sex tonight that I almost suggest we immediately return to the hotel room.

"Ask me anything you want." I close my eyes and nibble his earlobe.

He brushes his lips on mine. "Do I have to ride the ones with loops?"

My eyes pop open. "Loops?" I exhale to the count of three, needing to get a grip.

"Yeah, loops." The glint in his eyes makes me wonder if that's really what he was going to ask.

"Why? Don't you *like* being upside down, hurtling through the air on a steel contraption?"

Laughing, he kisses me again. "Doubt it, but I'm willing to try it for you."

"Let's start with rides that don't attempt to reverse gravity and work up to the intense ones."

We run from one rollercoaster to the next, joking and flirting with each other.

I receive a kiss before each ride, and we hold hands in the air, fingers entwined. I'm like a junkie for the anticipation of each hill the coasters climb, the thrill of big drops.

The adrenaline rush is addictive, almost as good as making out with Alex last night. But I'm glad we stopped. Glad he's looking out for my best interests.

After a ride with a long, steep drop, he says, "Wow, I had no idea you're such a screamer."

"Sorry. Am I busting your eardrums?"

"No, and don't apologize. I love it. I love *you*." It's the first time either of us has said it today and hearing him say it catches me off guard—in a good way.

I throw my arms around him. "I love you too."

We share one of those big salty pretzels, and I tell him, "It's time."

"For?" His eyebrows pinch together.

"The Goliath." I tug his arm in the direction of the ride I've been waiting for.

"Oh, God help me," he mutters.

It has loops, drops, and corkscrews. He keeps his eyes closed almost the whole time, but he's laughing by the end. "That was mind blowing."

"Yay, I knew I could make you a fan of the loops. I need a break now." I smooth my hair back in a tighter ponytail. "Let's eat lunch."

"How can you be hungry again already? Where do you put it all?" He scoops his arm under my legs, picking me up.

"I love it when you carry me." I nuzzle his neck but pull away with a *bleah* from the bitter taste.

"What? Oh, sunscreen. Sorry. Try again after we shower tonight."

He sets me down, and my stomach dips, swarming with butterflies like I'm on another ride. Did he mean "after we shower" as in *together*? I can't wait to be alone with him after this.

There are more people in the park now, and it's gotten hotter.

We ride a few more rollercoasters before we decide to leave.

I'm so happy I haven't worried about the SLY stalker, and Alex hasn't acted like he's concerned either.

Back at the hotel, I scan the parking lot, keeping a wary eye out. Thankfully, there's no sign of Carla.

Alex glances around. I guess he *has* been thinking of what happened this morning. It'll suck if pictures of us show up in other places besides Carla's SLY pages. I wish there were a way to keep Alex out of it.

As we wait for the elevator, I glance around the lobby. A lady in one of the chairs is looking at her phone. I can tell she's photographing us.

Chapter Forty-Nine
Alex

Eva and I return to the hotel, and dread from this morning's run-in with Carla returns full force. I'm pretty sure I saw someone downstairs taking photos of us.

"Aren't hotel guests entitled to better privacy than this?" I ask as we enter our room.

"My experiences at hotels always included FU's security team. Would you feel better if we went home now?"

Leaving might be the smart thing to do, but I've anticipated this all day, being with her tonight. "No, we can stay. Unless *you* want to leave."

"No, I don't. Let's order room service and stay in. Will you order some burgers or something while I shower?"

"Sure."

She goes into the bathroom, closing the door. If I weren't distracted, I'd have suggested we shower together. I don't think either of our minds are on anything like that right now. I order room service. Once I've placed our order, I sit back, taking deep breaths. I want to snap out of this funk and make the most of tonight.

Eva emerges a few minutes later wearing a hotel robe.

My mind goes to what's underneath, and I'm done worrying about reporters.

"Food's on the way." I kiss her forehead. After my own quick shower, I put on the other hotel robe.

Room service arrives, and I pay the tip before Eva has a chance to.

"I was gonna cover that," she says, putting her wallet away. "You already paid for our food today."

"You've covered the hotel and park tickets. Let me pick up the tab on some stuff or I'll feel like a kept man." I joke, but there was a nugget of truth to the comment.

"Fine." She lifts the lid on the food tray.

The burgers, despite smelling good, are disappointing lumps of charcoaled meat, accented by wilted lettuce and thin pickle slices. We end up eating the popcorn we picked up at the park and lie propped on pillows in bed to watch TV.

"Is this what your life was like traveling with FU? Hanging out in nice hotels, ordering room service, and watching premium channels?"

"Pretty much. Long bus rides between hotel stays."

"Why not fly?"

"Ohhh, no, the Undertakers do *not* like to fly. They'll do it for the overseas tours, but in the States, it's wheels on the ground. The twins hate flying."

She clicks off the TV. I turn on my side to face her, my head propped on my hand. Her back is pressed into a pillow against the headboard. She looks cozy and cute in the thick robe and taps her toes on my arm a couple times until I can't resist anymore. I run my hand from her ankle to her knee, and she jumps.

"You're tickling me." She leans forward to grab my hand.

The popcorn spills. I help her pick up the pieces. More gets knocked out from her wiggling. Everything I do makes her more ticklish. She squeals, and it's adorable.

"I'm trying to clean this up. *You're* making it worse," I joke. "Be still." I try to pluck a piece of popcorn nestled at the V of her robe. The popcorn slips further in and disappears.

"Oops," I say, but I'm not sorry. Her chest rises with a deep inhale, and I want more than anything to dive after that lucky kernel. She tucks one end of her robe's belt into my hand.

I look into her eyes, hopeful. Oh, so hopeful.

She helps me untie the belt. The single piece of popcorn tumbles onto the bed. I brush it aside and pull her robe open. My breath hitches. She's completely, blessedly naked.

"You're beautiful." I kiss her, brushing my tongue over her lips. They're a little salty, and I want more. I'm eager to taste all of her and lie beside her to nuzzle her neck, breathing in the scent of her shower gel. Her skin's soft and silky smooth. She arches her back as my lips move over her breasts.

Her hips squirm. "Touch me," she pleads.

Unable to wait any longer, I slide my fingers into the warmth at the apex of her thighs. We gasp at the same time, breaking a kiss.

"Oh my God, Eva, you're so wet." I take my time touching her in subtle, different ways, and find a rhythm that has her breathing hard and fast, moving with my hand.

When she climaxes, the noises she makes almost send me over the edge. I want to be inside her, to have every inch of her bare skin on mine.

With swift movements, I pull my robe open, and we work together to tug my underwear off. She wraps a hand around me. I moan as she strokes me, my eyes closing.

"I want you, Alex," she says, breathless.

My eyes open and peer into hers. "Are you sure?"

"I'm sure. If you didn't bring any condoms, I have some in my bag."

"I love how you came prepared. So did I." I leave her side to get one from my bag and catch her looking at how aroused I am.

She bites her lip, watching me roll on a condom.

"Are you still okay with this?" I ask, pausing.

Her lips curve upward. "I'm more than okay with it, just admiring the view."

I lower myself between her legs, gentle as I enter, kissing and caressing her. "I love you, Eva."

Chapter Fifty
Eva

I awake in the morning, naked and warm next to Alex. My stomach flutters at the memory of last night. Incredible doesn't even begin to describe it. He made my first time special.

We fell sound asleep, holding each other. Sometime during the night, I dreamed of him whispering in my ear. The dream was so real I could feel his breath on my neck. Then it wasn't a dream anymore. I woke to him murmuring in his sleep. I kissed him until he was awake.

His eyes fluttered open. "Oh, Eva, I want you again." He led my hand under the sheet to show me how ready he was.

Now, I yawn and stretch beside him. His eyes open, and his face lights up as he looks into my eyes. He dips his head, giving each of my breasts a kiss and then nuzzles my neck.

"Are you sore?" he asks.

"Maybe a little, but I want you again," I say, repeating his words from last night.

"Hmm, yes, please. Let's shower and take our time."

We lather each other up and rinse under the gentle spray of warm water.

As we towel off, he dips his head and kisses my chest. I arch my back and catch our reflection in the mirror. I can't take my eyes from how hot we are together, both naked and him so aroused. Before my brain has time to process what's happening, he's on his knees in front of me.

Looking up at me, he nuzzles one of my inner thighs, then the other. His lips move higher. I shiver and gasp as his mouth does the most amazing things to me. Closing my eyes, I moan and run my fingers through his damp hair.

"Oh, God, yes," I cry out at the building of an orgasm.

My body trembles, and he slides a supporting hand to the small of my back.

He slows what he's doing as my climax subsides. I'm almost too sensitive for any more touching. As I'm about to pull away, he hums. The vibration of his lips brings on a whole new, delicious sensation. Another orgasm builds within seconds. Somehow sensing it, he adds the perfect pressure. My hands grip his shoulders, urging him on, and I have a third orgasm.

"Alex." I'm breathless. "I can't stand anymore."

He stands and wraps me in his arms. "Let's go back to bed. We have one condom left."

"I'll put it on you." I take it from the nightstand, and he lies on his back. With a little help from him, I put it on and say, "I want to be on top this time."

He lies back, and I straddle him.

"Be careful." He guides himself into me. "Last night, I didn't want to hurt you and didn't exactly, you know, go all the way in."

"Seriously?" I had no idea, but I lower myself and figure out what he means. I'm completely filled and stretched by him. "Maybe this won't work. I can hardly move."

"Try leaning forward." He draws my hands up to rest on each side of his head and runs his own hands down my back. "How's this?"

"Better. Is it still good for you?"

"Perfect." He lifts his head to kiss one of my breasts, then the other.

I grind my hips. Another orgasm didn't seem possible, but this position gives me perfect control with everything—angle, speed, depth. His hips match the rhythm of mine. I explode around him, my entire body thrumming.

As the intensity subsides, my upper body collapses onto him. He bucks beneath me, and now he's the one making hot, uninhibited noises. He loses control, and I love knowing I've done that for him. I smother him with kisses, whispering, "I love you."

"I love you too. You're incredible." His chest rises and falls with each deep breath.

I move off him, and he discards the condom, lying back beside me.

I snuggle into the crook of his arm, and I'm ready to explain why I took off for Louisiana. "Can I tell you what made me freak out on

Sunday?"

"I was hoping you would." He seems relieved I'm bringing it up, and he's been sweet to not pry, but I don't want to keep anything from him anymore.

I start with what Lor told me about Mom and Franklin and finish with the fact she was a band groupie. "She went from having a child with a man old enough to be her dad, to hooking up with guys from at least two different bands."

"Damn. She's faithful to Spike *now*, right? I mean, aren't they getting married?"

"Already did. Last Saturday in Paris."

"Are you sad you weren't there?" He brushes a strand of hair from my face.

"No. The thing is…on their last night in Austin, I saw her…with Ike."

"You *saw* them? Like, having sex?"

"It was headed there until he pushed her away, but I overheard them talking, and now I know they've hooked up before. Not just the time that may have gotten her pregnant with me. I'm not sure if Spike knows. Finding out Mom and Ike are cheaters just hit me really hard. It's why I reacted like I did about the picture of you and Jessica. The thought of *you* being a cheater—"

"Oh, Eva, I'm so sorry. I'd never cheat on you."

I kiss his temple. "I know. The other problem is the triangle thing between Mom and the twins. It makes my skin crawl. It's like she's been cheating on my dad with my *other* dad. And I can't understand why the guys are interested in her. She's so much older than them." I roll my eyes.

Alex looks away, grimacing as he sits up and swings his feet to the floor.

"What's wrong?" I take his hand.

"Nothing." His posture straightens. "You're my sexy Hungarian girlfriend. I feel…cultured."

"*Half* Hungarian. I'm thinking of looking for my relatives in New York or wherever they've scattered over the years."

"Do you think they know about you?" He starts to dress.

"Doubt it. Mom turned her back on the whole family and even changed her name. It used to be Sarika Szabo. She called me on my way home from Louisiana and ordered me to leave Austin and arrange for all new disguises. Threatened to cut me off—"

"Damn." The color drains from his face. "You're not gonna leave me, are you?"

"No way." I get up and put a T-shirt on. "I told her I'm done letting her call the shots."

He hugs me. "I bet that was hard, but I'm glad you're not going anywhere."

"Nope, you're stuck with me."

After checking out of the hotel, we reach Alex's truck without another Carla Kinsey encounter. We have breakfast and head back to Austin, listening to playlists of California Nine and some of Alex's favorite country songs.

He steers into the parking spot beside my truck at his apartment complex. "What are your plans for the rest of the day?"

"I want to spend some time with Lor, then Blair and I have plans later tonight. Can I use your bathroom before I head home?"

"Of course."

I put my bag in my truck, and we go inside.

Cassidi's at the kitchen table with her laptop and a grim expression. When I exit the bathroom, a conversation between Alex and Cassidi halts. The tension in the kitchen is thick.

Alex looks at his phone, nostrils flaring.

"What's going on?" I ask.

"SLY." He shows me his phone and taps the screen, playing a video clip of yesterday's incident outside the hotel.

"I'm sick of this. Why won't that woman leave me alone?"

"It isn't just about *you* now," Cassidi says. "You've dragged Alex into your publicity."

He sighs and takes my hand, leading me to his room. "Ignore Cassidi, please."

"Okay." I hug him, and he wraps his arms around me. "We sort of expected this, right?"

"Yeah." He kisses my forehead. "I had a great time in San Antonio."

"So did I. I'm tempted to stay, but I should take off now. I haven't spent much time with Lor this week. You want to walk me to my truck?"

In the parking lot, we're kissing each other goodbye beside my truck when we're interrupted by someone slow clapping. "Well, isn't this sweet?"

Alex and I break apart. I look around to find the source of the voice. A woman stands a few parking spots away, near a van. Expecting someone with a camera to emerge, I grit my teeth and step toward the woman at the same time she approaches me.

"Um…Eva…wait." Alex takes my hand.

"No, they've crossed a line." I address the stranger. "It's one thing to come at me in public, but this is where my boyfriend lives. Aren't there harassment laws for reporters?"

"Whoa, blondie. I'm not a reporter." She holds her hands up. They're empty. No mic.

"You mean you aren't here with *them*?" I point at the van. Its sliding door is now open, and Carla peers out, grinning, but she stays put. "I don't understand," I mutter and return to Alex.

The woman says, "Alex, do you want to tell your girlfriend who I am or should I?"

He's turned to stone, still and pale.

Ice runs through my veins at the woman's wicked smirk. It reminds me of the joker cards on Lor's living room wall.

She settles her gaze on me. "I'm Angie."

My head rears back. The dots connect. This is Alex's ex, but she's older than him. More like mid-thirties. Is this why he didn't tell his family about her?

He could've told *me*. My eyes plead with him for some explanation, but his eyes aren't on me. He's glaring daggers at Angie, at her freakin' *perfect* figure in a filmy blouse and tight pencil skirt.

She brushes her hair over her shoulder, looking so bold. Disgusting. "I've been following SLY about you, *mystery* girl." Her eyes take me in, head to toe.

She makes my skin crawl. How was *my* Alex ever with *her*?

"And Alex." She sidles closer to us. "Imagine my surprise to see photos of *you* with her in San Antonio yesterday. Your brother gave me your new address, in exchange for...hmm. No, that's between me and him." She laughs and bites her lower lip. "I called Carla Kinsey last night and told her she could find you two lovebirds right here. Then I got the best idea for how to make this into a total shit show for you."

I shudder, like something slithered up my spine. The woman is diabolical.

"What have you done?" Alex's voice rasps.

"Oh, you'll see, but this wasn't all *my* doing. The photographer at my place the other day shared his photos with SLY." She waves at Carla, who gets out of the van, microphone at the ready and camera guy in her wake.

Alex snaps into motion, marching toward Angie and Carla, as if to block them from me.

Carla dodges him and thrusts the microphone under my chin. "Eva, were you aware of Alex's ties to Angie Forsythe, wife of San Antonio Mayor Sonny Forsythe who's running for governor?"

Wait…what? Angie's *married*? To a *mayor*? Who's running for *governor*?

I can't move. Can't breathe.

Numb, I fix my eyes on Alex. Angie touches his arm. He jerks it away.

"Have you forgotten Sonny will destroy me if our past goes public?" he seethes.

"Why the hell should I care? You've moved on from me, and since Sonny and I split up, I don't care about him *or* his reputation. I don't need his money, either. I found out my uncle left me loads of cash."

Carla shoves an iPad in front of me. "These were taken a few days ago at Angie's ranch."

At Angie's *ranch*? What was Alex doing there?

I almost puke at what's on the screen. In a series of photos, Alex and Angie seem to be kissing.

Alex tries to lead me off by my elbow, but it's too late. I already saw Angie's hands all over him. She was kissing his face and neck.

The picture of Alex asleep with Jessica flashes in my mind. I was so naïve to believe that was nothing. How many women is Alex seeing while claiming I'm the only one?

With bile rising in my throat, I find the strength to turn away from Carla and her iPad and discover that a camera's been pointed at me, catching my reaction. The earth tilts. I stumble back a little.

Angie pretends to brush something off her hands and takes a couple steps back. "My work here is done."

"Eva…let's get out of here." Alex takes my hand.

I bristle at his touch and pull away.

"Oh, one more thing." Angie looks over her shoulder, right at me. "Alex is a great lay, isn't he? I taught him everything. *You're welcome.*"

My stomach churns, sending a sour taste to my mouth—*my* Alex—with her.

She walks to the van and leans against it, facing him and me, like she's watching a show—a shit show, as she called it. I want to scratch her eyes out. Wipe the smile off her face.

Finally, numbness morphs into red hot rage. I whirl on Alex. "Did you sleep with her? The other day? At her ranch?"

"*No.* I left. I ran off, but they didn't show you that now, did they? Don't fall for this shit."

"Why were you there in the first place? Was it because I left town and wouldn't call you back?" I cover my mouth to stifle a sob.

"No. The only reason I saw her that day was because I came

across her on the side of the road with car trouble."

"How far did it go? Did you kiss her?" My voice rises, full of searing anguish. I don't even care who hears. "It sure looked like *she* was kissing *you*."

He tucks his chin and shoves his hands into his pockets. I wrap my arms around my middle, trying to hold myself together. His silence is deafening. He won't even look at me.

Chapter Fifty-One
Alex

"How far did it go?" Eva asks again. The sadness and regret in her voice tear at my insides.

How should I answer? I don't want to tell her Angie kissed me, but what if the photographer got a shot of us lip locked too?

I can't deal with this, not here. If only the ground would open and make Angie and Carla disappear. How will I fix this? Is it even possible? I'm such a dumbass!

Eva's face is fifty shades of red. And, *shit*, now she's crying.

I open my mouth to say something—what, exactly, I have no idea. Nothing comes out. I squeeze my eyes shut.

"You better say something, Alex," Eva demands. "Because my imagination is filling in the blanks. I can't *believe* you went to San Antonio with me—*slept with me*—right after you—"

"I didn't sleep with her!" I blurt and turn my back to Carla's camera guy and take my hands from my pockets, clasping them in front of me. "She tried, but..."

"*Tried?* What the hell does that mean?"

"Look, Eva, I can't think straight with these people watching. I need time—"

"You need *time*? After last night?" She scoffs and drags in a ragged breath. "How about I give you plenty of time? *Alone*. I don't like being lied to, and as far as I'm concerned, that's what you did. You should've told me what happened with her."

My heart squeezes painfully. I can't bear the torment on Eva's face but everywhere else I look I find an audience. Angie, Carla, the cameraman, and now Cassidi's outside our apartment.

"Eva, I *have* to get out of here. Let's go." I walk toward my truck, and thank God, she follows. We'll talk somewhere quiet, without an audience, where I can explain everything.

The tendril of hope that she'll listen dies as she stops beside her own truck and opens the driver's door. "Screw you, Alex. I poured my heart out to you this morning. Told you all my secrets." She clutches her chest. "Now I find out you've got a bunch of your own. I'm not going anywhere with you."

"Eva..." My chest cracks open as she gets in her truck. Slams the door. Drives away, tires squealing. She's really leaving. I can't believe she left. I can't believe it. It's my worst freakin' nightmare, amplified by a thousand.

Brushing past Cassidi, I enter the apartment and lock myself in my room.

After pacing back and forth, trying to decide what to say, I call Eva.

No answer. I try again. It goes straight to voicemail. "Eva, I'm so sorry," I say. "I freaked out, but I want to explain now. Angie made what happened sound like something it wasn't. Call me back. Please. I love you."

I hang up and send a text.

Please call me. I'll explain everything. I'm so sorry.

I love you.

A while later, my phone starts blowing up with texts and calls, not one of them from Eva.

Brady asks if I'm okay and sends a link. Carla's already posted the whole ugly scene on SLY.

There's a voicemail message from Mom. "Please tell me this stuff isn't true." There's a long pause. "Call me when you're ready to talk. I love you."

No way can I handle talking to Mom right now.

All these months since calling it quits with Angie, I've worried about Sonny's threats, but I'm not sure even he could've wrecked me the way Angie herself has. I have to make Eva understand that when Angie and I got together, I had no idea she was married, much less to whom.

Sean, my old asshat roommate from the dorm, texts to congratulate me on my "primo conquests." Great. Like I want props from that tool.

Devin sends a row of laughing emojis.

I block his *and* Sean's numbers.

Never...have I ever...been *so* alone.

Well, not exactly. There's still Cassidi to contend with. I finally leave my room for something to eat and drink several hours later and brace myself for her I-told-you-so parade, but she surprises me. As I scarf down a sandwich, she doesn't say a thing.

"What are you waiting for?" I ask. "This is your chance to say, 'I told you so.'"

"You're an idiot."

"There it is." I storm back to my room. "I bet you're happy now."

"Hey, wait." She sounds apologetic, but I don't care.

A few seconds later, she knocks. "I'm sorry. Can I come in?" She gets nothing but silence from me because I'm about to break. My throat's tight. My eyes sting.

"I'm coming in anyway." She opens the door.

I refuse to look at her. I sit on the edge of my bed, eyes on the floor. Tears brim, threatening to fall.

Cassidi sits beside me. "I watched the video on SLY already. I called you an idiot for how guilty you acted about Angie when she implied y'all...got reacquainted."

"Nothing happened! My God, why won't anyone believe me?"

"I believe you, but I don't blame Eva for driving off."

"I couldn't hash it out in front of an audience. I wanted Eva to go with me, to talk somewhere privately. She wouldn't. She walked away—*drove* away and didn't give me a chance."

"Um, from what I saw, she *did* give you a chance. And you just stood there."

I'm surprised Cassidi's sticking up for Eva. "What's your deal? I've wanted you to give her a chance all along, and now you're willing to when it's too late."

"I'll admit I've been unfair about Eva. Focused on the wrong things. Obviously, her life hasn't been full of rainbows and unicorns. And I wasn't paying enough attention to how happy she makes you."

"Gee thanks. Does me no good now."

"You should tell her everything, but don't wait too long."

~ * ~

Eva never calls or texts me back. I wait, hope, and sulk for the whole weekend.

My days consist of going to work, returning home, and going to bed. Get up the next morning. Repeat.

People at work who've watched my life implode online either ask carefully worded questions to dig for details, or give me dirty looks, which they probably figure I deserve.

The last thing Angie said to Eva—about me being a great lay

thanks to her—haunts me. I won't blame Eva if she never gets over that.

Monday night, I call Eva again. The call goes straight to voicemail. At least she hasn't blocked my number.

Mom calls again, and I answer. I'll have to talk to her at some point.

"Hello, Alex." Her voice is cold and distant.

"Mom, I'm sorry."

"I have been so…blindsided and shocked by you. More than I ever thought possible."

The disappointment in her voice breaks something inside me. I could've sworn there was no way to hurt worse than I already did. I choke up and press my fist to my mouth. Mom's silent for a moment. There are a couple of sniffles on her end.

"I'm sorry," I say again.

She clears her throat. "I'm sorry you made certain choices and never felt you could talk to your father or me about them."

"I was embarrassed. I didn't know Angie was still married when we got involved."

"Well, that's some relief."

"Are people in Florence talking about it? Saying anything to you?"

"Uh…*yeah*, people have had quite a lot to say and ask about." She sounds bitter.

"Shit," I murmur, not even caring she disapproves of swearing. "Okay, I guess there's no coming back from this. I gotta go."

She says something as I hang up, and she tries to call me right back, but I can't talk to her anymore. Can't take the shame in her voice for another second.

Cassidi keeps quiet and gives me space. Small blessings there.

Brady checks on me Thursday night. There isn't much for me to say besides what he already knows: I've hurt Eva, and I'm screwed.

The next day Carlos lets me leave early. I try calling Eva again but get her voicemail. I drive to Casa Lor. The access code I last used for the security gate no longer works and nobody responds when I push the call button.

I have one last hope. ACR. I drive there, intending to grovel for forgiveness no matter who's watching, but she isn't here. Blair isn't around, either.

Nadine tells me Eva asked for the week off. I can't help wondering if she's gone MIA again.

Chapter Fifty-Two
Eva

The Alex-shaped hole in my heart gnaws at me every waking moment—and a lot of sleeping moments as well. I dream of him every night. Of our nights together and how we said *I love you* to each other. Then, I remember Angie in his arms, putting her lips on him. And her hateful parting words. I worry again about what happened between her and Alex right before San Antonio.

A glutton for punishment, I keep monitoring SLY and have waves of nausea from watching Carla interview Angie one-on-one. It's clear she thinks only about herself. I wonder if Alex knew what a mean streak she has when he hooked up with her.

There's also an interview of Mayor Sonny Forsythe with a San Antonio reporter. He says, "No comment," a lot, but when asked about the "scandalous affair his wife had with a teenage boy," he tells the reporter that he and Angie were separated at the time and have since filed for divorce, so it's none of his business what she does, but for the record, he makes it clear the teenage boy was of age. A consenting adult.

The reporter persists. "Your wife stated you previously threatened Alex Marshall with public humiliation of him and his family if he ever went near your wife again. Do you plan to follow through with the threat?"

"I never made any threats. Why would I waste time and energy doing any such thing? Besides, he's suffered enough humiliation already, don't you think?"

That's one good thing—Alex doesn't have a mad husband out to get him.

Even so, he's gotta be catching hell from family and friends. I bet his brother is having a field day at Alex's expense. It's hard not to feel like he deserves it.

A couple of days later, Vanessa calls, having heard of my public humiliation.

"At least you didn't run away this time," she says.

"No, but I've ignored Alex's calls. I don't really know why. Like for some twisted payback or whatever. Stupid."

"It's understandable. After you move past your anger—and you will—you'll have some perspective and hopefully reach the right frame of mind to talk things out with him."

Blair and I have also talked on the phone. I've told her everything about my messed-up family and how things fell apart with Alex. She's great at commiserating, but my only real solace is Lor. I sometimes sit in on his therapy sessions, and he's made great progress toward walking on his own again. He had Darnell set up his room with a bunch of rehab equipment.

Lor sweats and strains, gritting his teeth through his endless exercises. I distract him with readings from *The Hitchhiker's Guide to the Galaxy*. I've never seen him this determined before. Today, he's on the platform with parallel bars. Arms braced, hands gripping the bars, beads of sweat streaking the sides of his face.

Darnell's right alongside to assist. "Your legs are stronger than you think. Don't overwork your arms."

I'm at the other end of the platform and set the book aside to cheer him on. "Come on, Lor, you can do this."

With more focus than ever, he relaxes his upper body and shifts his weight into a proper standing position.

Darnell coaches him in a low, encouraging tone through first one step.

Then two.

And three.

Lor's steps are more of a shuffle and take time. He finally reaches me, exhausted but beaming from his accomplishment.

"You did it!" I hug him, careful not to disrupt his balance.

His chest puffs up with pride.

"Great job!" Darnell claps. "Now rest. You can do it again tomorrow."

While Darnell helps him shower and change clothes, I bring the mosaic-tiled guitar into his room. I place it on a guitar stand in a spot where he'll be able to see it from his bed.

"Whoa, what's this?" Lor asks as soon as Darnell wheels him

out of the bathroom.

"A surprise." I take over for Darnell and push the wheelchair closer to the guitar for my brother to have a better look.

"It's beautiful. Where'd you find it?" He runs a finger across the colorful tiles. "Wait…is this—"

"It's yours." I spin the guitar around and show him the cracked neck. "An artist came across the broken guitar and saw it as something worth keeping. It was at ACR the first day I went there. I saw it as a sign I was meant to be there. I didn't show it to you at the time in case it reminded you of what you've lost. But now, I hope it'll represent something positive."

"Second chances," he whispers, catching my hand in his. "It's awesome, Eva. Thank you."

Hector makes a celebratory dinner, which Lor and I eat in his room. We segue into our usual card game of Spite and Malice.

He wins the first hand and shuffles for the next. "I talked to Spike today. He's worried you and Mom haven't patched things up."

I cut my eyes away from him. "I'm not ready. You wouldn't blame me if you knew everything she said."

Lor talks me into rehashing the conversation from when I was returning from Shreveport.

"She went nuclear on you, huh?" He deals a new hand. "Don't worry. If she disinherits you, you'll still have *my* estate." This was said with a smirk and playful shove on my arm.

"Whatever." I shove back. "I'm not worried about it. She's the one who brought it up."

He taps the scar on my hand. "The day this happened, I wasn't even supposed to be in charge of you. Had I known I would be, I wouldn't have been drunk. Mom dropped you off with me by surprise so she could hook up with some guy."

My heart pounds in my ears. "It tracks with what I know of her now. But I never held the finger accident against you."

"You're a good person." He gives my shoulder a light squeeze.

"What was it you wanted from your father?" I ask, curious again what upset him the day he almost told me.

He takes a long time to answer. "I wanted him to *be* a father to me. That's all. You're lucky, Eva. You've got two father figures who love you."

"Counting you, I have three. I love you, Lor."

"I love you too, little sis. I'm glad you're here. Sorry I made it hard at first. And I'm sorry things went to shit with Alex."

Later, in bed with my laptop, I torture myself by searching online for the photos of Angie and Alex. I study each one and begin to see a different story than I did the day in front of Alex's apartment. Angie's arms are around him, but his arms are by his side.

His face is turned away from her, and in one of the shots, he looks repulsed.

Then I find a video clip Carla *didn't* show me.

Chapter Fifty-Three
Alex

Friday morning, I find I missed a call from Eva last night. There's no message, but damn, she finally reached out, and I didn't answer. I must've already been asleep.

I call her back. No answer, but I can't take this anymore. I have to see her. I *have* to fix this.

The only other thing I can think to do is call Lor.

"Hi, can I talk to Eva?" I ask voice cracking. "She won't answer my calls."

"She left last night."

"She what? She...left?"

Shit. Did she run away again?

"I can tell you where she went," Lor says, "if you promise to stop breaking her heart."

"Okay, yes, please." My heart stutters with hope. "I promise. Where is she?"

"Martin and Rosy's, but I don't have their address. Do you?"

"I can find it. Thanks, Lor." I hang up and call Dad.

I've avoided talking to him for a week and feel bad calling him now that I need something, but he can tell me where I'll find Eva.

"Hi Dad, it's Alex."

He chuckles. "Son, you called my cellphone and I *do* have your name saved with your number." He doesn't sound mad. I can't believe it. "I wondered when I'd hear from you."

"I haven't exactly felt like chatting. As I'm sure you're aware, I hid a bunch of stuff from y'all, and it caught up to me."

"We've been trying to give you space to work through things. Maybe I should've called to check on you, but it's not that you haven't been on my mind. How're you doing?"

Wow. I've tarnished the family name, and yet he sounds happy I called. "How are you not furious with me? Haven't I embarrassed you all over town?"

"There's been some embarrassment. Including with a few of my clients, but you're our son, and we love you. Everyone makes mistakes. You've just had the misfortune of having yours made available for the world to scrutinize."

"You could say that again."

"How's Eva?"

"She hasn't been talking to me, but I found out she's at Martin and Rosy's. Could you give me their address? I need to see her, and I'm already on my way to Georgetown."

"I'll forward it to you. Good luck, son."

Twenty minutes later, I pull into Martin and Rosy's driveway. Eva's truck is at the end of it. Relief floods every part of me. She's right where Lor said she'd be, but now...will she talk to me?

I park and get out. Give her truck a gentle pat like an old friend— I'm that desperate to reconnect with her. I ring the doorbell and wait a minute. Nobody answers.

I'll camp beside her truck if I have to, wait until she comes out to drive home if I need to.

I hear voices and laughter from around back. One of the laughs is Eva's. It's music to my ears, but I freeze, feeling like an intruder. She sounds happy; the opposite of the last time she saw me.

Something within me spurs my feet forward, in the direction of the sweet sound of her voice. I make my way around the left side of the house, glad there's no fence but also worried about trespassing. Wonder what Martin's stance is on firearms.

"Hello," I say in a tentative voice as I round the corner.

And there's Eva.

She's on the back porch with Rosy and Martin. They're seated around a patio table.

Eva looks my way. Stands up but sits again, like she's unsure of herself. I understand. I'm also unsure of myself, unable to decide if I should approach or not.

An eternity passes, with us staring at each other, not moving. I could stare at her forever, but will I ever be able to hold her again?

Rosy says something to her I don't hear. It puts Eva in motion. She gets up, steps toward me. I walk toward her, uncertain if I should jump for joy or prepare for more pain. Is it wrong to hope she'll throw her arms around me and kiss me? I *really* need that. I need to touch her, hold her.

She's more beautiful than ever, in a bathrobe and flip-flops. No makeup; she never needs it. Her hair's damp, like she recently showered. And her scent weakens me as she stops in front of me.

"Hi." Her voice is low and dull. It's not the warm greeting I crave, but I'll take it, and her eyes look at me in a hopeful, rather than hostile, way.

"Hi." I stupidly extend my hand, as if we're going to shake. I'm quick to slip it into my pocket. "You must be Eva. My name is Asshat."

"Yeah, it is." A slight smile dances across her lips.

My heart swells at the promise in it, but we're silent as we study each other. This is awkward.

Rosy and Martin go inside.

I take Eva's hand. She doesn't pull away.

"How have you been?" Idiot. What a crappy question.

"Not great." She clears her throat. "I'd be better if my boyfriend hadn't kept me in the dark about so much."

My ears perk up—she called me her boyfriend.

I'm tongue-tied, trying to decide if I heard right.

"I called you last night because I saw the video online," she says.

I blink. "What video?"

"The one the photographer took after the photos of you and Angie at her ranch. You told her off and left."

My eyes widen. "I haven't seen it. I'm glad *you* did. Do you believe me nothing happened with me and Angie that day?"

"Yes, I'm sorry I didn't trust you before."

"No, *I'm* sorry it happened at all. When I came across her beside the road, I should've left her stranded."

"Yeah, you should've." She slides her hands up my arms. And in the next second, she's *in* my arms. She lets me hug her.

It's hard not to squeeze too hard. "I love you so much, Eva. I never meant to hurt you." I try not to sob.

She clings to me, crying against my shoulder.

Then she tells me what I need to make my world right. "I love you too."

Chapter Fifty-Four
Eva

Alex's arms tighten around me. I love the way his body molds to mine.

Resting my face on his chest, I inhale his spicy aftershave.

God, I've missed him. The world's right again.

He kisses my cheek. "Eva…will you be able to trust me again?"

"Yes…" I gaze at him. "But let's talk. I need to know what happened."

There's something in his eyes. A hint of the look he had the day when everything went sideways. Is it fear? Shame? Dread?

"I'll tell you whatever you want to know," he says resolutely.

"Let's go to my tiny house."

His jaw drops. "*Your* tiny house?"

"What's built of it so far." I lead him behind Martin's workshop where the tiny house frame is on a trailer, shaded by some big oak trees.

"This is great, Eva. What's with the air mattress?"

"I slept here last night. I needed to feel like I was—"

"In a smaller space?"

"Yeah." We sit on the mattress.

I sigh. "Let's rip off the Band-Aid. Did Angie manage to land a kiss on your lips?"

He grimaces. "She did. I wasn't expecting it. I couldn't…I didn't—well, it *happened* but not because I wanted it to, and I turned away. Felt like hurling."

I swallow hard against a wave of nausea. "Why didn't you tell me before the shit show? I think I would've understood. Didn't I prove that when I heard about you and Jessica?"

"I'm an idiot. I panicked. There were reporters and cameras and people walking by with their cellphones pointed at us… I was freaking out, but it's no excuse." Deep worry lines crease between his eyebrows. "Helping you understand what was going on should've been my number one priority."

"Damn right."

"And you *will* be my number one priority, if you still want to be with me."

I can't imagine my life without him. "I want to be with you, but no more secrets, okay?"

"No more secrets." After a moment, he says, "For the record, I thought Angie was divorced. I found out she was married at the same time her husband found out about me. He went ape shit."

"Did he hit you?" I stroke his cheek, horrified at the idea of someone punching him.

"No." He covers my hand with his. "He threatened me in other ways. He knew details about my family. Said if it got out his wife had an affair with a teenager, it would screw up his campaign. He swore my 'wholesome, upstanding parents would never be able to show their faces again in their small conservative town.' His words exactly. I'll never forget them. Of course, now, he claims to have never threatened me."

"Yeah, I watched the interview. No wonder you didn't want your family to know, but Devin knew. Didn't Angie say he's the one who gave her your address?"

"Yeah, I'm not sure how he figured out I'd been…with Angie."

"Did you love her?" I stare at my lap, not sure I can handle looking him in the eyes for this.

"I *thought* I did but never said it, which I'm glad about. It would have been stupid and wrong. I had no idea what it meant to love someone…until you."

I give his hand an encouraging squeeze.

"Eva, believe me, I'd change so many things if I could. I've been lost without you." He puts a finger under my chin and tilts my face toward his.

Those gorgeous eyes plead with me, and in this moment, I trust him and love him more than ever. My heart swells. "I've been lost without you too."

He gives me a sweet kiss on my lips. "I don't ever want to be without you. Please tell me you aren't planning to move away in this tiny house."

"I'm not moving anywhere, but I do plan on traveling some. Will you come with me?"

"I'd love to. Where do you want to go?"

"Lots of places, including Hungary." I giggle at the bug-eyed look he gives me. "Not in the tiny house, of course."

"I can't afford—"

Putting a finger to his lips, I say, "Money's not an issue."

"It wouldn't be right. I'll feel like I'm taking advantage."

"*You* will, or you're worried Cassidi will think that?"

His brow furrows.

"We'll make a deal," I say. "No five-star hotels or dining in the finest restaurants."

"Can we slum it and stay in hostels? I've always wondered what that's like."

"Yes, as long as you're willing to fly first class. It's an awful long way to go in coach."

We laugh, and he says, "Okay, I can't wait to travel everywhere with you. I love you, Eva."

"I love you too, Alex."

~ * ~

When I return to Casa Lor after visiting Martin and Rosy, I tell Lor I'm ready to talk to Mom. I don't want to do it on the phone, though, and he puts his scheming skills to good use.

He enlists Spike and Ike, who are anxious for Mom and me to mend fences, and together they hatch a plan.

Mom's flying to Austin for the filming of a cameo appearance in a movie, and Lor "needs" her to sign something.

Lor and I wait in the living room for her to arrive.

She enters, pure style and grace, glowing from the attention at the filming, no doubt.

"My dears, good to see you." She kisses my cheek, then Lor's.

"Hi, Mom. Bye, Mom." He gestures to Darnell that he's ready to return upstairs.

"Where are you going?" she asks. "You said there's something for me to sign."

"I lied. Talk to your daughter." He waves as he's wheeled into the elevator.

She scowls and stays standing, as do I.

"How long are you staying?" I ask.

"I'm not. There's a car here, ready to take me back to the airport. Eva, you've stayed in Austin out of your sense of obligation, but why don't you join us in Europe?" She acts like our phone fight never happened. "The guys miss you. Overseas tours are a different fun from the U.S. ones. You don't know what you're missing."

"No thanks. My life is here now."

"If you're anything like me, you'll become restless. I'm shocked you haven't already."

"I'm *not* anything like you, Mom, and I don't want to be." I pause for a moment. "I know about your past. Lor told me."

"Wha—what do you *think* you know about me?" She turns toward the window. I can't see her face, but I can tell I have her attention.

"For starters, your real name is Sarika Szabo."

I lay it all out between us, not in an accusatory or blaming way, but matter of fact. She doesn't deny any of it and remains quiet until I'm done.

She keeps her eyes averted. "I have no regrets. Everything I did…I did it because it was right for me and what I needed. This is how I've chosen to live my life."

"Fine. But I'm not going to live my life like that. Whether you want to admit it or not, the choices we make affect other people. Unlike you, I can't selfishly ignore that."

She clears her throat and adjusts her purse on her shoulder. "I should be going."

"I love you, Mom." My tone is cool, and I walk toward her. Eye to eye, I tell her, "I don't love the things you've done, but I do love you. And if you'll do *one thing* for me, I'll let this go and never remind you of any of it again."

"Well, speak." She gestures, impatient. "What is it you want? Because I must leave soon, or I'll miss my flight."

"I want to meet my extended family. Tell me how I can get in touch with them."

"How should I know? I haven't spoken to them in forty years," she mumbles.

"Give me names then." I refuse to back down. "Last known whereabouts. Cities. Street names would be great if you can remember." I hand her a pad of paper and pen from the coffee table.

"What, right now?" she asks, incredulous. "You expect me to do this now?"

"Yes. Now." I don't trust her to follow up with me later.

She reluctantly plops onto the sofa's edge and scribbles off a list.

I hug her goodbye, and I'm relieved when she tells me she loves me. It isn't the love I want from her, but it's all she has to offer, and I'll find way to make peace with that. After she leaves, I box up my wigs. There's an organization that'll take them for cancer patients who've lost their own hair from chemo.

Chapter Fifty-Five
Alex

While Eva's having a tough conversation with her mom, I drive to Florence to talk to *my* mom.

I enter the house and find her in the kitchen, washing dishes.

"Hey, Mom," I say, my voice cracking.

"Alex? Oh! You startled me." She hurries to dry her hands.

"I'm sorry for everything. I didn't mean to make you cry." My throat tightens. I tear up without warning. She hugs me and sheds a few tears.

"It's okay. This family might go down in Florence's history as the most scandalous, but so be it." She laughs and dries her eyes.

We sit at the table.

"Why didn't you tell us about Angie?"

"I…had no business getting involved with her. Then I found out she'd lied about being divorced. I didn't want y'all to be disappointed in me, like I'm sure you are."

"Learning of this in the way I did was the biggest shock I've ever had. I won't lie, I was disappointed."

I cross my arms and keep my eyes down. She's never read me the riot act, but I feel it coming.

She's quiet for a minute, folding and refolding a napkin on the table. "Alex, the thing is, disappointing people is only human. It's bound to happen. The good thing is *forgiveness* is also human."

I look up at her. "Are you saying you forgive me?"

"I do, and so does Dad. You're too hard on yourself."

My shoulders suddenly feel lighter.

I uncross my arms and take her hands in mine. "Thank you, Mom."

We chat until it's time for me to head back to Austin.

She walks with me to my truck. "What are your plans tonight?"

"Going to Eva's."

"I take it y'all worked things out." She hugs me. "Have fun. Invite her here again sometime. We'd like to get to know her better."

"Okay, Mom. See you later."

I listen to California Nine on the way to Casa Lor and can't wait to spend some time chilling with Eva after the crazy last couple of weeks.

She waves to me from the porch where she sits alone on a wooden swing.

"Hey, beautiful." I sit beside her and pat the wooden armrest. "This is new."

"Yep. It was delivered and assembled today. What do you think?"

"I like it." I'm loving the serenity in her expression. "How were things with your mom?"

"As I expected." She relays their conversation. Sounds like Eva finally spoke her mind and cleared the air.

"I'm proud of you." I drape an arm across her shoulders, and she cuddles closer to me.

"It's the first time I didn't let her have the upper hand." There's no mistaking the hint of satisfaction in her voice.

We swing lazily until she invites me into the house to escape the heat. Inside, Hector has an amazing stir fry dinner ready for us.

We take our plates to the guesthouse and eat while watching a movie. Eva falls asleep before it ends. I scoop her up and carry her to her bed. As I pull the covers up for her, I notice in the dim light the top of her dresser is bare. The wigs are gone. I'm glad I'll never have to see Eva as anyone other than her beautiful self again.

I lean down to kiss her cheek.

She takes my hand and whispers, "Stay."

Her eyelids drift shut again as I lie down and hold her close.

Epilogue
Eva

My unwanted debut into celebrity gossip news was several weeks ago, yet the frenzy hasn't died down as I'd hoped. The vultures— I mean *reporters*—are still trying to get a piece of me. Because of them, I'm recognized almost everywhere I go. Strangers ask me personal questions and make unsolicited comments.

In some ways, Alex has had it worse. He was being recognized and called a cheater so often while giving UT tower tours that he requested a different campus job. He's working in one of the libraries now.

Today, I'm on my way to see him for his lunch break. I'm wearing a ball cap and thick-framed, nonprescription glasses to somewhat disguise myself. The trick is to walk with purpose, avoiding eye contact with people.

While he finishes up some work, I busy myself unpacking our lunch. That's when my eyes fall to Alex's open sketchbook. He's done a series of drawings, like a comic strip. I'm featured in almost every frame, either at ACR or overseeing the building of my tiny house.

He and I chat while we eat, but my mind stays on his drawings. They're so good and tell a story about me that I'd much prefer people obsess over instead of the other stuff.

We finish eating, and he walks out of the library with me. Even though I put the ball cap and glasses back on, a cluster of girls nearby stop and gawk at us.

"Shit, here we go again," he mutters.

One of the girls calls out, "Hey, Eva, I can't believe you didn't dump his cheating ass."

The other girls nod and make noises of agreement.

The air leaves my lungs with an invisible punch to my gut. His grip on my hand tightens. He says nothing, but this isn't the first time a random person has said something like that to me, and I can't take it anymore.

"Alex *didn't* cheat," I say loudly. My voice isn't as strong as I'd like, but I stand firm and continue, "Stop acting like you know the whole story and try minding your own business."

"Eva don't engage," Alex says quietly, reminding me that's what we agreed to do.

The girls exchange eye rolls and move along.

I face him, tears stinging my eyes. He folds me into his arms. He's my shelter in this ongoing shitstorm.

"It isn't fair," I say. "To you, I mean."

"None of it is, but we'll be okay. People will eventually lose interest." He presses his lips to my forehead.

"But they'll always remember unless..." I think of Alex's drawings again and pull my head back to look up at him. "What if we give them something else to focus on?"

His eyebrows rise. "I don't know. Like what?"

"I have an idea. Can you come over after work and bring your sketchbook?"

He agrees, and we part ways. Returning to Casa Lor, my mood lifts as a plan takes form in my mind.

I go looking for Lor as soon as I arrive home. These days, he spends less time in his room. I find him in the dining room, seated at the table with another guy.

Lor takes a swig from a water bottle and introduces me to Randall. With a smirk, he adds, "He'll be my biographer."

"Hmm, déjà vu." I laugh because, unlike last time Lor tried to pull a fast one on me, I know this is legit. For one thing, Randall has a laptop open in front of him. For another, I helped Lor pick Randall from a long list of writers.

The public interest in me brought new attention on Lor and his current situation, but he doesn't mind. He's decided to do something he swore he wouldn't: hire a biographer to write about his life, rise to fame, pitfalls, and ongoing recovery. I'm so proud of him and admire how he wants his biography to raise awareness about addiction and alcoholism in the music industry.

"I don't want to interrupt you guys," I say, "but I might need your help with something."

"Sure, have a seat," Lor says, and Randall pulls a chair out for me.

They help me develop a narrative, and when Alex arrives, he joins us at the table.

His face lights up as I bring him up to speed.

"Count me in," he says, opening his sketchbook.

Before long, we've created a short video. It features pages of Alex's drawings being slowly turned, one after another. In it, there's voiceover of me saying, "This message is directed at gossip mongers like Carla Kinsey and her followers: How sad it must be to have no life, so you're forced to chronicle and feed off the lives and hardships of others who want nothing more than to live their life in peace. Why not do something more with your life? May I suggest looking into organizations like Austin Creative Repurposing. ACR takes things that are in shambles, like the lives you callously destroy and discard, and turns them into something new, fresh, and positive. Their website is www-dot-austincreativerepurposing-dot-org. Stop in to look for yourself and tell them Lil' Eva sent you!"

We post the video on all the major social media platforms, tagging SLY and their competitors, and adding lots of hashtags to optimize exposure.

It goes viral. Soon, ACR's website has more visitors than ever. People start asking how to make donations, not only of supplies but also money.

There's real power in what we've done, and more video ideas start flowing.

The next video will be about building another tiny house using all repurposed materials. Martin, Alex, and Mr. Marshall are going to help me with it. The finished house will be placed on the Marshall's property in Florence as a surprise for Alex's sister Lena. While she may never be able to live on her own, the tiny house will give her a place *of* her own.

My new "celebrity" status isn't so bad after all. Not when I can use it to help others.

Acknowledgements

I started writing this novel in 2016 and so many people have played a part, big and small, along the way. First and foremost, I want to thank my husband Tim. You're my biggest supporter, and you've been with me through all the ups and downs. Your background as a professional musician came in handy too. Second, and just as dear to me—our amazingly talented daughter, Chloe, who illustrated the Eva and Alex characters for the book cover. Thank you, Chloe, from the bottom of my heart, for your artistic touch on this project.

Critique groups and partners make all the difference! My local group, fondly known as the Cuppa Austin Group (because that's where we met in-person before the pandemic) are invaluable: Lorraine Elkins, Sheryl Witschorke, Gayleen Rabakukk, Louise Byrne, and Jen Rassler. Former members and those on hiatus from the group who were also a big help: Naomi Canale, Lori Keckler, and Lindsay Leslie. Thanks for all the years of support, encouragement, and camaraderie. Other writers and authors who've critiqued at various stages: Susan Fletcher, Kristine Munden, Wendra Lynne, Herb Long, Melanie Miner, Rachel Gozhansky, and Heather Harwood. These are all people I've met through the Society of Children's Book Writers & Illustrators (SCBWI). While *Whiskey on Our Shoes* isn't kidlit, SCBWI is where I've found my writing friends, and the organization has been instrumental.

There are a few long-distance critique partners I've never met in person, but we found each other anyway. Faydra Stratton, Laura McFadden, Kit Forbes, Jocelyn Vitale, Marie Garay, and Ashley Martin. Credit goes to Ashley for the title of *Whiskey on Our Shoes*. Thank you to all of you!

Mentor Haleigh Wenger selected *Whiskey on Our Shoes* in the 2019 #WriteMentor program, and I thank you for helping me through revisions that helped make the story what it is today. Thanks to Brandy Woods Snow as well, who provided much needed advice at just the right time. Others who've helped on a developmental level: Naomi Hughes and Cate Courtland.

Thank you, Savvy Authors, for your semi-annual pitchfests. My participation in one of them led to request that turned into a "yes." And thank you to my publisher, Cassie Knight and the whole Champagne Book Group team. I'm so grateful to you for giving this story, and me, a chance. It's been great working with you and my fabulous editor Dawn Barclay. Also, a heartfelt thanks to designer Sevannah Storm for incorporating my daughter's character illustrations into a great cover.

There are many other organizations and resources I've found helpful: The Author's Guild, Writers League of Texas, WriteOnCon, Author Mentor Match, RevPit, Pitch Wars, and YARWA. Your roles in the industry are important and appreciated.

The idea for Eva's missing finger stemmed from a Leander High School classmate, Paula Meyer Aucoin. Paula's loss of a finger wasn't from an accident like Eva's, but she was so helpful with providing useful details for this book. Thanks, Paula, for letting me pick your brain about your own missing digit experience!

Finally, I thank my sister, Wendy Meyer, for being willing to read first drafts. Aside from Tim, you know me better than anyone, and I'm so glad to call you sister.

About the Author

Tonya Preece writes romance and contemporary young adult fiction and incorporates music into all her books in one way or another. She lives near Austin, TX where she's a small business manager for a forensic engineering firm. She and her husband enjoy traveling, live music, wine, and spoiling their fur babies.

As an active SCBWI member since 2015, Tonya has volunteered for several conferences, and has served as a critique group facilitator. She joined Writer's League of Texas and The Author's Guild in 2021. She's serving as the 2022 WriteOnCon Financial Administrator and Critique Boutique Coordinator.

Tonya's 2022 debut, *Whiskey on Our Shoes*, was selected for the 2019 #WriteMentor program. One of her YA novels, THE MISSING MEMORIES OF CORDY O'REILLY, earned her a 2020 scholarship/mentorship with Austin SCBWI and was a finalist at the 2018 Houston SCBWI conference.

An avid consumer of written stories, Tonya reads and/or listens to an average of 75 books a year. Some of her favorite YA authors include Jeff Zentner, Julie Buxbaum, Sarah Dessen, and Robin Benway. In adult romance—Kate Clayborn, Christina Lauren, Helena Hunting, Emily Henry, and Abby Jimenez. Series she tries to keep up to date on: Rhys Bowen's *Royal Spyness* and Janet Evanovich's *Stephanie Plum*. Recent mainstream faves are *Where the Crawdads* Sing by Delia Owens and *Daisy Jones & the Six* by Taylor Jenkins Reid.
Five Fun Facts about Tonya that aren't reading or writing related:

1. She volunteers at a local food pantry, where she's enjoyed serving weekly since 2017.
2. Her travel bucket list includes Italy, Ireland, and Bora Bora. Australia would be awesome, too!
3. She loves ziplining, indoor skydiving, and rollercoasters.
4.. She's a fan of bands like With Confidence, Broadside, All Time Low, State Champs, Sleeping with Sirens, and As It Is.

5. In her free time, she can be found indulging a jigsaw puzzle habit and/or binging shows like *Outer Banks*, *Never Have I Ever*, *Downton Abbey*, *Bridgerton*, *Good Girls*, *Veronica Mars*, and *iZombie*.

Tonya loves to hear from her readers. You can find and connect with her at the links below.

Website/Blog: www.tonyapreece.com
Facebook: https://www.facebook.com/tonya.preece.1
Instagram: https://twitter.com/TonyaPreece
Twitter: https://www.instagram.com/tonyapreecewrites/

Thank you for taking the time to read *Whiskey on Our Shoes*. If you enjoyed the story, please tell your friends, and leave a review. Reviews support authors and ensure they continue to bring readers books to fall in love with.

And now for a look inside *Some Assembly Required*, a fun and quirky story about a woman embarking on the new stage in her life after a divorce by Robin Winzenread.

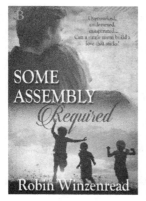

Can Ro Andrews, an overworked, undersexed, exasperated single mom, find love with Sam–a man allergic to chaos and crumbs—and make it stick, not sticky?

When new divorcee Ro Andrews moves her pack of semi-feral children to a run-down farmhouse, helping her brother restore the moldering homestead and living an authentic life—per the dictates of Instagram and lifestyle blogs everywhere—tops her to-do list. But romance? Hell, no. Between hiding from her children in baskets of dirty laundry, mentally eviscerating her cheating ex, and finding a job, Ro has a full plate.

Until she meets Sam Whittaker, a hunky Texas transplant with abs of steel and a nameplate that reads Boss. Clad in cowboy boots and surfer curls, this child-free stud has Ro on edge—and rethinking her defective Y chromosome ban. Somehow, this overworked, undersexed, exasperated single mom needs to find time to fall in love with a man allergic to chaos and crumbs and make it stick, not sticky.

Chapter One

As my young son's cries echo through this diner, I'm reminded again why some animals eat their young.

It's because they want to.

"Hey, Mom! Nick farted, and he didn't say excuse me!"

Normally when Aaron, my spunky six-year-old, announces something so crudely, we're at home, and his booming voice is muted by the artfully arranged basket of dirty laundry I've shoved my head into in hopes of hiding like an ostrich from a tiny, tenacious predator.

This time, however, Aaron yells it in the middle of a crowded diner in the small, stranger-adverse, southern Illinois town we're about to call home and, frankly, we don't need any more attention. Thanks to my semi-feral pack of three lippy offspring, we've already lit this place on fire, and not in a good way.

Despite our involuntary efforts to unhinge the locals with our strangers-in-a-strange-land antics, this dumpy, dingy diner, minus its frosty clientele, has a real comfortable feel, not unlike the ratty, stretched-out yoga pants I love but no longer wear because a) they don't fit any more and b) I burned them—along with a voodoo doll I crafted of my ex-husband (see my Pinterest board for patterns), after I forced it to have sex with my son's GI Joe action figure (see downward-facing dog for position).

Crap. I should have put the pictures on Instagram. Wait, I think they're still on my phone.

"Mom!" Aaron bellows again.

Right now, I'd kill for a pile of sweaty socks to dive into, but there's nary a basket of tighty-whities in sight, and that kid loves an audience, even a primarily rural, all-white-bread, mouth-gaping, wary one.

Frowning, I point at his chair. "Sit."

More than a bit self-conscious, I scan the room, hoping for signs of defrost from the gawking audience and pray my attempt to sound parental falls on nearby ears, earning me scant mom points. Of course, a giant burp which may have contained three of the six vowel sounds just erupted from my faux angelic four-year-old daughter, Madison, so I'll kiss that goodwill goodbye. I hand her a napkin and execute my go-to look, a serious I-mean-it-this-time scowl. "Maddy, say excuse me."

"Excuse me."

belch

Good lord, I'm doomed.

"Listen to me, Mom. Nick farted."

I fork my chef salad with ranch dressing on the side and raise an eyebrow at my youngest son. "Knock it off, kiddo."

"You said when we fart, we have to say excuse me, and he didn't." Finally, Aaron sits, unaware I've been stealing his fries, also on the side.

Kids, so clueless.

Nick, my angelic eight-year-old, is hot on his brother's heels and equally loud, "We don't have to say it when we're on the toilet. You can fart on the toilet and not say excuse me. It's allowed. Ask Mom."

Aaron picks up a water glass and holds it to his mouth. "It sounded like a raptor." He blows across the top, filling the air with a wet, revolting sound, once again alarming the nearby locals. "See?" He laughs. "Just like a raptor."

I point at his plate and scrutinize the last of his hamburger. "Thank you for that lovely demonstration, now finish your lunch."

Naturally, as we discuss fart etiquette, the locals are still gawking, and I can't blame them. We're strangers in a county where I'm betting everyone knows each other somehow and, here's the real shocker, we're not merely passing through. We're staying. On purpose.

We're not alone, either. My brother, Justin, his wife, Olivia, and their bubbly toddler twins kickstarted this adventure—moving to the sticks—so we're eight in total. Admittedly, this all sounded better a month ago when we adults hashed it out over too much wine and a little bit of vodka. Okay, maybe a lot of vodka. Back then, Justin had been headhunted for a construction manager job here in town, and I was in a post-divorce, downward-spiral bind, so they invited the kiddies and me to join them.

For me, I hope it's temporary until I can get settled somewhere, as in land a job, land a purpose, land a life. When they offered, I immediately saw the appeal—the more distance between me and the ex and his younger, sluttier girlfriend the better—and I decided to move south too.

Now I can't back out. I've already sold my house which buys me time, but I've got nowhere else to go. Where would I land? I've got three kids and limited skills. Plus, I don't even have a career to use as an excuse to change my mind or to even point me in another direction.

In other words, I'm stuck. Whether I want to or not, I'm relocating to a run-down farmhouse in the middle of nowhere Illinois to help Justin and Olivia with their grandiose plans of fixing it up and living "authentic" lives since, according to Instagram, Pinterest, and lifestyle blogs everywhere, manicured suburbs with cookie-cutter houses, working utilities and paved sidewalks don't count. Unless you're stinking rich, which, unfortunately, we, most definitely, are not.

Let's see, Justin has a new career opportunity, Olivia is going to restore, repaint, repurpose, and blog her way to a book deal, and me…and me…

Nope. I got nothing. No plans, no dreams, no job, nada. Here I am, the not-so-proud owner of a cheap polyester wardrobe with three kids rapidly outgrowing their own. I better come up with something, and quick.

Where's cheesecake when you need it? I stab a cherry tomato, pluck it from my fork, and chew. The world is full of people living their dreams, while mine consists of an unbroken night's sleep and a day without something gooey in my shoes. I take aim at a cucumber slice, pop it in my mouth, and pretend it's a donut. At least I don't have to wash these dishes.

Across from me, Olivia, my sometimes-vegan sister-in-law is unaware I'm questioning my life's purpose while she questions her lunch choice. Unsatisfied, she drops her mushroom melt onto her plate and frowns. I knew it wouldn't pass inspection. She may have lowered her standards to marry my brother, but she'd never do so for food. This is why she and I get along so well.

Olivia rocks back in her chair and smacks her lips, dissatisfied. "There's no way this was cooked on a meat-free grill. I swear I can taste bacon. Maybe sausage too." Her tongue swirls around in her mouth, searching for more hints of offending pork. "Definitely sausage."

Frankly, I enjoy finding pork in my mouth. Then again, I have food issues. Though, if I liked munching tube steak more often, perhaps my ex wouldn't have wandered. The bastard.

Justin watches his wife's tongue roll around, and I don't blame him. She's beautiful—dark, luminous eyes, full lips flushed a natural pink glow, cascading dark curls, radiant brown skin, a toned physique despite two-year-old twins. She's everything I am not.

She tells me I'm cute. Of course, the Pillsbury Dough Boy is cute too. Screw that. I want to be hot.

Regardless, I expect something crude to erupt from my brother's mouth as he stares at his lovely bride, so I'm pleasantly surprised when it doesn't. Instead, he shakes his head and works on his stack of onion rings. "What do you expect when you order off menu in a place like this, babe? Be glad they had portobellos."

Across from me, she frowns. Model tall and fashionably lean, she's casually elegant in a turquoise and brown print maxi dress, glittery dangle earrings, silky black curls, and daring red kitten heels that hug her slender feet. How does she do it? She exudes an easy glamour even as she peels a corner of toasted bun away from her sandwich, revealing a congealed mass of something.

"This isn't a portobello. It's a light dove gray, not a soft, deep, charcoal gray. I'm telling you this is a bad sandwich. I'm not eating it." She extracts her fingers from the offending fungus and crosses her bangle bracelet encased arms.

Foodies. Go figure. No Instagram picture for you, sandwich from hell.

Fortunately their twins, Jaylen and Jayden, adorable in matching Swedish-inspired sweater dress ensembles and print tights, are less picky. Clearly, it comes from my chunky side of the family. They may be dressed to impress, but the ketchup slathered over their precious toddler faces says, "We have Auntie Ro's DNA in us somewhere."

I love that.

Justin cuts up the last half of a cold chicken strip and shares it with his daughters, who are constrained by plastic highchairs—which I can't do with my kids any more, darn the luck—and, in addition to having no idea how to imitate raptors with half-empty water glasses like my boys or identify mushrooms by basis of color like their mother, they are still quite cute.

Love them as I do, my boys haven't been cute for a while. Such a long while. Maddy, well, she's cute on a day-to-day basis. Yet, they are my world. My phlegm covered, obnoxious, arguing world.

Justin wipes Jaylen's cheek and checks his phone. "We need to get the bill. It's getting late."

I survey the room, hunting for our waitress. Despite the near constant stranger stares, this place intrigues me. It feels a hundred years old in a good, cozy way. The diner's creaky, wood floor is well worn and the walls are exposed brick, which is quaint in restaurants even if it detracts from the value in Midwestern homes, including the giant moldering one Justin and Olivia bought northeast of town. Old tin advertising posters depict blue ribbon vegetables and old-time tractors in shades of red and green and yellow on the walls, and they may be the real antique deal.

They're really into primary colors, these farm folks. Perhaps the best way to spice up a quiet life is to sprinkle it with something bright and shiny. As for me, I've been living in dull shades of beige for at least half a marriage now, if not longer. Should I try bright and shiny? Couldn't hurt.

Red-pleather booths line the wall of windows to the left, and a row of tables divides the room, including the two tables we've shoved together which my children have destroyed with crumbs, blobs of ketchup, and snot. Of course, the twins helped too, but they're toddlers so you can't point a finger at them especially since all the customers are too busy pointing fingers at mine.

Bar stools belly up to a Formica counter to the right, and it's all very old school and quaint, although I would hate to have to clean the place, partly because Maddy sneezed, and her mouth was open and full of fries.

Kids. So gross.

Three portly gentlemen in caps, flannel, and overalls overflow from the booth closest to our table and, clearly, they're regulars. They're polishing off burgers and chips, though no one is sneezing with his mouth open, most likely because his teeth will fly out in the process. I imagine the pleather booths are permanently imprinted with the marks of old asses from a decade's worth of lunches. Sometimes it's good to make an impression. The one we're currently making, however? Probably not.

Nearly every table, booth, and stool are taken. Must be a popular place. Or it may be the only place in this itty, bitty town. It's the type of place where everyone knows your name, meaning they all stared the minute we walked in because they don't know ours, it's a brisk Tuesday in early November, and we sure aren't local.

Yet.

Several men of various ages in blue jeans and farm hats sit in a row upon the counter stools, munching their lunches. A smattering of conversations on hog feed, soybean yields, and tractor parts fills the air. They all talk at once, the way guys tend to do, with none of them listening except to the sound of his own voice, the way guys also tend to do, like stray dogs in a pound when strangers check them out and they're hoping to impress.

Except for one of them, the one I noticed the minute we walked in and have kept tabs on ever since. Unlike the others, this man is quiet and, better yet, he doesn't have the typical middle-aged, dad-bod build. While most of the other men are stocky and round, square and cubed, pear shaped and apple dumpling-esque, like bad geometry gone rogue, he isn't. He's tall with a rather broad triangular back and, given the way it's stretching the confines of his faded, dark red, button-down shirt, it's a well-muscled isosceles triangle at that. Brown cowboy boots with a Texas flag burned on the side of the wooden heel peek from beneath seasoned blue jeans, and those jeans cling to a pair of muscular thighs that could squeeze apples for juice.

God, I have a hankering for hot cider. With a great big, thick, rock-hard cinnamon stick swirling around too. Hmmm, spicy.

This Midwestern cowboy's dark-brown hair is thick with a slight wave that would go a tad bit wild if he let it, and he needs to let it. Who doesn't love surfer curls, and his are perfect. They're the kind I could run my fingers through forever or hang onto hard in the sack, if need be. Trust me, there's a need be.

His body is lean, yet strong, and beneath his rolled-up sleeves, there's a swell of ample biceps and the sinewy lines of strong, tan forearms. It's a tan I'm betting goes a lot further than his elbows. His face is sun-kissed too, and well-defined with high cheekbones and a sturdy chin. A hint of fine lines fan out from the corners of his chocolate-brown eyes and, while not many, there're enough to catch any drool should my lips happen to ravage his face.

Facial lines on guys are so damn sexy. They hint at wisdom, experience, strength. Lines on women should be sexy too, even the stretchy white, hip-dwelling ones from multiple, boob-sucking babies, but men don't think that way, which is why I only objectify them these days. Since getting literally screwed over by my ex, I'm the permanent mascot for Team Anti-Relationship. I blame those defective Y chromosomes myself. Stupid Y chromosomes.

Regardless, it's difficult not to watch as this well-built triangle of a man wipes his mouth with a napkin. I wouldn't mind being that white crumpled paper in that strong tan hand, even if I, too, end up spent on the counter afterward. At any rate, he stands, claps the guy to his left on the back, and I may have peed myself.

The sexy boot-clad stranger pulls cash from his wallet and sets it on the lucky napkin. "I've got to get back to the elevator, Phil. Busy day."

Sweet, a Texas accent. How very Matthew McConaughey. Mama like.

A pear-shaped man next to him raises his glass. "See ya, Sam. You headed to George's this afternoon?"

"I hope so. I need to get with Edmund first, plus we have a couple of trailers coming in, and I've got to do a moisture check on at least two of them." His voice is low, but soft, the way you hope a new vibrator will sound, but never does until the batteries die which defeats the purpose, proving once again irony can be cruel.

And what the hell is a moisture check?

I zero in on the open button of his shirt, drawn to his chest like flies to honey, because that's what I do now that I'm divorced and have no husband and no purpose—I ogle strange men for the raw meat they are. Nothing's going to happen anyway. Truth be told, I haven't dated in an eternity and have no real plans to start, partly because I've forgotten how; just another unfortunate aspect of my life on permanent hold. I've been invited to the singles' buffet, but I'm too afraid to grab a plate. At this point in my recently wrecked, random life, I would rather vomit. Hell, I barely smell the entrees. I'm only interested in licking a hunk of two-legged meatloaf for the sauce anyway. There's no harm in that, right?

Where was I? Right, his chest, and it's a good chest, with the "oood" dragged out like a child's Benadryl-laced nap on a hot afternoon. It's that goood.

Of course, as I mentally drag out the "oood," my lips involuntarily form the word in the air imitating a goldfish in a bowl. While I ogle this particular cut of prime rib, I realize he's noticed my stare not to mention my "oood" inspired fish lips, which is not an attractive look, despite what selfie-addicted college girls think. Our eyes lock. An avalanche of goosebumps crawls its way up my back and down my arms and, I swear, I vibrate. Not like one of those little lipstick vibrators that can go off in your purse at the airport, thank you very much, but something more substantial with a silly name like Rabbit or

Butterfly or Bone Master.

That, my friends, is the closest I've come to real sex in two and half years. Excuse me, but we need a moisture check at table two, please. Not to mention a mop. Okay...definitely a mop.

For a moment, we hold our stare—me with my fish lips frozen into place, vibrating silently in my long-sleeved, heather green T-shirt and jeans, surrounded by my small tribe of ketchup-covered children, and him all hot, tan, buff, and beefy, staring at us the way one gawks at a bloody, ten-car pile-up. All too soon, he blinks, the deer-in-the-headlights look fades, and he drops his gaze.

C'mon, stud, look again. I'm not wearing a push-up bra for nothing.

Big, dark, brown eyes pop up again and find mine. All too soon, they flit away to the floor.

Score.

Damn, he's fine. Someone smoke me a cigarette, I'm spent.

I scan the table, imagining my children are radiating cuteness. No dice. Aaron imitates walrus tusks with the last of his French-fries, Nick is trying to de-fang him with a straw full of root beer, and Maddy's two-knuckles deep into a nostril. And I'm sitting next to Justin.

Figures. My big, burly, ginger-headed, lug of a wedding-ring-wearing brother is beside me. Does this hunk of burning stud think he's my husband? Should I pick my own nose with my naked, ring-less finger? Invest in a face tattoo that reads "divorced and horny?" Why do I even care? He's only man meat. After all, was he really even looking at me? Or Olivia? Sexy, sultry, damn-sure-married-to-my-brother Olivia? I whip back to the stud prepared to blink "I'm easy" in Morse code.

blink *blink* *bliiiink*

With a spin on his star-studded boots, Hotty McHot heads toward the hallway at the back of the diner, oblivious that my gaze is rivetted to his ass and equally clueless to the fact that I have questions needing immediate answers, not to mention an overwhelming need to scream, "I'm single and put out, no strings attached" in his general direction.

Olivia pulls me back to reality with her own questions. "I mean, is it that difficult to scrape the grill before you cook someone's meal?"

She's still honked off about her sandwich, unaware I'm over here having mental sex with the hunky cowboy while sending my kids off to a good boarding school for the better part of the winter.

"I didn't have many options here," she rattles on, "even their salads have meat and egg in them. Instead of a writing a book, I should open a vegan restaurant. I was going to give them a good review for the ambiance, but not now. Wait until I post this on Yelp."

Eyeballing the room, Justin polishes off the last of his double-cheese burger. "Sweetie, we're moving to the land of pork and beef. Vegan won't fly here, and I doubt the help cares about Yelp. Did you notice our waitress? She's got a flip phone. Time to put away your inner princess and stick with the book idea."

Long fingers with bronze gel manicured nails rat-a-tat-tat on the tabletop. She locks onto him with dark, intelligent, laser-beam eyes. "Would it kill you to be supportive, honey bunch? You might as well say, uck-fay u-vay."

Apparently channeling some weird, inner death wish, Justin picks up an onion ring, takes a bite, then pulls a string of overcooked translucent slime free from its breaded coating. He snaps it free with his teeth, then offers it to her. "Your book is going to be great, babe, and it will appeal to a larger audience than here. Remember the goal, Liv. As for me, I'm trying to keep you humble. No one likes high maintenance."

The limp, greasy onion hangs in the air. She ignores it, but not him. "Okay, this time, sweetie, I'll say it. Uck-fay u-vay with an ig-bay ick-day."

Jaylen looks up from her highchair and munches a chicken strip. "Uck-fay?" she repeats through fried poultry. "Ick-day?"

Behind her an older woman, also fluent in pig Latin, does a coffee-laced spit-take in her window booth. I hope she's not a new neighbor.

Justin chuckles and polishes off the offending string of onion. Olivia stews. Time to implement an offense. Clearly, we need an exit strategy.

Where's our waitress? I spy her delivering plates of food three booths down and wave. She nods, so I use these few moments to ward off any drama. "Suggestion, you two. Let's not piss off the help. This may be the only place where we can hide from the kids and eat our feelings. Not to mention drink. Agreed?"

Justin snorts, but says nothing. Olivia rolls her eyes, but also says nothing. Success, although it's tentative. Time to leave.

Water pitcher in hand, our waitress returns to our table. She surveys the left-over lunch carnage, unaware my sister-in-law is both unimpressed and pissed off, and it's fairly obvious that, if we're all going to be regulars here, a sizeable tip, different children, or the offer of a kidney is in order. A middle-aged woman in jeans, T-shirt, and an apron with short, no-nonsense, dishwater hair, she refills our water glasses, possibly so I'll have something with which to wipe the seats or drown our young. Or both. I can't be sure. But I'm open to options.

She sets the water pitcher on the table and starts stacking dirty plates. "Ready for dessert?" She's a bit harried, and, with the possibility of an eruption from Olivia hanging over our heads, I pick up a napkin and start wiping. "We have cherry cobbler."

An indignant cry erupts from the booth behind us. One of the three portly gentlemen hollers—this is the kind of place where you holler— "Save me a piece of cobbler."

"Yeah, yeah, in a minute, Ernie." The waitress scowls. "What else can I get you? Pie? Cake? The coffee's fresh."

"Yeah, but it ain't good though," barks the man named Ernie. A fresh wave of snorts erupts from his companions.

I stifle a laugh, but it's a challenge, especially since Aaron's been flicking my salad croutons in their general direction throughout most of the meal and, despite my scolding, he's getting quite good with his trick shots.

"I bet you've done this before," I say to the woman whose name tag reads "Anna."

She glares at the booth. "Yep, they're regulars. Of course, I call 'em a pain in the butt, myself."

"Good to know, Anna."

"Name's Sarah. This is the only tag we had left."

Of course. Naturally, the crusty old guys are regulars in a diner where everyone knows your name, so you wear a tag that isn't your own, presumably for strangers who rarely show up on a Tuesday. I like this quirky town, even if it doesn't like me.

"Where are you all from? Chicago?" pries the waitress formerly known as Anna.

Olivia avoids eye contact and spit shines her twins. "Is it obvious?"

Curious, Sarah takes in the dress, the earrings, the bright red shoes. "Yep. What brings you through town?"

Backs stiffen throughout the room. Heads swivel in our direction. The general roar of conversation drops a decibel or two, all the better to eavesdrop, I assume.

I confiscate Maddy's spoon and add it to the pile of flatware on my salad plate, then plunge on before anyone at our table offers an unwelcomed critique of the menu. "We're moving here. They bought a place on Stockpile Road, Thornhill."

Eyes stare from all corners of the diner. Bodies sit taller. Ears bend toward us, and whispers swim across a sea of faces.

"Thornhill?" Sarah cocks her head. "You mean old lady

Yeager's place? I hope you're good with a hammer."

"It needs a bulldozer," shouts a voice from the back.

"Stick a sock in it, Ernie. Men," she mutters.

"I've got a toxic ex and a lot of frustration, so…" I imitate a manic hammering motion, but, getting no response from the masses, I load up Aaron's spoon with croutons and keep talking. "Justin's in construction—he's starting a new job here next week. He'll put us to work on the house. Should be fun."

Olivia stares at the hunk of sandwich left on her plate before looking pointedly at our waitress. "I plan to blog about the experience— articles on reclaiming the house, restoring the gardens, growing our own vegetables and herbs, recipes, homemade soaps. Think avant-garde Martha Stewart. It's what I do."

Sarah blinks rapidly as she digests Olivia's words. "Ah." She hesitates. "Want a doggie bag?"

Justin chokes on the last bite of his burger as he examines his phone. "Not necessary, but thanks. Can we get our bill though?"

A finger-painted, ketchup rendition of a farting raptor rambles across Aaron's plate. Sarah sets down her stack of dishes, rips our bill from the order pad in her apron pocket, and picks up my son's plate without so much as an appraisal. "So, you all are moving here. Good to know. I haven't been up there in years." She adds another plate to her stack, obliterating his finger art. "I hear it's a real project. Anyway, good luck, and welcome to town." She spins on her heels with arms full of dirty dishes. "You can pay at the register."

Justin tucks his phone in his pocket and wipes his mouth, pleased with his greasy, meaty lunch. "We need to get going. The movers will be here within the hour."

My heart does a double thump. Time to head to the new homestead. True, I'm a hanger-on in this adventure of theirs, just a barnacle on their barge, but I'm excited too even if I haven't been to the place yet. Desperate to reignite my life, the promise of a thousand potential projects, plans, and ideas leap to mind, calling out to me with hope. Maybe this is where I'll find myself. Or a purpose beyond wiping tiny hineys. Something. Anything, really.

Ready to settle the bill, I toss two twenties at Justin. "Here's my cash. Can you pay mine too? I'll run to the restroom, and then we'll get out of here. Sound good?

He grabs the cash. "Yep. Get going, sis. I got this."

My imagination whirls with anticipation as I rise. Roughly fifteen minutes from now, we should be there, home. Can a fresh start be far behind?

Oblivious to my growing excitement, Aaron considers me for a moment as I push back from the table, ready to roll. "Mom, if you fart in there, are you going to say excuse me?"

Nick polishes off his root beer and sets his glass on the table. "I bet she won't. I bet she'll sit there, fart, and say nothing."

Good gravy, will they get off this topic already? My stern gaze falls on blind eyes. Ignoring them, I make a hasty exit to the restroom, but Aaron once again sends shockwaves through the diner with his cry, "Will you tell us if you fart?"

sigh

Maybe I can outrun his voice. I rush away and turn the corner sharp, seeking sanctuary in the women's room. Instead, however, I spy something even better. Speeding toward me from an open door at the end of the hall is Hottie McHot-Stuff, the good-looking cowboy with moisture on his mind.

We both stop short. I sidestep right, as he sidesteps left into my path. We chuckle. Immediately we both dance the other way, blocking one another yet again.

I flash him a smile and grin. "Sorry about that. How about I stop, and you walk on by?"

Hints of vanilla, pine, and leather waft my way. He nods agreement, and our eyes connect. For a moment, we hold yet another stare.

Damn, he's even better looking up close and personal. I could get used to this. Heat rises in my face—where'd that come from? Moisture rises in my jeans—I know where that came from.

All too soon, he breaks our gaze and sidesteps around me. "Excuse me and thank you." Boots clack on the wooden floor, and he saunters away, dragging a steam cloud from my body in his wake. It's a wonder the candy-striped wallpaper in the hallway doesn't peel.

Happy to have a new hobby, I peek over my shoulder and gape at each swaying butt cheek. "You're welcome," I mumble as his blue-jean clad McNuggets disappear around the corner. "You are very welcome."

Into the diner restroom I go, daydreaming about hot cowboys and diner sex. A random inspection of my breasts, hoping they impressed, halts my midday revelry. Because, naturally, there's a hunk of crusted ketchup clinging to my left boob.

Perfect. At least there isn't a French fry in my cleavage. Or is there?

I scrape at the hardened blob with marginal success, preferring to study this fresh new stain on my old, dumpy T-shirt rather than the current flustered face in the mirror. I hate mirrors. The view always disappoints, even now after I've dropped a few dozen post-divorce, pissed-off pounds. But, as I de-crust and wash my hands, I finally look up.

Stain or no stain, I want to see what the cowboy saw.

A round, pixie face with a smattering of freckles that in twenty years when I'm pushing fifty everyone will assume are age spots. Bright green eyes with ex-husband anger issues and a twinkle of insanity. A hint of frown lines spreading across my pale, translucent forehead, explaining my new-found love of long, wispy bangs. Reddish blonde hair thanks to a box from the grocery store. A great big mouth built for yelling and eating. Yep. That about sums it up.

I pinch my cheeks for color because, nowadays, for sheer self-respect alone and in spite of my self-imposed dating ban, I'm making an effort. The truth is, in my full-time baby-making years, I'll admit I didn't most days. A relentless, nonstop tug of war between keeping it together or giving up and letting everything go to seed waged inside me as I confronted dirty diapers, dirty dishes, dirty underwear, and dirty socks. Clad in sensible shoes and something stretchy most days, I only wanted to be comfortable.

News flash. Husbands hate comfortable.

Which is why I am comfortable no more. Time to flush and flee. My old chubby life swirls down the crapper, and my new, uncomfortable, slightly less chubby, but even less focused one awaits. Halle-freaking-lujah, I'm a stalled work in progress.

Drowning in my personal funk, I toss a paper towel in the trash and bolt from the bathroom, far away from the mirror when—slam!

A tall, thin, elderly man sways, reduced to a sapling in a strong breeze, threatening to collapse to the floor under the weight of my rapidly advancing body. He's bundled up in a thick coat, and thank heavens, too, because his right lapel is the only thing that kept him upright.

I cling to it now, gripping with all my might as he steadies his skinny legs beneath himself. His dusty brown bowler hat tilts far forward on a patch of thin silver hair, and there's a spare quality about him.

A tired, watery stare falls upon me, and his initial alarm gives way to anger. "Young lady, watch yourself!"

Why couldn't I have slammed into the cowboy? I could have grabbed something more substantial than this old man's coat.

Letting go of the gentleman's lapels, I lurch backward. "Oh, my gosh, I'm sorry!"

He stands erect, but even with his dignity restored, his anger grows. "You, young people. You don't think, none of you. You have no concept of your own actions, no sense of responsibility!"

Holy crap. What do I say to that? I'm tongue-tied. After all, I did mow him down with my mom thighs. Plus, he thinks I'm "young people," and he sounds like he means it, possibly even enough to pinkie swear.

However, neither of us whips out a tiny digit. Instead, we stand there, locked in stony silence. "Sorry," I repeat for want of anything else to say.

Finally, he turns with a huff and disappears around the corner into the dining room.

Great. We've barely been in town an hour, and I am far from making friends.

Shaken, I hesitate. Please let this move be the right decision. Please?

It has to be because, right now, I'm a freaking mess. Somehow, I managed to abdicate control over my life to a man who eventually chafed under the responsibility. Now? Now, post-divorce, I'm a rudderless ship, a floating piece of flotsam bobbing downstream, willy nilly, with no real goals or plans other than to make this move, which may or may not be a smart move. What if this proves to be a dead end too? I can't have any more dead ends. Wasn't my marriage enough?

Everyone else has it together. Why the hell don't I?

Desperate for hope, I settle for a plea to the universe instead. Alone in the hall, eyes closed, back against the wall, I give it a go.

Hey, universe, will you please let this move be the right decision for me and my kiddies? Please? With sugar on top?

No one answers, God, Karma, the universe, or alien overlords for whom I am a rapidly failing SIMS avatar, nothing.

Was I expecting an answer?

sigh

No.

I'm alone in the hallway. No skinny old men or hot, buff cowboys walk my way. Regrets, fear, and second thoughts burn behind my eyelids, threatening tears. Steeling myself, I open my eyes, ready to swipe them away before any should fall when I notice it.

A bulletin board anchors the opposite wall, demanding my attention. It's plastered with everything from hay for sale (first cut too, which I assume is the deepest) to pictures of mixed-breed puppies alongside notices for church chili suppers. Bluegrass music drifts in from the dining area, and I drink it in, savoring the ambiance, searching for a sign.

Wait, what's this? An employment ad? For an actual job? Who

in the hell advertises on bulletin boards in this digital age? Better question, is it a sign from the universe? A random act of coincidence? A magical stroke of luck?

Who cares? It's an ad. I lean forward and read.

"Local businessman with multiple enterprises seeks organized, responsible individual to serve as part-time office manager with potential for full time available. Knowledge of basic accounting a plus. Requires good communication skills, customer service, and an ability to type. Pleasant office demeanor a necessity."

Oh my. It's a real job.

Snapping a picture with my cellphone, I give thanks to my short-lived pre-baby history of minimum-wage, part-time jobs at gas-stations and mini-marts. Customer service? No one rang up a carton of Marlboro Lights faster than me. Responsible? The Circle K condom dispenser in the men's restroom was never empty on my watch.

Is this my sign? It sounds like a stretch. Can I really do all that? I, mean, I wasn't exactly bred for this job, was I?

Bred for it? Ick, parent sex. There's an early Saturday-morning memory from age ten I don't need to recall right now.

Scratch that. It's time to be bold and bring on the next chapter of my life.

Lord knows, I need it.

Out Now!

What's next on your reading list?

Champagne Book Group promises to bring to readers fiction at its finest.

Discover your next
fine read!
http://www.champagnebooks.com/

We are delighted to invite you to receive exclusive rewards. Join our Facebook group for VIP savings, bonus content, early access to new ideas we've cooked up, learn about special events for our readers, and sneak peeks at our fabulous titles.

Join now.
https://www.facebook.com/groups/ChampagneBookClub/